MW00325497

UNCANNY

STOUT

Also by J. Elliott

Short story collections:
Ghost Lite
Uncanny Stout

Novels:

Monkey Mind

UNCANNY

STOUT

A DARK, FORTIFYING COLLECTION OF MACABRE STORIES

J. ELLIOTT

hedonistic hound press

This book is a work of fiction. Names, places and situations are all creations of the writer's imagination and are not to be construed as real. Any resemblance to actual persons or events is entirely coincidental.

Hedonistic Hound Press

Copyright © 2020 by J. Elliott
Book cover and interior artwork by J. Elliott

Please visit: **hedonistichoundpress.com**

All rights reserved. This book, or parts thereof, may not be reproduced in any manner whatsoever without permission except in the case of brief quotations in critical articles and reviews.

Printed in the United States of America

Acknowledgements

Thank you to the Writer's Alliance of Gainesville: Wendy Thornton, Joan Carter, Richard Gartee, Dan South, Mike Kite and James Singer for your advice, guidance, patience and handholding. To the Writer's Group of the Alachua Branch Library: Art Warner, Peggy Cogar, Martha Bustamante, Jessica Jaeger, Rachael Raulerson, Ricardo Gonzalez, Joseph Leverette, Amy Gresock and Harry Mason, thank you for sharing your time and insight. Many blessings and much success to you all, always.

Additionally, a great thank you to the M. R. James Appreciation Society and Classic Ghost Story Tradition members on Facebook for wisdom, humor and inspiration. My people! Particular thanks to Yan Balthazar for encouragement and feedback, and James DelVecchio for inspiration on ghostly activity.

Thank you to Jan Schumann, Janet Iannantuono, Tally Johnson, James P. Nettles III and Alex Matsuo for a great Atomacon experience and inspiration for "The Hoarder House".

My gratitude to beta readers Jo Ann Lodahl, Mark Davidson, , Peggy Cogar, Elaine Young and Pat Piper.

Special thanks to Rick for your love, encouragement and support. I could not have done this without you.

Jessica Elliott   2020

Author's Note

My previous collections have featured a seed note prior to each story with a comment about how the story came into being. As this book already has a bit of a story before each main story, the seed notes have been moved to the back of the book.

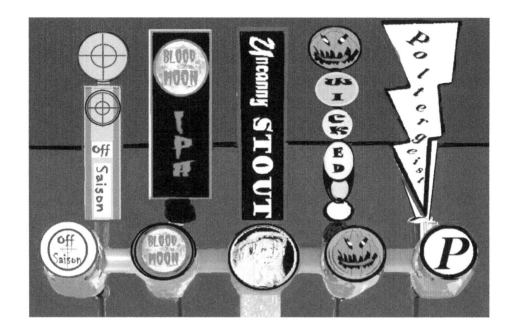

Table of Contents

Nothing Like A Strong Pot of Tea

BW&S

ONE

Finally released from duty after twenty-eight hours of post-hurricane line work, Zap was beyond exhausted. As he drove home through a cold, drizzling rain, he kept himself awake by trying to find some part of his body that wasn't aching, tight, or hurting. His feet felt like lead-- he was sure he had a collection of blisters on his toes. His legs and back ached, his stomach growled, hands were raw, his neck was stiff, his eyes burned. There wasn't enough hot water on earth to ease his body's complaints. Oh, wait. His nose. *Well there you go*, he thought, *my nose doesn't hurt. I've got that going for me.*

The windshield wipers were beating out a hypnotic rhythm sure to put him to sleep if he wasn't careful. He popped on the radio and hunted for something attention grabbing.

The last job had been the worst. His hands so tired he'd lost dexterity and couldn't get the power lines attached on the power pole properly; it had taken twice as long as usual. His tools had slipped like eels in his hands. He'd finally got it though, by gum. He'd felt that small bit of satisfaction when he saw lights spring on at homes nearby.

Zap's GPS was routing him through a little town he wasn't familiar with, a town called Fleeting. Likely to be one of those old Southern towns just a few blocks long with a jiffy store, a laundromat, a thrift store and maybe, if he was lucky, a tiny restaurant. His house was forty-five minutes away. He couldn't remember when he'd wolfed a thin sandwich. It'd sure be great if he could find a bar that was still open that served food. A beer and a half-decent burger would do him a world of good. Chances were slim he'd be so lucky.

Radio reception was poor; he couldn't find a station that would come in clearly without either static or that annoying fade-in fade-out effect that happens in stormy weather. Zap tried to think of a song that he could sing to the beat of the windshield wipers, but he was too tired.

The road zig-zagged through countryside with no landmarks or structures. Zap felt his eyes get heavy and once or twice he nodded off, coming back with a jolt. Then up ahead he saw some lights. At least he might get some junk food at a convenience store. He shifted in his seat and gripped the steering wheel to stay awake. His headlights hit a rustic sign welcoming him to the town of Fleeting.

Welcome to
FLEETING
Population 847 8!
Plus 19 dogs
20 cats
and a mess of
chickens

Well, the sign was entertaining at any rate. Welcome to Fleeting: population adjusted from three hundred and forty-seven to three hundred and forty-eight. Nice. Someone had had a baby recently. Zap felt his heart lift a little at the town changing the sign for the new addition.

The lights ahead grew brighter and buildings came into view. Hey, this town had a bank and a post office! *I'm in the big time now!* Zap chuckled to himself. There was a tiny grocery store, closed of course. Then he got excited. The BW&S Pub--a dive bar with its lights on and a red neon sign on the fritz that blinked O P E N with the P and the E dim and flickering.

There was one vehicle in the parking lot, probably belonging to the bartender, he guessed. As Zap parked next to it, he looked it over. It was a Chevy pick-up truck with a custom paint job, two-tone, black with orange stripes, a late 60's model that looked like it had been sitting for an extended period of time. The plate was 247HWN.

Zap turned the engine off and made a dash for the bar's entrance. It was a peculiar establishment, an old brick building with a sign by the door that looked like a pub sign from Britain.

The BW& S Pub. The front door even had an old-fashioned door latch. He was relieved when the door opened. He walked in, shut the door behind him and shook the rainwater off his head.

"Welcome!" said a husky female voice.

The interior was dark with a low ceiling. It took Zap's eyes a moment to adjust to the dim lighting. Following the voice, he stepped forward to a gorgeous bar counter with brass bar stools with red and gold striped upholstery. The bar smelled of cigars and something else, something familiar and pleasant in an odd sort of way. What was it?

As the attractive middle-aged barmaid came into view, he recalled the smell. It was much like a smell from his childhood, the smell of the backseat of the stagecoach in his grandfather's barn, a musty combination of old fabric, soil, and leather.

"Boy, am I glad you are still open," Zap said, "you *are* still open I hope?"

"Aye!" The woman said gliding closer to him. She was wearing an off-the-shoulder peasant blouse that clung to her buxom bosom revealing perfect skin so white she almost glowed.

"Hey Sugar, my name's Gracie, and I'll be your server. What'll ya have?" she asked, tucking a hank of hair behind her ear. The way she wiggled as she asked the question implied that she was available for the asking.

"I should drink some water, and I'd love a beer. I just got off an endless shift repairing power lines. I'm so hungry I could eat a horse. Have you got any food?"

"Fix you right up!" Gracie said, reaching for a menu and a drinks list sliding them across the bar top to him. She held onto them until he reached for them. When she let go, she winked at him before sliding away. He glanced down at the drinks list. He felt a presence in front of him and heard the glass touch the bar. The barmaid had returned with a large glass of ice water.

"Thanks," he said, reaching for it. *My mind must be going, he thought, I could have sworn she was just at the other end of the bar. How did she pour this so quickly?* He nodded again and took a deep welcomed drink. The water was like pure mountain water. He felt his body craving more and he guzzled it down.

Gracie smiled and patted the drink list. "I'll be right back to check on you."

4

He nodded.

He heard her asking "Can I get you another drink?" Dang if she wasn't at the other end of the bar already.

Zap's eyes were used to the caliginous[?] lighting by now and as he glanced around, he realized he was not the only customer. The bar maid was waiting on an old man with a white beard and thin white hair in a short buzz cut sitting alone before a huge plate with a fish cascading off it, dead eyes and gaping mouth toward Zap, tail touching the counter on the other.

There were quite a few occupied tables, too. Mostly single people at tables barely lit by hurricane lamps that looked like real antiques, not reproductions, and possibly not electrified. A dowdy gray-haired woman regarded him through her glasses, sizing him up. She was hunkered over a bounteous salad. Without taking her gaze from him, she stuffed a great forkful of greens into her mouth and chomped with the grace and decorum of a half-starved donkey.

Zap thought it was odd that he'd not seen other cars in the parking lot, but then again it was dark and raining and he had focused on the door.

The portion sizes were enormous at any rate. He would be well fed.

He glanced at the drinks list:

[?]Sorry. Not meaning to be tricky or clever, I just love antiquated words. **caliginous** kuh-**lij**-uh-nuh s--adjective from the Latin from cālīgō: darkness, dim, murky

5

HOUSE WINES
RIPPER'S ROSÉ
MURKY MIRE MERLOT
SHIVERY CHABLIS
BLOOD LETTING RED
BELL WITCH WHITE
GIVES ME SHUDDERS CHARDONNAY

DRAFT BEERS
OFF SAISON
POLTERGIEST PORTER
BLOOD MOON IPA
HAUNTED HILLS PILSNER
LEATHER FACE LAGER
WICKED JACK PUMPKIN ALE
UNCANNY STOUT

"Whoa!" he said. "That's different." He needed a cold beer and he liked porters, so poltergeist porter was the choice there. He looked at the menu:

OFFERINGS TO START:

Ultimate Sacrifice Nachos: $8.00
choose chicken or chilli
comes with cheese, jalapenos, tomatoes and sour cream

Stuffed Skins: $7.50
six hot potato skins stuffed with bacon, cheddar
chives and sour cream

Suck on Them Bones: $9.00
short ribs to die for, a house favorite

Ritual Rings: $8.95
sweet vidalia onions glazed with honey
deep fried in killer batter with ranch dressing

CAULDRON OF THE DAY:

Bloody Mary Please Come Out: $7.95
tomato basil soup with deviled egg
finger sandwitches

SANDWITCHES:

Dead Body Wrap: seasoned chicken or tempeh $8.95
fajita, sauteed mushrooms, green peppers, onions,
salsa and sour cream preserved in a garlic herb wrap

The Beastie Burger: 13-ounce angus beef patty $12.95
grilled onions, swiss or provalone cheese,
lettuce, pickles on a homemade bun

Gracie was before him again, leaning forward, displaying a munificent cleavage while refilling his water glass. "What'll you have, Sugar?"

Zap startled and glanced up. "Uh, the porter, I guess."

"Oh, shit, Sugar, the Poltergeist has been acting up. I'm not sure if it's tapping out or if there's air in the line. It's been real ornery tonight. The Uncanny Stout's real good. How 'bout that?"

"Yeah, okay, I guess. That'll do."

"Know whatcha want to eat?"

"Uh, I haven't looked at everything yet, this is an interesting menu…"

She laughed, "Thanks! Me and my husband just *love* Halloween and anything to do with the classic monsters, so it's Halloween in here all year round. We met working at a haunted house and got married on Halloween. Our bridesmaids and groomsmen were all dressed in monster costumes. I was dressed like the Bride of Frankenstein of course, with my hair all out to here…" she waved a hand about a foot over her head. "And Franky, my husband was of course Frankenstein. His best man was a werewolf. Oh, man, that was something else."

"Sounds like it…well, guess I'll do the Beastie burger."

"Want to go all the way?" she asked with a wiggle.

"Huh?"

"Pickles, lettuce, tomato, mayo and mustard?"

"Oh, yeah." Zap said, exhaling.

"Hon, are you okay? You seem nervous. I won't bite you," Gracie said, patting his hand. "Oh, I *love* a man with them big ol' workin' hands."

Zap laughed uneasily, "No, just tired I guess." Zap pulled his hand back to the menu. Looking into Gracie's eyes was unsettling. He didn't want to stare at her breasts, so he looked down at the menu. The upside-down pentagrams bothered him, as did the words that popped out "skins," "dead," "ritual," and "bloody." He wondered about the pub name. Was that some satanic thing he didn't know about? Gracie was still hovering.

"Ya ought to look around before you leave. The whole place is decorated in Halloween and macabre stuff we collected over the years," she said waving a hand. While she was gesturing to look around, her torso took up a lot of his immediate view despite keeping his eyes down.

"I'll do that," Zap said, still focused on the menu. Say, what's BW&S stand for, anyway?"

"Beer, wine and spirits, Baby."

Zap looked up to find Gracie staring at him with a flirty smile. "I'll get your order in right quick. It'll be up in no time." She winked and glided away.

Zap heard a small bump on the bar in front of him. He looked up from the menu to see his perfectly poured stout. Gracie was nowhere in sight. He drank a few deep sips. It was malty, almost chewy, with a hint of chocolate at the back. Zap swiveled on the bar stool to survey the room and other patrons. The old woman was chewing her salad aggressively.

She must be hungry, he thought, *or that salad is really good.*

Coral Ardisia

It was the first day of sunshine in over two weeks. One of those glorious, glossy days after rough storms that seem especially blessed by God. After two weeks of rain and gloom with night temperatures heading towards freezing, it now felt like spring, delicious spring in the first week of February in North Central Florida.

"Global warming," Coral muttered, bemused.

She'd run her errands after lunch dashing to the post office, the library, the grocery store. With already an hour or more of daylight than just a few weeks before, there was plenty of time for some gardening before dark. Coral, an ardent gardener, itched to work in the yard with the intense need of an addict overdue for a fix.

Coral had been a middle child in a large family with an abusive father. Raised on neglect and disappointment, she'd survived by developing an insular steeliness. Perhaps her Germanic heritage contributed to her sense of self-sufficiency and order. Since her brief but disastrous marriage to a shifty man who left her and their young son for a woman half his age, she'd become wary of men in particular and people in general. She kept her house tidy with little clutter and everything in its place.

She enjoyed her cats and her solitude.

Working in the soil, puttering in her flower beds and the greenhouse fed her soul. But her vast knowledge of plants and landscaping and her earthy nature made her a natural instructor. She was a fixture in the University's Institute of Food and Agricultural Services, the go-to source for the best way to propagate vegetables and on early detection of root rot, fungus or parasites. Though she had few true friends, she was well-respected with a reputation for being honest, knowledgeable and straightforward.

Out on one of her constitutional walks just after the holidays, she's spotted some tell-tale coral ardisia berries along her favorite trail through her woods. She stopped and scowled, hands on her hips. "Oh no you don't. I'm not having it."

Birds ingested the berries and redeposited them, so to speak. Left unchecked, the woods would soon be overrun with hardy new plants. But between the horrid weather and a whopper of a head cold that had lingered over a week, Coral had hardly been out of the house since Christmas.

This irked her. So much time wasted!

January was the time to get out there, to work on the pathways, scan for the first signs of poison ivy, cut the vines and green briar. And oak tree seedlings! Nothing wrong with an oak tree, though the live oaks were the most desirable. She had to keep the laurel oak seedlings in check, or they'd be everywhere. Yes sir, this was the time. Once early spring came, it would be too late—all at once the new leaves would cloak the bare woods and make it harder to find the undesirables.

‖

Why, last year she'd rescued a native plum tree bent over double pulled down by vines. The poor thing had looked like a gymnast doing a back bend. She'd rescued it just in time to recover. So deprived of sunlight, it had lost most of its leaves even before winter set in. Since then, she'd watched the tree reach-reach-reach to right itself to a proper standing position. She looked forward to the seeing the delicate white flowers explode like popcorn come spring.

She'd had difficulty getting to sleep some nights just thinking about all the work to be done. And that ardisia in the woods! The berries dropping into the soil and taking root or birds feasting, seeds dispersing, *plop, plop, plop*! She'd even had a Nyquil-induced nightmare about pulling weeds. The more she pulled, the more appeared. She'd jolted awake fighting for breath. Her nostrils were completely blocked up; her pillow was wet with drool; her sheets damp with sweat.

But today, by golly, no excuses. She felt up to a bit of exercise and fresh air and see what was what.

"I'll just do a bit before it gets dark," Coral rationalized, changing into her yard clothes. She fetched a pair of gloves, a tarp and a shovel, and set off. Soon she was scowling over an extensive patch of the offending ardisia.

She'd once thought it was beautiful. Back in the day, she'd taken pity on one hearty plant covered in berries. It had appeared just before Christmas in a corner of her yard looking like a Christmas gift, a faux holly, all bright leaves and jolly berries shining out from the mulch--the one bright plant on a wintery gray day.

She'd learned the hard way. The next December there were twenty adult plants with tiny pups peeking up from the leaves.

"Just spray it with Rid-Up, that's what I do," someone had said.

"Right!" She'd countered. "Put more pesticides in the soil. You'll be drinking Rid-Up soon enough. Might's well mix it in your orange juice now like the orange juice growers. What do they care if you get cancer?"

The irony was not lost on Coral that she, Master Gardener and long-standing president of the Flower Power Garden Club, shared a name with her nemesis, one of the top invasive plants in Florida. She'd staged eradication events in local parks and given lectures about the havoc this well-adapted, insidious creeper could create in a woodsy habitat. And here it was in her own back yard.

Coral got down on her hands and knees and worked at pulling out the peripheral offenders. Younger with shallow and comparatively small roots, they pulled out easily.

Coral grunted with disgust as she discovered that under this juvenile ardisia hid a half-dozen baby pups all clustered together.

Yank…yank…yank.*Ya-annnk*!

Yank.

Yank, yank, yank YA…AANNNK!

The pile of pulled weeds on the tarp beside her quickly grew.

Coral grunted again and sat back on her heels.

"Whew."

She should have brought out a bottle of water with her, but, no matter, she wouldn't be at it much longer. She wiped a bead of sweat from her temple.

"I'll get this bunch and the ones there covered with berries and I'll stop," she said aloud. Coral, now in her early seventies, had long tended to speak out loud for company.

"Right. Out YOU come," she said, eyeing a particularly bushy specimen. She stood up and grasped the shovel, taking a moment to catch her breath. Her body reminded her of the month of relative inactivity. She felt achy and tired already.

"Come on old girl," she encouraged herself. "Just a bit more. Can't leave *that* out here. We'll get this monster then go in."

She pushed the shovel in and wiggled it around searching for that perfect access up under the root ball. The point of the shovel hit something hard with a dull *thunk*. She tried again. The shovel tip veered off of an invisible ledge.

"Must be an oak tree root there," she grumbled.

She stood back. A leggy beauty berry bush blocked her access from this direction; a hickory seedling was in the way for an attack from that side. She shifted the shovel and tried again. This time, she felt roots breaking under its pressure.

"Aha! Gotcha!"

She tipped the shovel; the plant keeled over. Coral reached down and snatched it down low towards the ground.

YAAAAA--AANK!

She lost her balance and tipped backwards when the plant came free. Righting herself, she tossed the plant on the top of the pile with a victorious flourish.

She took a breath and clapped some dirt off her gloves. There were still so many. Where had they all come from? Three large ones were *covered* in berries. She'd have to be extra careful with those. Just one lost berry and the game would start all over again.

"Oh my. Where did you come from?" How had she not noticed those before? This was awful. She'd have to come back out tomorrow and make a day of it. She leaned on the shovel handle regarding another little community of baby ardisias with dismay. They were snugged up against the base of a dead oak tree, crisscrossed by green briar.

"I knew I should've brought the clippers," she said with a disapproving cluck.

She knew she was over-tired, close to that tell-tale dangerous place of fatigue where one could get sloppy and have an accident.

"Just this last bit, then I'm done."

The sun was lower through the trees and the air was getting chilly. But Coral didn't notice the cooler air, in fact, it felt good. She'd worked up quite a sweat. With satisfaction, she regarded the tarp she'd put down to contain the pulled weeds. It was invisible under the great mound of roots reaching up at all angles from the pile like crooked fingers, some fat as carrots. The snarl of green leaves and berries looked like a holiday holly display hit by a hurricane. She turned her attention to the next offender and raised the shovel.

"I'm...going...to get you...evil thing..." Coral panted, working the shovel under the motherlode of plants. By far the tallest she'd ever seen, this plant had stems shooting out in all directions, and each stem was loaded with berries. Coral just couldn't seem to get under it. It must have grown over a tree root. She kept hitting something hard. The plant shook as if mocking her.

Sweat beads ran down her flushed face. Her back and arms ached.

"You...are... the... last... one." She puffed.

15

The shovel handle snapped in half, throwing Coral off balance.

"Oh! Ow! Ow!" She yelled, tumbling into a long wild blackberry vine that grabbed and tugged at her skin like tiny vicious fishhooks, ripping jagged holes along her forearms. One particularly nasty strand reached around the back of her head, grabbing her neck.

"Ow!" she howled. "Oh, Mercy!"

She struggled to stay calm and work herself out of the strands of blackberry. It seemed that for each bit she extracted from her skin, somewhere else, another strand grabbed her. She'd often had the creeping suspicion, a niggling fear, really, that plants had a collective consciousness, a cross-species sympathy, such that while she was digging up and cutting out an invasive, sympathetic plants nearby would grab and poke at her to impede her progress. These thoughts usually came to her when she was approaching exhaustion.

She twisted slowly towards an opening in the snarl of briars.

Thunk!

A dead branch fell on her head.

Her hands flew up defensively. Coral fell hard on one knee. A briar sliced her face like a razor. She felt the blood run on her cheek.

"Ow! Ow!" she screamed, her mind caving to the irrational thought that the plants were teaming up against her in earnest, getting their revenge.

The pitch of her screams changed abruptly; the pitiful cries of pain become shrieks of hysteria. Had a neighbor heard her cries, so shrill, so agonized, he or she would have called for the police on instinct, sure a vicious assault was in progress. Alas,

Coral was in the midst of her woods at dusk, acres away from the nearest neighbors who were in for the night, lighting their wood fires, cooking supper or watching football on their widescreen televisions.

Coral's left shoe was somehow coming off--no being *pulled off*, by a rubbery, probing mass of finger-like tubers: tenacious root balls reached up her foot and grabbed hold of her ankle. She struggled to stay upright but the shocking pain lacerating her everywhere—hands, face, ankles, midriff all at once--was too much.

She collapsed into darkness.

Coral's son Dan arrived at her house shortly before nine the following morning to take her to her doctor's appointment. He left the car running and went to the door. Normally, she came out as soon as she heard the car. He'd expected her to come out, handbag in hand.

Odd, he thought. She's always on time.

The door was unlocked; he stepped inside. "Mom, it's me. Are you ready?"

No answer.

The light was on in the kitchen but there was no sign that she'd had breakfast. The Mr. Coffee pot was empty. That wasn't like her either, he thought with growing concern.

"Mom?"

She'd planned a full day of it. After the doctor's appointment, they'd go to lunch, then a camelia show she'd been talking about for weeks. Where could she be?

He dashed through the house and upstairs, hoping to God she hadn't fallen in the bathtub or something.

"Mom?"

She was not upstairs. He scurried back downstairs and outside, calling as he made his way around the house. He ran a hand through his hair and gazed out beyond her perfectly landscaped *House and Gardens* yard towards the path to the woods. He trotted along the path looking side to side for her. Dread shot through his body when he spotted the broken shovel off the path. He recognized it as her favorite "Jersey shovel" as she'd called it, because it was short and easy to put in the trunk of a car. He didn't really get the implication until later while binge-watching old episodes of "The Sopranos" and watched Paulie dispose of a body.

He called out, "Mom? Mom!" knowing with a sick feeling in his gut that he wouldn't hear a reply. Turning to go back to the house, when he saw a bit of shoe sticking out from under a patch of deep green leaves.

"Oh, God, Mom!" he said, slowly realizing her body was twisted in a thicket of briars that looked like razor wire wrapped around her legs, arms and body.

Dan struggled with his speech for the funeral. Several times he began to scribble out, *she died doing what she loved, gardening,* but the look of sheer terror on her face kept coming back to him. He crumpled page after page.

The official cause of death was dehydration and hypothermia. Though in the seventies during the day, the temperature had plummeted into the forties during the night. She must have overworked herself then succumbed to the damp ground and cold air was the official report. It sounded plausible, and yet how had she gotten so thoroughly tangled like that? She'd looked trussed and hogtied…

Dan had directed that in lieu of flowers, a donation could be made to the garden club. The funeral was small and simple. As Dan had expected, a modest group from the University came out of respect, but no one demonstrated any true grief. The service was brief. Dan felt like a zombie at the podium reading his speech knowing he was the only one who would really miss her. It was all he could do to stand before the wooden-faced gathering. His heart wrenched by conflicting emotions while he looked out at a sea of flat expressions. Some checked their watches. Some had the audacity to be texting or scrolling on their cell phones. He gripped the podium and addressed a spot on the back wall. He got through it without breaking down. Then it was limp handshakes and condolences at the door and on to round two of this awful process: the cemetery.

Just a handful came to the grave site. Coral had always said the Micanopy cemetery was the most beautiful she'd ever seen with old oaks, camelias and azaleas amidst the old tombstones. Of course she was being interred in the newer section which was not as established with flora, but it was still pretty. She'd pre-paid for her spot decades before, making the final arrangements easy for him. So typical of her to be so organized.

It hadn't been Dan's idea to bury her on Valentine's Day, but it was when the funeral director could schedule it. The cemetery director said that Dan could have an azalea planted near her headstone if he wished, after the funeral. He'd willingly paid extra for that small tribute.

The weather had turned grim again. Frost and freeze warnings for several nights running, bone-chilling cold mornings with blustery gray days as a cold front swept across the southeast.

Not optimal conditions for a grave-side service.

The few attendees huddled under the canopy looking uncomfortable as the bushy-eyebrowed minister droned on about grace, life everlasting and heavenly rest.

Dan cast the first pile of dirt onto the casket. He could hardly see through his tears. Coral's voice echoed in his head. "You have to have good soil. Good soil is the key."

Lost in his world of shock and bereavement, he was slow to notice the nervous twitter of suppressed giggles from a few ladies huddled together under an umbrella. Dan pulled himself back from childhood memories of planting annuals with his mother. He and the minister swiveled their heads toward the rude interruption. The women looked up with looks of sheepishness mixed with concern.

What on earth were they going on about? Dan wondered, glaring at them. How could they be so callous? A private joke? Tasteless. He followed their glances. There was the headstone Coral had preordered, a practical, modest stone with just room enough for her name and the key dates. Was that it? Perhaps it was unusual to have the grave marker in place so early, but it was ready so why not? Hardly something to laugh about. There was the wreath that Dan had ordered and some other flowers… and *what was that?*

This area of the cemetery was mostly a field of dead grass. Yet, surrounding the stone and the cascade of funerary mums, there was a glossy ring of green leaves with jaggedy little edges like a fairy circle. He'd not noticed that before. Well, he'd been in such a horrible numb fog, it made sense he'd missed it. But it was peculiar, this bold outcropping around the head stone. In fact, looking around, he spotted more. It was like the funeral party was surrounded. Dan scanned the other grave sites and the open field. Dead grass. This seemed to be the only place with the holly-like greenery. In fact, looking again, there seemed to be even more than he'd just noticed. There. And there.

21

He heard one of the women whisper, "Look. Coral ardisia. How ironic is that? Coral would just *die* if she saw —"

Realizing Dan was staring at her, the woman's mouth stretched out in an oops-you-caught-me grimace. "Oh, sorry," she mumbled with an awkward laugh. She covered her mouth with a hand and turned to hide amongst the other women.

TWO

Zap had finished the second glass of water and was almost finished with the Uncanny Stout when Gracie appeared in front of him with his plate. Well, one could hardly see the plate as it was loaded with the biggest burger Zap had seen, plus a mountain of fries and extra lettuce and tomatoes.

"Here you go, Baby," she said, setting it in front of him. "The Beastie. Say, Sugar, what's your name, anyway? You look like a Dave. I bet your name's Dave, isn't it? I'm good with guessin' names." Her eyes gleamed in expectation of being correct.

"Zap. Real name's Zachary, but I got electrocuted a few times when I started out, so I've been Zap for years."

Zap eyed the burger unsure of how to attack it. This was the kind of burger you had to pick up and squeeze tight, you'd never be able to set it down again, or all the layers of goodies would tumble out.

Gracie laughed out loud, "Well, ain't that somethin'? Zap. Oh, I like that a lot. Ready for another Uncanny?"

"Yeah," Zap said. He gulped down the rest of the beer and passed her the empty glass. As he negotiated the massive burger, he heard Gracie in conversation with a lone man at a table for two behind him.

"Good to see you, Lester. Been to the market lately?"

"Naw, been feelin' poorly."

"Aw, I wondered. Haven't seen you around much."

"My brother Bill came to visit for a while, up from Florida."

"Oh? Didja have a good visit?"

"Yeah. Good to see him again. He and I ran a pawn shop together for years before he and Debbie moved to Florida. We were both born pickers. Used to bring home stuff from the dump all the time. Drove our mother nuts."

Zap gripped the burger and took his first bite. Even if he hadn't been ravenous, it would have been the best burger he'd ever eaten: cooked to perfection, a hint of pink on the inside, and so juicy. He felt like a hyena attacking its prey as he sank his teeth into the burger again and again.

Mr. Fanshawe: "...and might you have any field glasses?"

Squire Richards: "I have, but they're not things I use myself, and I don't know whether the ones I have will suit you. They're old-fashioned, and about twice as heavy as they make 'em now. You're welcome to have them, but *I* won't carry them."

--from "A View from a Hill" by M. R. James

Night Vision

Only the hardcore vendors had braved the grim morning to set out their wares in the dark. And it was *dark*. The pole barn structures of the Can-Doo Flea Market might protect one from rain, but they also trapped the cold air that clung to the impartial concrete slabs below them. The meager bulbs overhead were far apart and offered up the kind of illumination that a firefly might offer to a lost camper on a moonless night straining to find his bearings on a well-worn map.

It was a blustery December Sunday, a wintery day by Florida standards with a kaleidoscope-of-charcoal sky and wet-cold gusts of wind that would pry at the collar and coat seams for access to one's heart. The temperature in the early hours of morning dove into the low twenties.

Bill was a picker. He canvassed yard sales, flea markets and pawn shops looking for odd things he might resell or salvage for himself. He was up early that morning, his body jabbing him with the familiar aches and pains reminding him of the various accidents on the road and in the garage over the years. Not the best time to have decided to get off the Tramadol, not that it had been working so well anymore. The side effects had been more annoying than the pain. He'd done his stretching exercises and drank two helpings of the "anti-inflammatory shake" his daughter had foisted on him. He swallowed an ibuprofen with the last gulp of "greeny goodness". It wasn't so bad. He liked spinach, and turmeric was supposed to be the miracle cure for everything. He took more time than usual dressing that morning, rubbing on the fragrant oil that seemed to ease his back pain before donning layers. He took a thermos of coffee with him to warm his wiry frame and spirits.

It was daylight when he parked his old pickup truck in the customer lot and ventured toward the most likely barn to hold hidden treasures. A crusty old vendor named Caleb specialized in funky fragments from history: butter molds, coal bed-warmers, old coins, military uniforms and suchlike.

Caleb was there as usual, a knit cap on his head, his hands in the pockets of an oversized bomber jacket. His Mark Twain mustache parted in a smile upon seeing Bill.

"Mornin', Bill."

"Caleb, how're you?"

"Creaky and cold."

"Same!"

"Cold as a Polar bear's nose," Caleb said with a half-smile.

"Not many vendors today, but I knew you'd show."

27

Caleb looked up and down the aisle. Most of the vendor stalls were vacant. "I'm always here. The day I don't show, well, you'll know I didn't wake up."

"I hear ya," Bill nodded.

"Whatcha lookin' for today?" Caleb asked, running a hand over his mustache.

"Same as always. A bargain."

Caleb laughed and pointed an elbow toward some shabby boxes under a table. "Got some new stuff at an auction on Thursday in them boxes down there. Haven't really looked through it all, to tell ya the truth, so none of it's priced. Figured I'd work on it some today. Don't expect to be overrun with customers."

Bill glanced down the aisleway of the barn. There was only one other customer at the far end buying a coffee at the food kiosk.

"Nah, don't guess you will."

"You're free to pick through it. I'll price it if ya see anything looks good to ya."

Bill nodded. He pulled a flashlight out of his pocket and set down his thermos. Flipping on the light, he crouched under the table and began rooting through the boxes. He perused the top layer of miscellany pulling out a small box of brass doorknobs, a boot jack, a pair of ice tongs and a clunker of a lamp that might have come off a Model T Ford. He set the unwanted items aside and kept digging.

Caleb stamped his feet. "Damn. Should have put on them merry-no socks."

Bill frowned. "Merry-no?"

"Yeah, you know them wool socks 'at don't itch."

Ah, he means merino, Bill thought. He'd reached the bottom layer of stuff in the box. Nothing there. "I hear you," he said rubbing his hands together partly to keep them warm but partly in anticipation of digging through the next box.

He put the items he'd pulled out back with care and moved on to the next box.

Nothing of interest there either. Perhaps today would be unfruitful. Could have slept in. But the axioms his grandmother always used to say, "The early bird catches the worm" and "You won't know until you try" niggled at his mind so he kept digging.

Hmm. What's this? A box full of yellowed tissue paper protecting small dense objects. He unwrapped the first one. A silver pocket watch with the fob. Good shape. He opened the next one. These were in great condition and he might be able to resell them at a steampunk event. The punkers with money ate that shit up. He opened a few more of the little bundles.

"Here… didja see these?" Bill asked raising one up. "Watcha want for 'em? I'll buy the box if the price is right."

Caleb squinted. "Lemme see 'at."

Bill pushed the box out toward Caleb who took it, grunting. He pulled off his thick gloves and pawed through the unwrapped bundles with his meaty hands, his fingers like blunt red sausages. He grunted again. "How many are there?" he muttered to himself counting the bundles. Seven. All different. All in better-than-average condition.

They haggled over the price for a while before coming to an agreement.

The box was set aside, and Bill went back to rooting through the remaining boxes.

"Ahh... well now," he said, pulling out a helmet with a contraption on the top that looked like the kind of optical apparatus found in an optometrist's examining room.

Caleb leaned forward and made a face. "Oh, whatcha got there? Pull it out. Here," Caleb shifted some rusty tools to make room. Let's have a look."

They set the heavy helmet on the clear spot of table.

"Never seen anything like this," Bill said with a hint of excitement in his voice.

"Gotta be military," Caleb said.

"Looks ancient! World War Two era, do you think?" Bill asked, peering at it front to back. "It's so beat up. Wonder if it's still got all the lenses and stuff..."

"Probably doesn't work," Caleb said. "Old binoculars don't hold up too well. I got a box somewhere here full of 'em. The lenses get all cloudy. The technology has gotten so much better--"

"Don't see any manufacture marks. Maybe inside--"

Caleb examined the exterior framework of lenses while Bill inspected the interior.

"Crazy," Caleb said, shaking his head.

"I *thinnk*..." Bill said in speculation, "that this is some kind of early night-vision wear. Wonder if they still work. I can't really tell, there's too much light."

"But night vision didn't come along until the Vietnam era, I thought," said Caleb, pulling on his brushy mustache.

"I think I read somewhere that the Germans were working on the technology during the war," Bill said, picking it up and looking inside. "Huh. There might be a stamp mark here... can't really tell… I'd need a magnifier. Man, this sure is a hefty. Look at all this stuff! He pointed to the metal extensions and setting adjusters. "I'm going to try it on, okay?"

"Go ahead, just be careful."

Bill took off his hat, laid it aside and eased the helmet over his head.

"This weighs a ton! Dang!"

Caleb touched a casing at the base of the helmet, "Looks like a battery pack there. Probably standard batteries…mm-hmm…weight at the back to counterbalance all the stuff up front. Smart."

"A-yup. Well, you'd need new batteries and a dark room, I'll tell you that for free," Caleb said with a snigger.

"Well, no way you'd be moving fast with this on," Bill said, adjusting the helmet. "I can already feel a headache comin' on." He eased the helmet back off. "I'd love to try this at night. Out by my place, it gets real dark."

"Somethin' like *that*, I'd need to do some research to price…"Caleb said. "Probably not rare if it's military, but—"

"Right, right, of course…" Bill said, reluctant to let go of the helmet. "But it isn't in great shape…looks at this dent here on the side—"

"'Course I could ask Jerry—"

"And like you said, it probably doesn't work, it'd be just the historic value—"

"—he's like a reg'lar walking encyclopedia about military equipment—"

"Sure, sure, I could come back in a little while if you wanted to think about a price—"

"Could look it up and see if I can find listings—"

Later that morning, the deal was made, and Bill took his treasures home. There would be a new moon in a few days. *Optimal for opti-cal*, he thought with a chuckle. He couldn't wait to get back to his computer to do some research. *Sure hope I can find batteries*, he thought.

The new moon came with a cold front and a frost warning. The insulation on the old mobile home was minimal, but Bill wasn't about to give one more cent to the power company than he had to, so as usual, he had an impressive fire going in the fireplace. Bill cradled the bowl of beef and barley soup in one hand and a beer in the other and set them on the hearth. He pulled his recliner closer to the fireplace and settled in.

As he enjoyed the warmth of the simple supper, he contemplated the best places to test his new find. He'd done a bit of research. Best guess was, the helmet was manufactured in the late 1950s or early 1960s—a time before the technology hit its stride. Its weight meant that a wearer would remain stationary under optimal conditions of lighting and battery charge: a sniper in position for his target to step into view. He'd studied all the dials and settings and thought he had a pretty good idea of how it worked, and boy, did he hope it worked. What would he be able to see?

Bill downed his soup and beer in haste, eager to get outside. He took his empty bowl and bottle to the kitchen, then bundled up in a coat, hat and scarf. He'd have to remain barehanded to make adjustments. He retrieved the helmet and put it on. Feeling for and finding a knob near his left ear, he clicked it on. A responding hum came from the battery pack at the base of his skull. He moved to the front door and turned out the hall light and outside light. The front door looked like a grainy-green fuzz with a blobby bubble in the bottom left corner. Turning what he thought was a focus dial, the view cleared marginally. It reminded Bill of the annoying eye test questions, "This…or this," when the eye doctor switched lenses and the difference was so miniscule, one wondered if they were really the same and it was a cruel prank. "Uh, the first one, I think. Wait. Can I see the other one again?"

Turning another knob sharpened the contrast. Ah! Door panel details replaced the blur except for the warped bubble in the lower left corner.

"Ho, ho!" he chortled. He opened the door and stepped out into the December night.

Driveway…grass…gate… Bill made his way to the side of the house, surprised and pleased with how well he could see. The appurtenance was primitive and there was that annoying blotch of vision to work around, but he could see in the dark. He thought of the story of Alexander Bell calling out, "Mr. Watson, come here—I want to see you!" He felt an inkling of the thrill of the discovery of new technology. He was seeing through an early version of night goggles — what a tickle!

A small dark blur dashed into a nearby bush close to his feet.

What was that? Bill jumped.

Probably a rabbit.

He wished it weren't so darned cold. He'd lived up north B.D.--Before Debbie — and had come close to hypothermia enough times that he'd lost all tolerance for cold weather. Despite all the layers, he could feel the wet cold trying to get to his chest. The hairs in his nostrils prickled when he inhaled.

The top of an oak tree shivered in a breeze *shwee-wee-shwee — weesh* like children whispering at night when they were supposed to be asleep.

Crack!

A branch snapped behind him. Bill swung his head to follow the sound. The helmet swooped forward and slid. A lens banged his nose.

"Ow!" Bill pushed the lens off his nose and rubbed it. It sure smarted, but it would be fine. He pulled on the chin strap, but it was already at its tightest setting.

A large owl from a branch overhead swooped down as if to swat at Bill for disturbing its hunt. It flew so close Bill could see its intense eyes. Without a sound, it glided toward the pasture ahead. While it was unsettling that he'd been unaware of his proximity to the big bird, he was excited to see it with the night vision. What a hoot it would be to see the coyotes he often heard late at night. Or a bobcat. He'd found a bit of scat a back in summer--mostly fur and not covered over the way a house cat rakes kitty litter. That was a bobcat poop, he was pretty sure. If there was frost, he might see tracks.

Shwee-wee-shwee-shee. As more trees joined the whispered conversation, Bill felt the cold settling on his nose and cheeks with the tenacity of a face mask. The cold pried at the thin gap between the scarf and the helmet.

Shuffling in the brush to his left. His nose reminded him of the helmet just in time. He turned his head, slower this time, and missed whatever it was. The grass swayed where something had disturbed it.

Probably an opossum.

He moved out toward the pasture, visually sweeping right to left, left to right. For a split second, he thought he saw a man standing to his left. Looking at it full-on, it was just a dark fencepost covered in English ivy. The ivy reached up into a tree above and did resemble a tall emaciated person. Stretched and distorted by the damaged lens, it had, for just that second, appeared to be reaching toward him.

He unhitched the gate lock and strode out in the open field. It was colder here, away from trees and buildings. He scanned right to left, left to right and saw nothing. There was a cold silence now: no breeze, no owls, nothing.

It's a cold night. This was stupid. All the animals are denned up now. You should go inside yourself. Try this again another night.

His nose hairs were beginning to feel taut; each hair threatened to become its own icicle. His inner ears hurt. His toes and the end of his nose felt like hardening ice cubes. His body urged him to go inside, to get warm, to stop this nonsense.

He remained still.

What was that?

As if he'd sprouted out of the ground, an old black man in overalls walked with a garden hoe over his shoulder toward the

35

opposite gate. He paused where the gate hitch was, then walked through the gate and disappeared.

Bill blinked.

Did I just see a ghost?

He reviewed what he'd seen. The man had just manifested--poof--like in a magician's trick. He'd been wearing a thin white shirt and might have been barefoot. If he'd had feet. The legs weren't distinct. There was *no way* anyone would dress like that let alone be gardening with a hoe at this hour. He *had* seen a ghost! He'd never seen one before. He wasn't sure what he felt: excited, frightened, confused, but above all, really cold. He put purpose into his strides and went back inside.

Bill woke the next morning with a whopper of a head cold and stiff achy joints. He spent the day huddled by the fireplace blowing his nose and drinking chicken broth. On more than one occasion, he found himself on autopilot, heading toward the medicine cabinet in search of the Tramadol. He took a hot shower and downed an ibuprofen and some cold medicine. He slept a lot.

At night, lying on the couch close to the fireplace, he thought he heard footsteps outside just under the window. *Most likely an armadillo,* he thought, knowing one can make enough noise to sound like a full-grown man in boots stomping around. Bill shifted position to look through the dirty window. For just a second, he thought he saw glowing red eyes looking back at him, eyes at the base of the window as if some creature was peering in as he peered out, eyes reflecting the red-orange from the firelight behind him, *but that wouldn't be possible,* he thought. *My body is blocking that light, isn't it?* He turned to look at the fireplace behind him, his mind sluggishly affirming that his body was blocking the light in the strange eyes. When he turned his head back, the glowing eyes were not there. *Had they been at all?* He rubbed his eyes. The window ledge was knee-high off the floor, so a creature looking in would have to be over two-feet tall to see in...

Had he not been sick, he would have been alarmed, would possibly have gone outside to investigate, but his head was heavy with congestion. Breathing took up most of his energy. He pulled the heavy drapes shut and sank onto the couch.

He fell into a troubled sleep, waking intermittently gasping for breath as his nostrils had blocked up. He woke, blew his nose and returned to disturbing dreams of shifting shadows and strange creatures with gaping mouths. In one dream, he wandered in dense woods at dusk, no sign of a path or landmark to get his bearings. Distorted, disembodied voices called out, unnatural sounds like the last syllables spoken from an old record player still running though the power had been turned off.

Bill's heavy cold and the cold weather lasted for several days but he was up and out of the house that Thursday feeling better than he had in over two weeks. He was off to a promising estate sale. He wanted to be at the front of the line, first to get to the goodies in the garage. Nothing of interest in the house he knew, he'd studied the preview photos in the emailed sales notice. But the garage and outbuildings were packed with tools, antiques and tantalizing old boxes. He just knew this sale would be a gold mine, and it was. Bill drove home with a truck bed full of treasures he could resell for triple what he'd just paid. He spent the next week sorting, pricing and listing items online.

He'd forgotten about the goggles until he almost knocked them off a shelf he'd set them on. *Oh, yeah! Hmm. Tonight would be perfect. Cloudy, not too cold. Not enough moon to be a problem.* He moved them from the garage to the bench by the front door and then went back to taking pictures and pricing.

Bill had two beers with dinner. Why not? No guilt now, no conflict with meds.

He was putting on his jacket when the thought of the ghost came to him. He eyed the liquor cabinet. A shot of whiskey for fortitude wouldn't hurt. Just a shot. He got a small glass, poured and gulped it down. *Arrr.* It was good. Why had he gulped it? No rush. He savored the warmth in his mouth and throat. *Maybe just one more.* He poured another. This time he drank it slower, letting the friendly flavor roll around in his mouth before swallowing it. When he was finished, he set the glass down and headed down the hall, picking up a flashlight before going out the door.

Bill picked up the helmet and eased it on his head, snugging the chin strap. The moon glistened through wisps of half-hearted clouds—it reminded Bill of his youth and girlfriends in sheer lingerie. The night was still, save for a chuck will's widow in the distance. Though he tried not to make any noise, Bill's steps sounded loud and clumsy to him, hardly stealthy. He walked with purpose toward the gate and opened it as quietly as he could. The metal *click--shwing* startled two doves in a cypress tree to Bill's right—they flew out and away, their distinctive cooing, flapping sound fading into the woods on the near edge of the pasture.

Something scuttled under a cypress tree.

Bill moved out into the open and turned in place. A bunny darted from a tump² of tall grass and sprinted pell-mell across the open expanse toward the trees.

Except for the blur spot, these things work pretty good, Bill thought with satisfaction. *Wait, what's that?*

Something had been chasing the bunny. No, not something. Several somethings.

Whoa! What are those? Giant fireflies?

Bill frowned and blinked.

A pack of luminous oblong shapes were six feet or so behind the bunny in hot pursuit. The bunny leapt into the brush out of view. As if realizing they'd lost their prey, the translucent things came to an abrupt stop. They weren't running on legs; They were *gliding* just above the ground. Bill counted nine of them. He could see dead grass through them, but there was a density about their

---

² I know tump isn't a word. My mom's best friend, an avid fisherwoman, once explained that my line snagged on a "tump" of grass. You know what it means. Wad. Clump. Lump. Gilda is gone. I want her word to live on.

cores that fluttered and pulsed with an ill-defined motion in lavender hues—organs moving? Lungs? Heart?

Bill was so stunned by what he was seeing that he dropped the heavy flashlight. The *clunk* as the flashlight hit the ground startled the things. Their heads whipped around in unison, then *pa-shoo!* They darted away in all directions and disappeared like shooting stars—bright bursts that disappeared into nothing.

Bill blinked again.

As newlyweds, Bill and Debbie had taken a week-long trip to the Virgin Islands on their honeymoon. One day, out snorkeling with a group, Bill dove down to follow a clown fish and found himself in a colony of jellyfish. He'd never seen anything like them. They were domed like two dinner plates stuck together and almost invisible but for their faint purple hues like pale cellophane. They hung suspended like clear naval mines or ornaments on an invisible water tree. Twisting his torso to avoid one near his chest, he bumped one with his forehead. It was surprisingly dense but did not sting. Another one bumped his stomach. He looked up, down and side to side searching for an open area. They were everywhere. He had to go up for air.

If they had been the stinging kind of jellyfish, he'd have panicked. Instead, he felt like Aquaman playing soccer, allowing them to bounce off him as he rose to the surface.

He'd somehow gotten separated from Debbie. When they met back up and took off their snorkels, he asked, "Did you see those crazy jellyfish?"

She frowned, "What jellyfish? No. Did you see the baby octopus?"

"But they were big as dinner plates! They were all around. Kind of purple, but see-through. You must've felt them."

Debbie shook her head.

Like then, he wished he had a witness. These things he'd just seen looked like flying ghost otters. Long sleek bodies. Fat graceful tails. Graceful and silent, fast and *hovering*. He hadn't felt frightened or alarmed, just astonished. He had really seen them, right? Yes. Right there. He bent down and picked up the flashlight. Now closer to the ground, he could see a faint depression of a bunny trail just where the bunny had been. The bunny was real. The bunny was definitely running from something. From *them*. He stood up.

The wigglings of the weird dreams he'd had while sick squirmed around in his memory. Strange beings. Dark shadows moving just at the edges of his peripheral vision.

Far away he heard the faint '*whip-poor-will, whip-poor-will*' call of a chuck will's widow. Bill wasn't a birder, heck, he couldn't identify most of the birds he saw or heard. But this particular bird caught his interest as he often heard them at night. Usually just one. The call was sing-songy and pleasant like any songbird, yet soulful, wistful. But this was no sweet songbird. Hardly. This small bird with plumage the color of dead leaves was a fierce predator, a terrifying monster of a bird. With large hawk-like eyes, it was able to spot prey from quite a distance. Unlike the hawk, it didn't rely on sharp talons. Its enormous mouth could expand to envelope insects, frogs and smaller birds down the gullet, just like that. Sweet song from a fiendish mouth.

This would have been great camping weather: not too cold, but great for talking by a fire or sleeping under a heap of blankets. But just standing there, he felt the cold creeping from his feet up to his ankles and in the gap between his scarf and the helmet. He gripped the flashlight and walked further out in the pasture.

Ah! Movement along the far fence line caught his attention. One, two… three deer hopped over the fence and strolled out heading away from Bill. They were upwind. Bill froze. They hadn't seen him.

Two does and a yearling. Same bunch as usual, Bill thought. He often saw them passing by his kitchen window early in the morning about the time he made coffee.

He watched them for a few moments. While it was fun to see them in the goggles, this was hardly anything new and it was cold. He changed direction to angle to the corner of the field and loop back to the house. Tromping across the familiar patch, his mind wandered to what might be on television when he got back to the house…maybe another beer…and what about the flea market this weekend, was it worth going? Now at the gate, he turned his head once more to scan the pasture. Nothing. All was still. Even the chuck will's widow was silent.

This was where the ghost man was. Right here at the gate. He glanced behind him. Nothing. *Wonder how often he shows up. Could be every night. Could be once a year…during a new moon. Who knows?*

A hot shower would be good, relax his shoulders and back muscles… Yes, a hot shower and some of that liniment stuff… He closed the gate behind him and walked back toward the house. The helmet felt heavier now and was giving him a headache. He was passing an old hickory tree when he stopped in his tracks and did a double take.

"What the hell are *you?*"

Hanging in the branches were cat-sized creatures with huge oval eyes. He had never seen anything like this before, though

42

they looked sort of like sloths—weird dopey faces and listless bodies.

He stared.

They hung upside down like hairy bats. A few turned their heads to look at him; most seemed asleep.

It's the goggles. Bill pulled the goggles off his head and turned on his flashlight, directing the beam at the hickory. Normal branches. No creatures.

He reversed the procedure and looked again through the goggles. One of the creatures opened its mouth in a great gaping yawn.

This can't be happening. I'm seeing things. You are a crazy stoonad.

'Stoonad' meant idiot. It had been a staple of his father's vocabulary and one of many unsavory names Bill and his siblings had suffered under his father's roof. Bill's father had been a disdainful Italian, holding few people with any regard.

He took the helmet off again and flipped on the flashlight. Nothing.

It was tempting to see if he could touch one of them, feel it, but it was all just too weird.

Ghosts, invisible creatures — what next? No, let's not go there. I'm done.

Bill quickened his pace, reached his house, went in and locked the door behind him. Later, beer in hand, by the warmth of the fire, he ruminated on what he'd seen. Surely, he'd imagined them. But why? He was one of the earthier people he knew. He wasn't like Joey or Derek who believed every bogus alien or Big Foot story, doctored videos of ghosts and ghouls parading around in jiffy stores after hours. No, Bill was a guy's guy. Okay, he'd had a couple beers. But he'd been drinking beer his whole life. And okay, he got into the weed on occasion, but still. He never dropped acid or did any hard drugs. He didn't hallucinate. What was going on?

It was only with the goggles. But how was that?

The weekend rolled around, but Bill stayed away from the Can-Doo market. He knew he'd run into Caleb and he'd be compelled to tell him about the crazy shit he'd seen in the goggles. Caleb would think he'd lost his mind. Hell, *he* wondered if he'd lost his mind. No, he stayed away and spent the weekend concentrating on his listings. There were a few sales right off the bat, that was good. He made two trips to the post office with parcels — brass dog bookends to North Carolina, an Art Deco humidor to Texas, a box of antique woodworking planes to New Hampshire.

Sweet.

Bill felt energized by the sales, eager to put more of his vast accumulation of stuff out there. On Tuesday and Wednesday that week the weather was just too gorgeous to stay inside all day. The clear skies and spring temperatures lured Bill out to take long walks in the woods of local parks. The exercise made him stiff the next morning, but by midday, after a shower and some movement, he felt pretty good. The stiffness abated enough to encourage more outings.

No hallucinations during the day or night. In fact, nothing out of the ordinary at all. He wasn't sure what to think about the weird episodes with the goggles. Perhaps if he got someone else to wear the goggles—see if they saw something weird. But what if they didn't? He felt torn between wanting desperately to talk about what he'd seen and not wanting to be perceived as a nut job, a *stoonad*.

Thursday night found Bill going through the television channel options for the third time and finding nothing. He felt the pull of the goggles down the hall as if they were calling to him. He wanted to try them one more time just as much as he was afraid to try them one more time.

"Oh, what the hell," he said aloud. He finished his beer and got out of the recliner.

The moon was close to full that night which aggravated the distortion in the lower left side of his view. This time, he decided to walk down the dirt road out to the paved road instead. This would give him a glimpse of the south end of the pasture before putting him in woods most of the way. A creek ran through a culvert under the road down close to the mailboxes. Maybe he'd see raccoons.

Bill strode down his driveway looking side to side. A bit of a breeze now and then whispered in the canopy overhead, *shwee-wee-weesh*.

He passed the entrance to his driveway. Debbie's concrete angel met him with its usual serenity. Deb had collected angels and had insisted on an angel at the property entrance. Out in the country, you could tell the social and anti-social, humorous and reclusive people by their driveways. Cutesy women put out cutesy WELCOME flags with bright colors and cartoony characters; fishermen had fish mailboxes; attention-seekers had six-foot metal chicken sculptures and Debbie the Sunday school teacher had a four-foot concrete angel at the gate. He hadn't appreciated it while she was alive, but now it was a link to her. While it once annoyed him, now he couldn't part with it, though just now it irked him that the angel's eyes were cast down. Why couldn't she have a reassuring smile? Why wouldn't she meet his eyes?

Sensing more than hearing movement overhead, his eyes were drawn upwards. He had to steady the helmet with one hand to tip his head back. To his astonishment, ducking and swirling around the bald cypress tree above the angel were at least a dozen golden orbs the size of Easter eggs.

No way!

Bill watched, mesmerized. He felt like a little boy in front of a cartoon with a pixie sprinkling fairy dust.

"What are you?"

As if catching an updraft, the eggs floated upward and disappeared.

"O-kay. Right. Seeing things again."

They couldn't be real, but they'd given him a sense of peace and wonder he rarely felt anymore. Pondering this, he moved down the road, passing leggy cypress trees on the right and rogue citrus, water oak and hickory trees on the left. Maybe it was a sign from Debbie...

Nah...nice thought, but that woo shit ain't real. Angels and fairies.

He was approaching a stretch he called 'the sluice' where bamboo and silver thorn made high impenetrable walls on both sides. While walking the three-hundred-yard length of constricted space, Bill felt a twinge of claustrophobia. Driving through it made him think of the Olympic bobsleigh event. Infrequently, Bill felt was more than mere spatial disquietude. Debbie, friends and family had commented on it over the years.

"Funny, I got the creepiest feeling, coming to your house just now."

"I've never liked this stretch of the road."

"I had the queer notion there was something in the bamboo looking out at me."

"There's a bad energy here... I don't like it."

"I always gun the engine to get through that part... don't know why..."

Bill had flashbacks to military training of how to move through a funnel—you had to move quickly to avoid an ambush. He picked up his pace. He thought of those haunted cornfields where maniacs with chainsaws jumped out of the corn. *RRR-RUMMM RUMMM-RUMMMM-RRROOOM!* He'd taken Debbie to the corn maze over on Route 121 once. She'd screamed and hugged him so hard, she darned near popped his ribs. They'd laughed about it afterwards while sharing a funnel cake. She'd looked so beautiful with powdered sugar on her lips and nose. She'd said she'd never go into one of those mazes again, it was too scary.

For reasons he could not explain, Bill felt uneasy, bordering on dread. Perhaps it was the shifting shadows as the moon, unrestricted by clouds, cast stark shimmying shadows under the bamboo that faded when new clouds passed overhead. Or the movement in the silver thorn — mice, rats or bunnies scampering away. Bill found himself looking over his shoulder as if for a lurking marauder. But that was ridiculous. He lived too far out in the country for the curious let's-see-where-this-road-goes road-trippers.

With the sluice behind him now, the road opened out to the right with a view of a neglected field. Bill leaned on the fence to scan for any activity. The fence gave some under his weight.

Hmm. Fence post is rotting out, he thought.

Several bats worked the sky over his end of the field. Bill wasn't sure if it was four or five; they swooped, darted and doubled back. Bill liked bats. So quiet and graceful. Watching them normally relaxed him, but this time, he couldn't get rid of the feeling that his back was exposed somehow. Something might come from the darkness behind him and attack...

A bat dove and turned passing very close to Bill's face.

"Hello! Excuse me!" Bill said, stepping back. As his weight shifted, he had the horrible expectation of stepping back into something, something huge and evil. He jerked around, forgetting to allow for the helmet weight.

"Dammit!" he yelled as it swiveled, scraping his nose. "This thing's gonna break my damn nose yet!"

He planted his hands on it to stabilize it.

Nothing had grabbed him. There was no skunk ape reaching for him, no evil demon dripping drool down his neck. He was alone on the road by the corner of the pasture.

But the feeling of being watched by something malevolent was getting stronger.

Were the shadows darker than before? Bigger?

Bill pulled his jacket closer to his chest and tucked his chin into his scarf. *I'll just go down the road and back. Lived here for damned near twenty years. Nothing to be afraid of.*

But he *was* afraid. Of what?

He walked. The road here was a car-width wide, mostly sand with a weedy mound of grass running along the center.

Shwee-wee-shwee-shee — weesh.

The top of the tree canopy ahead whispered and swayed. The road came to a T at old man Edgerton's frog pond. During non-drought summers and all through hurricane season, the pond was loud with frogs chorusing, some in high helium voices, *Weeee — Werrrr, Weeee- Werrrr* and others with baritone *ROOORT-ROOORT ROOORTs.*

There were no frogs singing now.

Sploonk! Something fell into the pond. The sudden sound made Bill jump in his skin.

Probably an acorn. Geez, why am I so edgy?

Seeing the bend in the road just ahead was a relief. There used to be a massive dogwood tree there. Its branches reached in all directions shading out the grassy patch of the bend. He remembered it covered in flowers with the palest hint of pink at the edges. Debbie had said the flowers were symbolic of the cross of Jesus, the four petals were the cross, white with purity, but the dark tips were like the nails, and the clump in the center was the crown of thorns. Debbie had been so clear in her devotion. But she'd been taken from him. He'd found her on the floor in the kitchen. Brain aneurysm they'd said. She was gone just like that.

The dogwood was gone too, having died a slow death by blight. Each year another limb failed to leaf out until the year it stopped leafing out altogether. Now, there was just the rotting stump left, a dark spot in the thick grass. This was the one spot along the dirt road where sunlight and moonlight were unimpeded by foliage. Bill felt more at ease in this open area.

He exhaled; seeing his breath fog made him aware he'd been holding his breath.

Probably a waste of time. I should go back. But...it won't kill me to go down to the road and back. There still might be something by the creek. Damn, I wish this thing fit better. I'm getting a headache. Can't imagine some poor jarhead having to wear this for hours.

His boots crunched on the uneven limestone. Perhaps it was because the night was so quiet or because the helmet channeled the sound to his ears, but his steps seemed abnormally loud, disturbing.

The road turned to the right then back to the left. Bill passed the Zullmans' new fence on the left. Strange people. He'd never had a conversation with them; they kept to themselves. If he saw them in passing, they never waved, just stared with distrust in their eyes.

There was motion by their electric driveway entrance. Slowing to get a better look, he gasped, "What on earth?"

A ghostly gray woman in a beaded dress was kneeling on the ground clinging to a filmy body. There was no sound, yet it was obvious by her gestures and the limp figure below her that she was crying over a dead man. Then more images appeared: bodies on the road, bodies slumped against trees.

Bill's foot connected with something. He tripped and grunted. The helmet wobbled forward. He adjusted it and regained his balance. Looking down, he was aghast to see he'd stepped on a hand. He was looking down at the bloody body of a dead man.

"AHHH!" Bill roared, scrabbling backward. He fell back onto his buttocks and continued scrabbling backwards like a crab. But now all he could see was the moon over his head and dappled moonlight on the road and across the Zullmans' driveway.

No bodies. No ghosts. No massacre.

The helmet had rolled off the road into a wild blackberry patch. A bit of lens reflected the moonlight like a leering eye.

Get up. Get out of here. Leave that damned thing where it is and go home! I'm done!

The eye seemed like a bad sign, like an evil eye working on Bill. Part of him wanted to sprint home and lock the door, then come back in the morning with a sledgehammer and bash the night-vision goggles into bits. But the part of Bill that loved salvage argued that he shouldn't leave the goggles for someone else to find. It was just a helmet and lenses. Nothing evil. Maybe he'd seen real ghosts. Maybe that explained why the Zullmans were so weird. Their property had bad mojo. But meanwhile, he was sitting in the road like a crazy drunk.

Get a grip. Just get it and go home.

With antipathy, Bill stood up and approached the helmet. The eye effect had been a trick of the light. It winked out when he stood up.

His father's voice in his head said, "Don't be such a *stoonad!"*

Picking up a stout stick, Bill whacked the helmet a few times to free it from the thorns, then dropping the stick, he picked up the helmet and tucked it under his arm like a football. The temptation to run was strong, but he forced himself to walk. For one thing, the tumble had jarred his lower back. For once, the pain was his friend. Focusing on the discomfort took his mind off his fear.

He backtracked, limping. Soon he was passing the dogwood stump.

He winced and sucked wind. *Screwed my back up again, dammit. No, no, maybe not. Cold pack and some ibuprofen'll fix it up.*

The sound of the wind in the canopy mingled with his breath. *Shwee-wee-shwee-Huh…huh…shee-wee-wee – huh…shee-weesh…huh.*

Turning right now. Right into the sluice. So close. Almost there.

But this time, the dread hit him like a shock wave. Something was waiting. Something powerful and terrifying. Bill froze with indecision. He had to get home. There was no other way. The road was a black hole of darkness and malice. There was no doubt this time. Real or not, wasn't it better to see what was coming than to go in blind? With enormous reluctance, Bill eased the helmet back on his head and adjusted it. He'd have to run with his hands on his head to keep the helmet locked in place. He was about to start, when way up ahead by the concrete angel, a light began to glow. It grew bigger and brighter, floating above the middle of the road.

Bill blinked a few times. At the heart of the glow was a familiar, beautiful woman.

Debbie?

Hovering in a glorious shaft of light, Debbie looked like she did when they first met, young and vibrant. She was gesturing for him to come to her, waving with urgency. She'd never come back in a dream. He'd not sensed her lingering around the house. Not once. But there she was, beckoning. Beautiful. Angelic. His heart ached. Why couldn't she come to him? Why was she so far away? Her motions were desperate now.

"Debbie, help me!"

He bolted toward her, dazzled by her glimmering form, arms outstretched.

Bill ran faster than he had in decades. In his peripheral vision he saw black forms with wide eyes emerging from the bamboo. He focused on Debbie, aiming for the safety of her arms. Black wraiths with vulture-like talons slid out of the foliage. Knees high, legs pumping, Bill ran all out, pain shooting from his tailbone and low back in protest. The evil shades closed in, all talons and teeth. They had vacant staring eyes, huge mouths and weird tufts of gray-black plumage on their heads like freakish show chickens which would have been amusing if the waves of pure evil weren't so horrific. Surely, they'd snatch him up and skewer, bite, claw, and break his body. The horrid vacant eyes! So many of them, he didn't stand a chance.

Oh, God, they're blind and hunting me by scent! I can't fight so many! I'm going to die!

Bill's bowels let go. Then his sanity left his body—he ran screaming and flailing towards his beautiful angelic dead wife's open arms.

He was sacked like a quarterback with no chance. He felt his legs go out from under him as something wrapped around his throat.

He woke smelling sand and excrement. He felt damp cold ground under him.

I must be at the beach. Oh shit, I hope I didn't fall asleep in the sun again.

He felt grit on his face.

Where's my towel? Why is it so cold? God, why do I feel so stiff and sore?

Bill opened his eyes to discover he was lying at the foot of the angel statue by his driveway. His left arm was asleep; he'd been lying on it. He sat up cautiously expecting sharp pains, had he broken something? Why was he lying here? Then it all came rushing back. The last thing he remembered was a foul smell and being surrounded by black shrouded evil things and knowing he was about to die.

Was he dead? If so, this was a let-down. He didn't think you got the numby pins-and-needles when you were dead. His coat was torn. His neck was stiff as all get out and touching it, he pulled away partially dried blood. Looking down the road, he saw lenses, bits of metal and tracks in the sandy road as if a major skirmish had occurred: drag marks, claw marks, a chaos of his footprints, a fragment of fabric from his pants.

A familiar uncontrollable trembling began in his body. It felt a lot like an advanced stage of hypothermia and shock. Bill shifted to get up and realized the angel was looking down at him with a perfect expression of grace.

It was about a month before Bill got back to see Caleb at the Can-doo flea market.

"Hey, Bill, where ya been? You okay? You don't look so good."

"Yeah. I had the flu," Bill rasped.

"Again?" Caleb clucked. "I heard it's been goin' around. Good to see you."

"Yeah, man."

"Sore throat, eh? You sound like shit."

"Yeah."

"So, whatcha lookin' for today?"

Bill shot him a playful grin, "Same as always. A bargain."

Caleb pulled on his mustache. "Got some stuff on that table over there 'ats new. Got it outtuva foreclosure. Have a look."

"Thanks," Bill said, eyeing the table.

Caleb cocked his head, "Say, didja ever get them night vision goggles to work?"

Bill stiffened. He rubbed his throat with a hand, "Yeah, uh— no." As if forgetting the question, he fingered a pair of sunglasses a moment then said quietly, "You'd never believe…I saw… I saw —"

"Mmm?" Caleb encouraged.

Bill exhaled, "Darkness".

He said it with such emphasis, Caleb took an involuntary step back. He wondered why Bill was acting so strange, so evasive.

Bill spoke again, this time his voice was so eggshell-fragile it cracked. "Darkness…and light."

57

BW&S

THREE

As Zap's initial hunger abated, he forced himself to slow down and savor the burger. He held it in both hands, afraid to loosen his grip on it.

The old man with the white beard was working over his fish and seemed to be enjoying it as much as Zap was enjoying his beastie burger. As the man worked his knife and fork, the fish seemed to twitch, its tail flipping on the bar.

It was just a trick of the light, Zap thought, because the fish was so large and draped over the plate, it looked like it was moving as the man cut bite size chunks out of it.

The burger was loaded with grilled onions and cheese — even the pickles were outstanding. Zap thought he'd be happy to drive back here for a burger like this. He glanced down at the menu still next to him and re-read the description of the beastie burger. A thirteen-ounce angus patty…Why thirteen ounces? Wasn't that odd… Oh, probably for Friday the 13th, a subtle joke. Whatever. It was to die for.

Zap glanced at the man again. The man seemed to be applying much force into his fork as if pinning the fish to the plate. Zap blinked. No, just his tired imagination. The man set down his knife and fork and leaned back in his chair giving his ample belly more room.

Zap chuckled realizing that there was a poster from the movie *Lake Placid* on the wall behind the bearded man. The poster featured a huge sea creature rising up from the lake with its enormous jaws open. When the man had leaned back, it looked like he'd put his head in the monster's mouth.

The Lost Island of Unsonsy

"Baltimore, Baltimore. Next stop Baltimore, Maryland," an authoritative male voice announced, startling me awake.

I'd gotten up at four in the morning to allow time to catch the 5:55 train out of Norfolk. Once the train left the station, the steady *chug-chug* and mild rocking motion put me right back to sleep. Baltimore already. Well, good-o. I drifted back to sleep and woke when the train stopped. Doors opened, disembarking passengers filtered past me. So far, I'd been lucky enough to have the space for four all to myself. I'd stretched out on my side, using my purse as a pillow and my jacket as a blanket. The seat opposite was vacant. The train whistle blew, and we began moving again. Though I'd seen a number of boarding passengers pass by, it seemed my luck might hold to keep my own private nook. I closed my eyes and began to nod off.

There was a rustle of fabric as something bashed my knee. I struggled to an upright position as a dowdy, heavy-set woman with short graying hair loomed over the vacant seats.

"Hope you don't mind," she said, looking up, "the train is getting full. Was there someone sitting here?"

"Not at all," I said, rubbing my knee, "be my guest."

I scooted closer to the window, angling my legs to give her more room and avoid further bruising from her various bags.

A heavy messenger bag slid off her shoulder onto the seat as she set a canvas bag on the other seat and dropped a hard suitcase on the floor. A haversack large enough for a maid to steal the silver set with, an old-fashioned, embroidered affair that brought to mind "carpetbagger" and "snake oil salesmen" fell off the other shoulder. My shoulders ached just looking at it all.

"Too much stuff!" She exhaled, brushing her hair from her face.

I bit my tongue, fighting the urge to ask, "Well, whose fault is that?"

She pushed the canvas bag aside and sat with force in the seat cattycorner to me. The seat groaned in protest.

"How far are you going?" she asked, not looking at me but struggling to stash the suitcase under the seat. "I'm going to Providence." The suitcase refused to cooperate. In a huff, she hauled it up and set it under the messenger and carpet bags.

"Are you? So am I," I answered with dismay. Her bulk and belongings gave me a twinge of claustrophobia. I'd have felt completely boxed in without the natural light and illusion of freedom from the window.

"Vacation is it?" she asked. "I'm sort of on vacation, business and pleasure. I'm doing some research for a book." She patted her hair.

"Oh? That's nice," I said to be polite. I hoped she'd settle down and stop talking but she kept chattering on.

"Legends and folklore of the Chesapeake Bay area," she said pulling a hefty old tome from the messenger bag. "Did the tour of the U.S.S. Constellation yesterday." She chuckled and looked at me expectantly, almost as if I too was fresh from a visit to the ship.

I returned a blank expression.

She frowned and fluttered a hand at me as if to dust off my middle-school history memory. "You know, the 'sloop-of-war', the last all-sail battleship from the 1850s. Remarkable. Patrolled the Mediterranean during the Civil War. Gorgeous ship, they've got her fully restored. And such history." She tucked a wisp of gray hair behind her ear and eyed me over her reading glasses. "And supposedly haunted."

"Haunted?" I kicked myself for engaging her further, but it had caught my attention.

"So they say," she chuckled again, "depends on who you talk to, I guess. I spoke with a tour guide who'd been there for years. Said he's never experienced anything at all. Suspects it's a ploy to drum up tourism. But then again, some people just aren't sensitive. Wouldn't feel a thing in the most haunted place in the world, ha-ha!"

The woman had a roundish face, the kind of chunky cheeks that grandmothers like to pinch and deep dimples when she smiled. Her bubbly chatter might have been infectious. She seemed nice enough, yet I felt conflicted—should I let my guard down and succumb to her chatter, or shore up my defenses and retreat to the privacy of my own thoughts? Companionship might be a nice change. After all, it was a long ride, it might help pass the time though the topic of ghosts and folklore was not my bailiwick.

"Do you believe in ghosts?" I asked.

"I sure do! I was raised by one!" She laughed out loud and brushed her hand dismissively as if brushing away a fly.

Oh dear, this woman is nuts, I thought. My expression must have reflected my suspicion.

"I say that because I grew up in a haunted house. My mother said when I was in my playpen, on many occasions she'd hear me cooing and giggling. She'd come in to find me fixated on a spot in the room and reacting as if I was having a conversation with someone. Sometimes I even bounced up and down with glee."

My mouth fell open.

"Oh, sure, mother was alarmed at first, but then she figured, well hell, as long as I was happy, what harm could there be? A free babysitter!" She laughed again and swatted her knee.

"I don't know," I said shaking my head. "That would be *awfully* weird. Do you remember any of it? How long did it last?"

"It's hard to say, I was so young…my memories and what Momma told me are kind of blurry, but I do remember a kind woman with a long white apron. And Momma said that when I learned to talk, I kept asking for Benda-Lee. Mother found out there was a *Brenda* Lee Chase who had lived in that house."

"Well that's spooky."

She waved her hand again, "Oh, no, not really, but let me tell you what *is* spooky!" Her eyes gleamed at this. "I'm so excited about this." She patted the great book beside her. A bit of the binding flaked off onto the seat. "The more I think about it, I've got material for a whole nother book. Are you from this area?"

"Not from here, originally, but I've lived in Norfolk for the last nine years."

"Well, you know something about the Chesapeake at any rate," she said, opening the book with care and flipping to a

63

bookmarked section. "That's good. Do you know then about the islands, Smith and Tangier?"

I frowned, feeling my ignorance. "No, I'm afraid I don't."

"Oh," she said, deflated. "Well, you must make a point to visit. Fascinating. Such a strange micro-culture, the watermen. And the language! Ever talk with someone from Tangier? Oh, ho!" she chirped. "You can hardly understand a word! 'At thar in thee boot on Poke-moke Soon!'" More laughter and knee slapping. I had no idea what she'd just said at all, though it might have been Pocomoke Sound.

"Uh-huh," I muttered.

The outburst subsided, she looked more thoughtful, "Hard way to make a living, that's for sure what with the pollution and more restrictions all the time. They have to work longer and harder to get fewer crabs and oysters. A damn shame." She shook her head. "Went out to Tangier. Got to interview a couple of them, not that I understood much. Took a tape recorder. Spent a LONG time trying to decipher what they'd said!"

I nodded dumbly.

She frowned, "You didn't read Michener's *Chesapeake*, then?"

"No, I'm afraid—"

"Oh, you must. It's your duty since you live here and all."

"Yes, I suppose so..." I said, looking at the floor. I was beginning to think maybe I should go find the club car; make an excuse, go sit by myself somewhere.

"Well! Guess what?" She asked with such gusto, I startled and looked up. She was leaning forward, eyes fixing me over the glasses.

I shrugged, clueless.

"Well, you know, Michener had a team of researchers for his books. I happened to hunt down one of them, thanks to poking about on the internet. She lives in Alexandria. She kindly let me conduct an interview. Boy, did I hit the jackpot!" She clapped her hands like a toy monkey on crack playing the cymbals. I leaned back into my seatback, out of range.

I could have slid over, made some lame excuse and left, but she had me stuck there like a mouse in front of a cobra.

"Marjorie Cartmill did extensive research on the islands. Look." She thumped the map with a chubby finger, "See here where the Potomac meets the Chesapeake?"

I followed her moving finger over the yellowed map.

"And this line of islands starting with Bloodsworth going south to Marsh Island, the refuge here, then Smith Island and Tangier…"

"Mmm," I agreed, feeling a bit like a first grader with a tutor.

"What do you see here?" She thumped her finger then rested the fingernail below the name.

Resenting her patronizing tone, but feeling helpless to resist her, I squinted. The map was faded and blotchy, but I thought I read it correctly, "Un-son-sy. That's kind of a strange name."

She beamed. "I've been searching for some shred of evidence of its existence and here it is." She said this with the triumphant look and puffed her chest like a sage grouse.

"Evidence of —"

"This map is from 1895. This is the ONLY map I've ever found with Unsonsy on it." Her cheeks expanded and the dimples set as she smiled. "Do you know what this means?"

I shrugged, "Well, I —"

"This is like finding the lost city of Atlantis! Well, okay, maybe not quite...but it wasn't just a legend. There really was an island!"

"Legend?" I asked. As soon as the word flew out of my mouth, I mentally kicked myself. What was I doing? Why did I continue to engage like a daft parrot? My moment to escape was lost; now she'd rattle on all the way to Rhode Island.

"An obscure legend at that — only it's not! That Cartmill woman was a gold mine of information. Lucky me, she kept all her research. Like me, she was fascinated with Unsonsy, but it was determined to be too unsubstantiated and off topic to be included in *Chesapeake*. Or maybe it got edited out. Do you know it's over 1000 pages in *paperback*?" She scrunched her nose and raised her upper lip in an expression of mock horror. "Don't get me wrong, it's a great book, but –woof, that's no light read!"

"I imagine –"

"You know how there are certain species that only exist in one place, like there are certain birds and fish and lizards that only exist on the Galapagos islands?"

I nodded.

"Well, back in the 1800's, this island, Unsonsy, was too small to populate. Not like Smith or Tangier that have tiny towns with shops and grade schools. No, Unsonsy – which means unfortunate, unlucky and even *fatal* in Scots English – was used by fishermen as a place to hole up during a storm or do repairs on their boats. There were little shacks out there on the little bit of beach. Some marsh grass and a few scrubby trees, that was all there was -- about ten acres at high tide."

I raised an eyebrow, "An island called 'fatal'?" This sounded ominous. How come I'd never heard of it before?

"Ahh," she said, eyes bright. "That's the tricky bit. You see, there was a species of fish that only spawned on Unsonsy for some reason, never on Smith or Tangier. Like locusts, these fish could be dormant for years, just eggs on the marshy side of the island. But when the moon and the tide and who knows what other conditions were right, they hatched."

I felt a lump forming in my throat.

"Now these fish were a terrifying combination of flying fish and mud fish with a piranha-like appetite. Imagine if you will, a poor fisherman running ahead of a storm. He gets to Unsonsy, secures his boat and huddles in the shack to wait out the storm. The storm rages. Lightning flashed and thunder cracked right over head. The sea and sky are black as hell except for the chop

67

of the waves—which you could see only if you were lucky enough to have a lantern."

I rubbed a hand over the back of my neck to chase the shiver that tickled my hairline. "Awful. I'd never go out there in the first place. I'm not a water person. I can't even swim well."

"Oh, but the storm isn't even the half of it! You wait it out and finally, the storm subsides. You probably didn't get any rest, but now you can go home. But wait! You look out at the water and the waves are still just as choppy! How can that be? The wind has died down, the sun is coming out from behind the clouds. You were about to head back to the boat and begin bailing out the water but wait! What is *that?*" Like an actress, she looked past me, raising a hand to her mouth, her face a mask of imagined horror.

My pulse quickened. I had the irresistible urge to look behind me.

"There's a horrible sound of thumping, gulping, swishing movement. A desperate wet sucking sound. And then you see *them.* The bigger ones are flying out of the sea toward you, gills, fins, and wings flapping. The young ones are wriggling in the wet soil, struggling, yearning, starving. And there you are! And in that way that swarms can react as one, they see you. You turn to run back to the little shack— a desperate race—first one to get to you gets the tastiest bits, you know."

I shuddered and cried out, hugging myself. "Oh, stop! Please—I have ichthyophobia."

Ignoring me, intent on her story, she plowed ahead, her eyes wild. "You start to run. It's not that far, you can make it, you kid yourself. If you can get to the door and shut it behind you—and that's when the first one hits you on the back of the neck. You feel the sharp bite, the gnashing jaws, the weight of the wet fish hanging on by its teeth, chomping, chomping. You scream, you thrash about and it falls away. You are at the door—you are in the doorway—" She clapped her hands together, making me jump four inches straight up. "Another one strikes! And another! Now they bite the backs of your knees. Another one chomps on an elbow. You are fighting to get the door closed but you can't! There are young ones writhing at your feet, jamming the door. Another flying fish hits you full in the face! You fall down. Covered in blood, the little ones, frenzied now, wriggle up your legs. You realize with horror that the wetness you feel all over your body is not rain. It's not raining. That's your *blood*. You scrabble and scream—"

"Oh, please! It's too much!" I cried, half standing up. My flight response was hampered by the close quarters. My legs weren't firmly underneath me. I wobbled and sat back. Nearby passengers turned to stare at me. Embarrassed, I gestured to them that I was fine. But I wasn't.

"Ichthyophobia," I said, patting my chest, "I have a *fear* of fish. Won't touch a fish. Won't eat a fish. Dead fish with those eyes freak me out—*Rrrlah*!" I said thrusting my tongue out as if throwing up. Maybe now she'd get the hint and at least change the subject.

"Sorry, dear, of course, but you see how thrilling this is," she said, pressing her hands on the material in a possessive gesture. "Proof! Why, I wish I had enough material, I could write a whole book just on Unsonsy! I'm keen on this story in particular because I was raised near Salisbury, Maryland. My family goes back a long, *long* way—generations—and my Gran used to sing me this song from her childhood. We never dreamed it was based on a true story! It's called, 'When the Toothies Come to Play'. Kinda like 'Ring Around the Rosie,' it's a cheerful sounding little ditty that's creepy as crap. It goes:

Oh, how happy you can be
Working out at sea
Wishin' and a fishin'
And a crabbin' every day

Until the chill wind blows
As every seaman knows
There will come a day
When the toothies come to play

The sea a-starts to swirlin'
The waves a-start to whirlin'
For three nights and a day
When the toothies come to play

The wind a-starts to blowin'
Their hunger starts a-growin'
Oh, child, heed what I say
When the toothies come to play

Now every son and daughter
Knows to stay out of the water
Go far away
When the toothies come to play.'"

She was sure right about the chilling. The tune was cheerful, her voice and pitch fine, but the understated message of warning was unnerving.

I grimaced. "The 'toothies' are those horrible fish?" *Oh, great, I did it again! Shut up, shut up!*

She bobbed her head, visibly delighted that she had me hooked into her story.

"But I have proof that Unsonsy was real. Here—" she tugged at the messenger bag and pulled out a manila folder covered in penciled notes, " and bless Mrs. Cartmill again, the book is long out of print, I'd never have found this--ah, here it is. Mentioned in a book on Colonial Maryland, from the diary of one Captain Roberts in 1661."

I read aloud:

1661-9th October

The storm came vpon us with svch blacke uengeance, the skye was as pitch and the baye wilde as a seething water monster hvngry to swallowe the earthe. It was mvch feared that Arno and his men were loste. Worde arrived this daye laste to the effecte that by happenstance their crafte had been sighted vpon the shoer of Unsonsy by an olde fisherman. Greatly uexed we were that this man had not uentured closer to the islande to determine if the grace of God had occasioned their suruiual.

At first lighte we set sayle in seach of them. Ovr hopes for their rescue too soone were dashed, replaced by a grisly discouery the likes of which my eyes haue neuer seen in all my dayes. The boat laye intact yet what remained of the wretched men was little more than chvnks of fleshe and bone couered ouer with a blankete of blowflies.

The Powhatans speake of 'zhaabonigan-namens babaami-bibide' a flying needle fishe that in my ignorance I attribvted to legend or fancy, likened to the kinde of tale told to frighten childrene into behauiors of compliance and thvs I dismissed their fears as svperstitiovs poppycocke.

Merciful God of Compassion, mine own eyes haue seen these monsters, deade thank Heaven aboue. Their bloating bodies lay abovte on the shoreline and in the boate and sheltere -- sheltere that did navght to saue vnlvcky Arno and his men. Vnseeing euil and glassed-over eyes watched vs come ashore. Their movths gaped wide exposing the hideovs fanges like sea vrchine spines, the sharpest of needles in greate snapping jawes. These hell fishe swarme, feede, spawne and die ouer just a fewe dayes yet they growe impossibly large. Many were the lengthe and breadthe of my forearme.

Father of Mercye, I cannot excvlpate the horror from my minde. At svch times as I close my eyes, I see the sterne of the boate and call out names< "Arno! Jameson! Thomas?" Then I see a boote and bit of lege. Soon I am vndone by the ouerpowering smell of deade fishe and bloode. My foote strikes against the boate and the cloude of buzzing flies billowes up...

"That's disgusting. I'm getting queasy," I said, thrusting the letter back. She showed no sign of empathy. Her face was lit up with triumphant satisfaction.

My mouth was dry. Breakfast had been ages ago. I wished I had some water and a granola bar or even a packet of crackers to overcome the lightheadedness that had come upon me. More than anything, I needed to escape from this overbearing woman. She reminded me more and more of the domineering Kathy Bates character in *Misery*.

Her face shifted from maniacal to concerned, "I'm sorry, my dear. I get carried away. Let me find that column from the fifties, that'll cheer you up. Another gem from Mrs. Cartmill. Let's see, where is it… somewhere here," she yanked a notebook out of a tote bag and riffled through it, "somewhere — oh, here it is, from the *Chesapeake Weekly Catch* from… "She adjusted her glasses and read the header before turning it towards me, "Friday, October 30, 1959."

"Could I just — " I began to say, hoping to escape and go get something cold to drink.

The train lurched as she shoved the plastic sheet toward me. I found myself leaning forward for balance and grabbing the sheet out of instinct. I glanced down. Something about the title "Small Potatoes" and the words Mischief Night lured me in. At least it didn't seem to be about those damn fish. At first.

Friday, October 30, 1959

Small Potatoes

by Edna Gleason Parks

It's Mischief Night tonight folks. The town council has warned that they will be strict with curfews and will have extra police patroling after 10 p.m. Let's hope we don't have any incidents of vandalism like we did last year. And Saturday is Halloween so don't forget to buy your candy. Haskell's market has a two for one sale on candy bars this week.

Say, here's something spooky. How many of you recall the legend of Unsonsy? Rumor has it that several watermen noticed some extra peculiar weather the other night after that humdinger of a storm we had. Extra chop in the water, strange sounds like fish thrashing in the water when there was nothing there. Thumps hitting the side of the boat. Carl Upjohn claims his black eye was from getting hit by something that almost knocked him down only he didn't see anything. Carl is 6'4" folks--now what do you think could have hit him when he was alone in his boat like that?

74

I remember my grandpa used to sit back in his easy chair, blow cigar smoke in the air and recite this limmerick:

> With the waxing moon crabpots belayed
> And the waning moon harvest delayed
> What'll turn you berserker
> Are the fangs of the lurker
> And finding your mateys filleted

Then he'd laugh and tell us about the unlucky watermen who were eaten alive by the "murklurkers" -- fish that spawned on an island south of Tangier that got wiped out by hurricanes and disappeared in 1896, the same year my father was born.

Carl--were you really hit by a ghost fish or did you lose a bar fight? Fess up, now!

Be safe out there and have a Happy Halloween everyone!

I finished reading the column and handed it back. A headache was forming above my ears like a prayer cap of pain.

"Isn't that priceless?" she beamed.

"Err, yes. But probably Carl really was covering for a bar brawl he didn't want to admit to, don't you think?" I asked, standing up. "Anyway, good luck with your research. I'm sure it'll all work out for you. I'm feeling light-headed and am going to the club car—"

"Before you go, I *have* to show you the *pièce de résistance*," the woman said fumbling again in a folder.

"No, I'm not feeling well, if you don't mind, I'll just squeeze by—"

"Yes, sure, just a moment," she said. She had turned to dig around with zeal, and in the turning had put her watermelon knees across the miniscule space between our seats.

A piercing metal on metal squeal came from the train tracks. Our car shimmied, throwing me backward into the seat as we plunged into a tunnel. The fall, the whooshing sounds and the abrupt darkness side to side combined to derail my thoughts and nerves. The woman swayed a bit but otherwise remained focused like a terrier on retrieving something from the depths of her bag.

"Ah, here it is!"

I focused on steadying my breath. Deep breath in, steady breath out. I'd let her show me this one more thing then I'd find a way over her knees and her bags, even if I had to call on my middle school track and field hurdling skills.

She squinted at another item in protective plastic.

There was another whoosh as we shot out of the tunnel back into the light.

"I feel sure that Unsonsy was once a few acres in size, but it was reduced by a bad hurricane around 1878. There were two more hurricanes in 1893 and 1896. After that, Unsonsy may have appeared as a hint of a sandbar on an extreme low tide but was essentially gone. And no further mention of the fish swarming occurs after 1896."

"What a relief," I said, clenching my purse. My slim suitcase was in an overhead bin, if I twisted to my right, I could reach it and pull it down. "Well, this has been very interesting, I wish you the best—"

"But what if they weren't as isolated as people thought? Hmm?" She asked, arching her eyebrows.

I stood. The handle of the bag just out of reach. I stretched and said with annoyance, "Surely we'd have heard of them then. Everyone knows about the Loch Ness monster, Nessie for example and that's a myth." Success! I reached the bag and pulled it down. I'd be free in an instant. "And now that I think about it, isn't there a Chessie, also? But these foul fish. No, just a disgusting tale for bored fishermen."

"Perhaps," she said puckering her mouth. "Perhaps. But see here. The Victorians were a peculiar lot with a grim fascination with all things morbid and freakish… did you know they kept deformed people in zoos so that rich people could ogle them?"

"No," I said with a grimace of distaste. I clutched the bag handle and considered my options.

"They posed dead people for *memento mori* photographs."

"Please—"

"They kept all *sorts* of oddities in jars and curio cabinets as well."

"Lovely," I said, "I really must—"

"Mrs. Cartmill found photographs from a doctor's private collection. As a man of science, he had a collection to rival Ripley's Believe It or Not—"

77

"Excuse me, if you'll just let me pass—"

"Yes, of course," she said moving her round knees to the side for a tantalizing second, then snapping them back to the blocking position. "Just look!"

I was so stunned to realize that she was in fact, blocking me deliberately, that my eyes rose from her knees to her face. Her eyes were insistent and powerful like Bela Lugosi in *Dracula*. Against my will, I felt compelled to look at what she held before me.

It was a hazy photograph of a display cabinet. It took me a moment to understand what I was seeing. A skeletal foot inside the skeletal mouth of a fish—a fish with countless needle-like teeth—teeth so embedded in the bone of the foot that they two could not be separated. I was paralyzed by the thought of a fish biting a man (on land or in a boat) like that. A *flying* fish at that.

"My proof!" She crowed.

There was a placard in the box that read, 'Grimlicus Diabolica or voracious devil, common name, Murk lurker with all that remained of Michael Freeman found on Tangier 1877'."

I faltered for a moment. *Those fish, the legend, the horrible songs. It was all real. And maybe Carl's story of being hit by a ghost fish wasn't a quaint lie.* Some self-preservation mechanism switch flipped in my head forcing me out and away from this woman and her dreadful stories. Imagining I was a restless colt in springtime, I raised my bag high, bumped past her hard suitcase and leapt over her knees.

"Wait! I didn't get to tell you—"

Closing my mind to her voice and her energy, I bolted forward as fast as I could. The club car was four cars away. I crabbed my way forward sideways. At the first door, I looked

78

back with dread. Would she follow me? No. I felt freer with each car that further separated us.

The club car at last!

I was out of breath when I found an empty table in the corner and stored my belongings. I ordered a large glass of water, a plate of sandwiches and a beer. Despite the queasiness I'd felt in the woman's presence, I now felt desperately hungry. I never drink beer midday, but I wolfed the sandwiches and savored the beer.

A small flat-screen television on the wall was a welcomed distraction. That crazy woman and her freakish stories! My heart was still racing. I tried to put it all behind me and focus on the weather report about a storm system coming. Even the jolly but inane commercial jingle was a welcomed distraction.

The rest of the train ride was largely uneventful though the weather soured as we reached New York. My nerves steadied. With effort, I shook off the sticky feeling of having been caught in a dysphoric web spun by that horrible woman. My eyes roamed to the door. What if the door opened and she appeared? She'd see me and start yammering all over again.

Rain pattered on the roof. Distant lightning flashed. I fell into a kind of trance staring at the water droplets migrating across the window connecting with other droplets. If I blurred my eyes, the patterns almost looked like characters of an ancient language spelling out an incomprehensible message of wretchedness.

By the time the train arrived in Providence, the storm raged. Sheeting rain, deep puddles, thunder, lightning, and dangerous gusting wind. I was soaked to the skin running from the train platform to the station. Providence was kind to me; I was blessed to catch a cab without even catching a glimpse of that woman.

Late that evening, hair up in a towel, grateful to be warm and cozy in my pajamas, I flipped through the television channels. The rain pounded overhead. The lights flickered a few times. I prayed the power wouldn't go out.

When I was very young, a tree close to our house was struck by lightning in a shocking bang. We saw a flash of purple as the bark on the pine tree sheared off. Another strike hit the house and travelled through the power lines. The telephone bells rang. White flashes like old flashbulbs shot out of the outlets. The refrigerator made an unholy groan as it got fried. The burnt smell lingered for days. Since then, violent storms have frightened me into a high state of anxiety. I'd taken my nerve pill. It helped. But I was still edgy. I hoped to find a good movie or show to distract me.

There was a depressing show about the mass extinction of wild animals on the planet. Global warming was disrupting the usual migration patterns of so many species from butterflies and hummingbirds to elk and whales. Unable to get to their breeding ground, they got lost and died. I clicked through commercials and reruns of *The Golden Girls* and *Murder She Wrote*. I paused on a news report.

"Police are asking for help regarding the identification of two bodies found in a panga-style fishing boat floating adrift in Rhode Island Sound over the weekend. Signs indicate that the boat had been crippled for at least a week. The passengers may have been caught in last week's thunderstorm that caused the massive power outages in our area."

Massive power outages. No, no, no, I thought. Was this an omen that the power would go out again? I'd be sitting here in the dark.

Alone. I would never have picked a beach cottage if I'd known the weather would be so bad. I wished now I'd picked a chain hotel. I'd feel safer in a hulking multi-story colossus with someone at the front desk all night than this lonesome cottage. I leaned back into the pillows against the headboard.

"Though foul play has been ruled out, what happened to the boat and its crew remains a mystery as the hull sustained peculiar damage," the reporter said. The camera zoomed in on a long narrow boat on a trailer. Most of the interior was covered by a plastic tarp. The exterior had dark marks as if it had been beaten with a sledgehammer. Awful. It must have run aground and gotten bashed about by something under the water.

"…bodies found in the boat had bite marks found resembled those of a small shark…If you have any information, please contact authorities at… "

Ugh! Fish again! Gruesome! I gripped the remote and punched the channel button.

"Coming up next, George Clooney in *The Perfect Storm…*"

Click.

An insurance commercial showed a suburban neighborhood where fires were breaking out, cars were crashing into each other, sirens blared, huge trees fell on houses. An authoritative male voice asked, "Will you be prepared when catastrophe strikes?"

Click.

A grainy film that seemed familiar. Oh, no way, Roy Scheider looking out at the ocean watching kids splashing around. Oh, for heaven's sake! It was *Jaws*!

Click!

Thank goodness. A cooking show. Fine. I relaxed a bit. Oh shit. A seafood dish with lime juice. Why'd it have to be *fish*?

A thud outside made me jump. There was a heavy scraping sound and another thud. I leapt out of bed. The towel fell over my eyes. I shook it off. Was there someone out there? No one would be outside this late in this weather.

I talked to myself. I know it's crazy, but hearing my own voice has a calming effect sometimes. I can pretend someone in authority is telling me what to do. "The door is locked. You're safe. You can flip on the porch light open the curtain and take a look."

I crept to the sliding doors and flipped the light switch. All I could hear now was wind and rain. I peered out.

"Oh, thank goodness!" I exclaimed in relief. There was a heavy-duty garbage can rolling side to side. It had blown over and struck a porch post. I probably should try to secure it better, but no way was I going out there. It should be okay until morning. No need to get soaked for *that*.

Lightning streaked across the sky turning the dark night to a silver toned day for a split second. Glancing out at the beach, the ocean was a frenzy of white caps and frothy foam.

What was that? Had I seen something thrashing about in the waves? No. Just wild patterns of spume.

I closed the curtain and flipped the light off.

I'd just raised my knee to get on the bed when another sound made me whirl around in fright. It began tentatively tapping at the glass, not just in one place like someone knocking but all over. Within a couple seconds it was more insistent. The sliding glass door rattled in its track from the impact of something striking it. I imagined an evil Little League boy with a whiffle bat using the glass door as a backstop for batting practice. *Swunk! Swunk!* The sound shifted from pelting to pounding, from whiffle balls to tennis balls. I could hear it in the bathroom, too. Something was pelting the bathroom window.

It can't be. It just can't be those damn fish. No, no, no, no!

I ran back to the sliding door to make sure the bar was in the track and the doors were locked. Terrified, I whipped the curtain back.

"Hail! Oh, for heaven's sake. You silly cow, getting all frightened." Golf-ball sized hail. That's all it was! Silly me! It was still unsettling but hail I could handle. Whew.

Letting go of the curtain, I returned to the bed and pulled the covers up over my shoulders, angling myself so my back was against the headboard and I could see the television. The woman was twaddling on about how easy it was to make scalloped potatoes in a crockpot. She had an annoying artificial smile. The potatoes did come out looking tasty. Maybe I'd try it someday.

The pounding hail gave way to tapping then to steady rain. My eyes closed as the woman on the screen garnished poached fish fillets with extra smiles, orange wedges and parsley.

Fish in a pan. Fishermen at sea. Flying fish. As I entered the dream world my thoughts staggered around like drunk fishermen. Carl? Were you really struck by phantom fish? Global warming. She had so much material she could do a whole book just on the flying fish. The fish spawned in peculiar cycles. Isolated on a tiny island with a name that meant unlucky. Or were they isolated? Her face had loomed with a gloating expression when she asked that. Were they isolated? Perhaps not. Migration patterns. Enough research to fill a whole nother book. "Wait! I didn't get to tell you!" Grimlicus Diabolica. Of the devil. What didn't she tell me? She was going to Providence too. Had she said why?

Research for a whole nother book. Police are asking for anyone with knowledge. Bodies in the boat with bite marks. Grimlicus. Washed away in the hurricanes. Anyone with knowledge… The storm subsides but the water is still choppy, how can that be? They cycle so fast…crawl from the mud to feed.

"The wind a-starts to blowin'
Their hunger starts a-growin'
When the toothies come to play
When the toothies come to play."

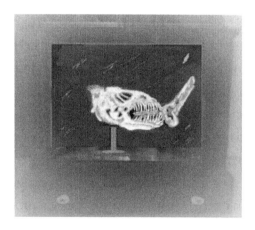

FOUR

Zap got up to find the rest room and headed slowly to the back

of the bar. He soon spotted a sign with a black cat with an arched back and glowing red eyes that read, REST ROOM FRIGHT THIS WAY directing him to a cave-like foyer. The décor of the pub was an eclectic mishmash of cheap Halloween decorations: skulls, skeletons, and black crows but also old framed newspaper articles with headlines like "10 Most Haunted Hotels in the South", "Bodies Found in Basement of Foster Care Couple" and " and "Fleeting Man Disappearance Remains a Mystery."

"Mommy, I'm tired," a child's voice said.

"Shh, I know, here, lie down. We won't be long. Sleep while I finish my soup," a woman's voice answered.

Zap hadn't noticed a child in the pub before. Seated in a booth about midway across the bar, a child lay on a small pillow on his mother's lap. A young Woody Harrelson wearing round red glasses stared down at them from a movie poster for *Natural Born Killers*. The mother patted her son with one hand while awkwardly holding out a spoonful of soup with the other. Zap could see the steam rising from the chunks on the spoon pulled from a black soup bowl in the shape of a cauldron. The mother blew on it and took a tentative sip. She was petite and attractive, probably in her mid-thirties. The child looked to be about eight. There was something sweet and sacred about the mother and child, like the Madonna and child that made Zap pause. They looked small and vulnerable in the large booth. It reminded him of his wife and child. He suddenly yearned to be home. It seemed he'd been away from home for weeks, not just two days.

The mother glanced up with a serene expression.

Zap said, "I have a boy about his age."

The woman smiled. "Good sleep is so important, don't you think?"

"Yes," he agreed. She couldn't know how tired he was and how he looked forward to getting home to a shower and bed. It was an odd thing for her to have said, but looking at the boy, he thought he understood what she meant. He was familiar with that tender feeling a parent got watching a child sleeping, a calm gratitude for their safety, a moment of appreciation when the child looked angelic. Rambunctious boys played hard and slept deeply. A moment of calm for the parent.

Zap nodded and continued to the men's room. He noted more of the decorations in the pub. A collection of small evil clown dolls peeked mischievously from between carved wooden partitions. There were posters of all the classic monsters: Dracula, the Wolfman, Frankenstein, Pinhead from *Hellraiser*, Freddy Kruger and Jason. Plastic bats with red eyes and fierce fangs hung from the ceiling. Hairy spiders hid in cobwebs stretched across the molding and heavy wooden ceiling beams.

The ladies' POWDER ROOM sign featured a skeletal woman dusting her forehead with a powder puff making her even more ghastly white. The door to the men's room was indicated by a life-size painting of a skeleton dressed in dapper Victorian clothing holding a sign that read ENTER IF YOU DARE.

Zap opened the door, started to go in; stood still.

The men's room was made to resemble a morgue. Close to the door was a mannequin partially covered by a sheet. There were faint red trails of blood going to a drain in the floor. The walls and stalls were a ghostly luminous white thanks to theatrical fluorescent fixtures in the ceiling. He forced himself to go in and approach a urinal. Having relieved himself, he moved to the sink to wash his hands. A cough from one of the two stalls made him jump. *This place is getting to me,* he thought. He'd been sure he was the only one in the rest room. Looking up in the mirror, he saw a lanky man with stringy hair pass him in the mirror.

"You scared me," he said, turning to look at the man.

But there was no one there, nor had the door opened or closed. He was alone.

Zap turned off the water tap and bolted for the door, wiping his hands hastily on his pants. Back in the pub, he looked around for the man with stringy hair. No luck.

Pillow Talk

"A ruffled mind makes a restless pillow."
— **Charlotte Brontë**

Humphrey waved goodbye to Whitney, the social worker from the Department of Children and Families and ducked into the back seat of the Ford Bronco. Once inside, he slid his backpack off and adjusted his seat belt. He sat in the middle so he could look out between the driver's seat and the passenger seat.

"We can go to UD first," Shelly Small, Humphrey's new foster mother said. Ultimate Destination was the latest mega store in town with everything from vegetables and party décor to computers and garden tractors.

Sam Small craned his head to look back at Hum. "We thought you'd like to pick out some toys and Shelly thought you might like to pick out some sheets—you know, maybe something with Ninja Turtles or Superman or something fun."

Hum nodded. That sounded good. "Can I have a new pillow?"

Shelly laughed and glanced at her husband. "A new pillow? Is that all?"

"Well, if that's as difficult as the kid gets—" Sam Small said with a puzzled look. "Of course you can. You can have a whole bed full of pillows." Lowering his voice and pursing his lips he muttered to Shelly, "Poor kid—he's been through so much."

Humphrey had been placed with four families in the last few years, five if you counted that brief disastrous stay with the Grungens. While he'd learned to have no expectations, he was relieved that the Smalls had not set off any inner alarm bells so far. They seemed like okay people. It could work. Anything was better than the Grungen household.

The Grungens had kept their charges in a windowless basement. The children had been allowed upstairs only when case workers came on wellness checks. The children never touched any of the toys scattered about the yard on appointment days. The sickly presentation of the children, lack of schooling, hygiene and some whispered pleas for help eventually landed the Grungens spots in prison. The children were returned to the care of the Department of Children and Families.

Fortunately for Hum, he'd only been there for three months and eight days.

True to their word, the Smalls bought all kinds of stuff for Humphrey: shirts, pants, underwear, toiletries, pens, notebooks. They'd passed through the toy section and encouraged Hum to select stuffed animals and action figures. Afraid to seem too greedy, he'd been careful to pick just a few toys to make them happy.

"Can I get a pillow now?" he asked.

"Yes, of course," the Smalls said, exchanging concerned looks when they thought Hum wasn't looking.

He was relieved when they got to the bedding aisle. He was allowed to pick out a super-long body pillow and a regular-sized feather pillow.

"Any sheets you want," Shelly said.

"Batman? Spongebob?" Sam asked pulling out colorful, packaged sets.

Humphrey looked at all the options. He liked the superhero ones, but they were red. He didn't like red. Transformers were strong, invincible with lots of silver, blue and black.

"Transformers," he pointed.

"Transformers it is," Sam said, pulling the set of sheets off the shelf and tossing them on top of the pile in the cart. "For transformation..." he said, thinking out loud.

Shelly and Sam observed that Hum was not a demonstrative child; he expressed satisfaction by relaxing his eyebrows and displaying the simplest of smiles.

That night, bathed, in his soft, new pajamas and new bedroom with Transformer sheets, Hum felt safe for the first time that he could recall. He liked this house, this room, these people.

This might work, he thought.

Shelly was sitting beside him with a selection of books. "Would you like me to read you a story?" she asked. "Did anyone ever read you a bedtime story before?"

"No."

"Well, here...let's get you all comfy in your pillows," she said, looking at the body pillow. It was longer than Hum, in fact, it occurred to her that he would probably fit *in* the pillowcase, he was so small. He grabbed at the pillows reflexively as if she were trying to get them away from him.

"I was just going to plump them up for you," she said, pulling back.

He nodded. "Sorry. I know. I just—" Not sure how to explain, he shrugged.

"You are, uh, particular about pillows, I noticed. Is there… a reason? Is there—?" Shelly wasn't sure how to ask the question.

He shook his head. "I just want my own pillow. Not someone else's."

"Oh…when you were in the other foster house, you didn't have your own pillow?"

He shook his head.

"No pillow?"

Closing his eyes tight, he shook his head. He felt safe here and almost happy. He didn't want to dredge up the memories, but then again, there was part of him that was crying out to tell someone. She seemed nice. She just might understand.

"In the Hootman house…" he began, "there were so many kids. Kids came, kids went. We got stuff from kids who'd gone, stuff got taken away and given to someone else. We didn't have anything of our own. Well, except our toothbrushes and hairbrushes."

Shelley had heard about the Hootmans. Some people hoard pets; the Hootmans hoarded children. They weren't cruel, just neglectful, overwhelmed and clueless about raising children. They wanted the children to be their friends but provided little structure or discipline. An accidental housefire reduced the house to a cinderblock shell. By a miracle, no one was seriously injured, but the Hootmans could no longer provide for their foster brood.

Shelly reached out a hand and brushed the hair from Hum's face. "Well, this is a new day, Hum. That will never happen again. You don't have to share or worry about your stuff getting stolen or taken away. This is your room. Your bed, your pillow."

"My pillow," Hum said, balling it up and hugging it to his chest, his eyes still closed. "not the nightmare pillow."

"Oh?" Shelly prompted.

Hum scrunched up his mouth. He'd never told any adult about the bad pillow. He was conditioned to keep quiet. But Shelley seemed like someone he could tell. Maybe. Would Cliffy know somehow and punish him? No. Much as Cliffy terrified him, he was pretty sure Cliffy couldn't get into your head when you were awake.

"If you got the nightmare pillow, you'd have scary dreams," Hum said with the matter-of-factness of a witness giving court testimony.

"The nightmare pillow? What was that?" Shelly asked, frowning.

"In the Hootman house. The mean boys would give the new kids or the kids they didn't like the nightmare pillow. If you slept on it, you'd have scary, bad dreams. It once belonged to a foster kid named Cliff. Cliff was sent to juvey because he was so bad."

"Oh, my," Shelly said. "Was he there at the same time as you?"

"No. He was gone before I got there. But I got his pillow a couple of nights. It was like, the longer you slept on that pillow, the more you felt *different*. Thought different. Mean. Bad."

Hum remembered the first dream. He opened his eyes wide to stop the sticky black feeling like psychic tar coating his body. Relief flooded over him to see that he was still in the cozy room with the bright colors, his new sheets and Shelly. He felt tears at the edges of his eyelids. He blinked to release them. The contrast of the two realities was jarring. This bright happy one might be real, might last.

"Oh, Humphrey, I didn't mean to upset you," Shelly said, reaching for the tissue box on the night table and pulling out a tissue. "Oh, honey," she said, wiping his eyes.

"You kind of…*became* Cliffy in the dreams. Like I was putting pins in little bugs and doing horrible things to animals…" Hum snuffled and wiped at his eyes. "I saw myself doing things I'd never do…once I was beating a dog in the face with a stick…"

Tears began to run down his cheeks. He sobbed and wiped at his face with his night shirt.

"Nightmares can seem real," Shelly said, trying to sound comforting but feeling uncomfortable with Hum's narrative.

"No. This felt different. I was mean and hateful. And… I killed things. I had a knife…"

"Oh!" Shelly covered her mouth. What had the psychologists said? It was important that the child be able to vent his memories but not to distort or lead him in disclosure? She wondered if Hum had ever talked this way to the social workers. She focused on wiping his tears.

"I…saw myself following this girl. She was walking home from school. She had long brown hair in two ponytails. In the dream, I was much taller than she was. I was big and strong and powerful. In the dream, the girl was in my school. Her name was

94

Lizzie. And I wanted to hurt her. I was on a black bicycle...I had a knife..."

Shelley frowned. "But this was in the dream, right? You didn't really do anything, did you?"

"No!" Hum yelled, thrashing his arms in the air and kicking at his covers. "No! I didn't! I didn't want to! She was pretty! I'd never hurt anyone!"

"Oh, Hum, shh-shh," Shelley said, alarmed at how quickly Hum had gotten almost hysterical. She heard Sam coming down the hall and looked up with relief. She felt frustration with herself for allowing Hum to get so distraught; she felt inadequate at calming him down.

"Hey, buddy? What's all this?" Sam asked, sitting at the edge of the bed near Shelley.

"Hum was telling me about bad dreams."

"But it was so real! The dreams were so real! I was going to hurt that girl. I had the knife! I called out to her, Hey, Skinny Little Lizzie!" He was shrieking now. Snot erupted from his nostrils. "But it wasn't my voice, it was strange. Big, like an adult and mean. And then I see the knife in my hand go like this—"

Hum's face contorted as his left hand fisted up and sliced the air between them. He shrieked again and fell back wailing and thrashing. "It wasn't me! I didn't do it!"

Shelly had flinched away from Hum's imaginary knife. She leaned into Sam and felt goosebumps rising on her arms and neck. She looked helplessly to Sam.

Sam stood up and scooped Hum up in his arms. He held him close in a hug as Hum sobbed into his shoulder. "Hey, shh-shh. It's okay. You're safe now. You're safe. Let's calm down. Sh-shh."

"You have to believe me!" Hum wailed. "I'm not bad!"

"Whoa, buddy! No one ever said you were bad. They told us you we were the luckiest couple in the world to get you because you are such a good, sweet boy."

Sam rocked Hum until his sobs subsided. Hum pulled back, his face a red mess of tears. Shelly grabbed a fistful of tissues and wiped Hum's face. Together, Shelley and Sam got Hum nestled back against his pillow, tucked into the covers.

"I'll read to you," Shelley said. "I'm so sorry I got you upset."

"No, I want to tell you. You have to believe me." Hum said sniffing.

"Okay, but not if you're going to get all upset again, okay buddy?" Sam said, patting Hum's leg.

Hum nodded. "Whoever had to sleep with that pillow had awful dreams. One girl woke up screaming. She never stopped. She went away in an amb'lance and never came back. Sometimes I when I'm trying to sleep, I still hear her screaming. She screamed down the hall. She screamed down the stairs. She screamed until the doctor gave her a great big shot. But she was still crying when they put her in the amb'lance."

Shelly hugged herself, "What happened to the pillow? Why didn't someone throw it away?"

"The older boys used it to scare us. They'd sneak it into your pillowcase if they didn't like you. They didn't like me," Hum sobbed. "But after the third time, I knew to look for the pillow. I looked into my pillowcase and saw it, old and stained with a red border around it. So that's why the last time I got it, I took it out to the fireplace to burn it. I didn't mean to start the fire. I wasn't trying to burn the whole house, just that pillow."

Hum was staring down at his hands clutching at the edges of the sheet. He missed the alarmed exchange between the Smalls.

"You? You started the--?" Shelley began.

"I found one of those clicker things you light the barbecue grill with. It was under the grill on the porch. I put the pillow in the fireplace and clicked. It rolled out towards me. I didn't know what to do. I tried to beat the flames out, but then the bottom of the sofa caught fire. And a spark went into the curtains." He covered his face with his tiny hands.

Sam shook his head and glared a warning at her. In his best imitation of an understanding therapist voice, he said, "That, er, that must have been very scary, that house fire."

"I didn't mean to. It was an accident," Hum said in a voice so soft they could hardly hear him.

Sam leaned back. "*You* started the..."

Hum nodded, somehow looking more vulnerable and even smaller, as if he'd shrunk a size, "The nice fireman said it was 'cause the Hootmans smoked all the time. It was prob'ly a cigarette, he said. But it was me. I never told nobody before."

"Well, maybe it was a cigarette, after all," Sam said, patting Hum again. "Don't blame yourself. It's not your fault."

Hum sniffed.

"Here, you get comfy and I'll read this nice story," Shelley said.

"Everything will be just fine," Sam said. "I'm going to check on something. Good night, Humphrey." He kissed the top of Hum's head and left as Shelley began reading Hum a story.

Eventually, Hum's jaw fell open and his body twitched. Shelley closed the book and slipped out, leaving a nightlight on and the door open.

She found Sam in his study, staring intently at his computer screen. He looked up, his face drawn and ashen. "How is he?"

"Sleeping. Sam, his story about the dreams and starting that awful fire. I don't know what to think."

"Look what I found," he said, pointing.

"What?" Shelley asked, coming around the desk to look at the screen.

"I've been hunting around on the internet." Sam said, his voice strained. "That boy's name was Cliffy, right? And the girl was Lizzie, right? Check out this article from last summer in the Red Bank Register. "

Shelley glanced down and read:

MONMOUTH COUNTY, NEW JERSEY Clifford Patrick Mullhaney, youngest serial killer in the northeast to be sentenced as an adult. The body of a neighbor was found in the woods off of Spoon Hollow Road…Eleven-year old Lizzie Benton was last seen riding her bicycle home from school…

Her head popped up. Her eyes locked with Sam's. "Oh, it can't be."

"Keep going."

… long-time neighbor Ashton Weeks reported that Clifford "Cliffy" Mulhaney had a reputation as a neighborhood bully and had been suspended from his junior high school… "I can't prove it, but I knowed that boy killed my Schnauzer, Mr. Wiggles and my cat, Hisser. I'm not at all surprised, but it scares me to death that he killed those three little girls. First poor little Lizzy, then Mabelle...

Shelley shook her head. "Does this mean that somehow those poor kids, sleeping on Cliffy's old pillow, could see into his mind? But that's not possible."

Sam looked up at Shelley with an expression Shelley'd never seen on his face before. She took a step back. His voice was grave.

"I know. But I noticed something. Do you remember when we first met Hum and got him to draw pictures with us?"

"Sure."

"I remember noticing that he held the pens in his right hand. I remember thinking, oh, that's good. He's a righty. You know I hated having to use a lefty desk when I was in school. I was pleased to know that wouldn't be an issue."

"So?"

"When he told us his dream and about Lizzie, he held the imaginary knife in his *left* hand. He slashed with his left hand. That's not normal. He did that because he was remembering it that way... because he was seeing it as a lefty in the dream. He was seeing it as Cliffy."

"No..." Shelley said. "It was a dream. A coincidence."

Rest easy, dear reader: The Smalls adopted Hum the following year. Though it took a while, with love and a bit of therapy, Hum's trust issues abated. The Smalls made sure that Hum had control and ownership of his belongings. He made friends at school and in the neighborhood; he ate and slept well. That Christmas was extra special—Hum relished the sense of safety and belonging as the greatest of the gifts he received. He grew stronger and happier over time.

Meanwhile, as the ink dried on Hum's adoption papers, the metal doors opened in cell block C at the New Jersey State Prison and Clifford Patrick Mullhaney was escorted down the barred hallway to meet his roommate Syck who sulked on the top bunk. He lifted his head off his hands as Cliffy scowled and shuffled toward the bottom bunk, curling a lip in disgust at the thin gray blanket and misshapen foam pillow. A thin smile worked its way across Syck's pockmarked face as Cliffy disappeared from his view. Below him, he heard the bedsprings creak in protest as Cliffy positioned the pillow against his back and leaned against the wall.

Adjusting to prison life took time. Cliffy had long enjoyed

the freedom the satisfying power that comes from bullying and intimidating others. There was a learning curve since Cliffy lacked protective connections with others, lacked the size or fighting skills to keep predators at bay. As you might imagine, he was the new prison toy.

But he was smart, mean and resilient.

What Cliffy found hard to tolerate was that in those few hours where sleep was possible late at night, he was bothered by vivid dreams. First-person dreams just like in those violent video games he used to play for hours, but so unlike his own, it was as if he was in someone else's mind. Sometimes, he was an obsessive-compulsive man of about fifty trapped in a world of repetitions and agoraphobia. Washing, washing, washing his hands, checking the locks on the doors and windows, pulling up his socks seven times each. It had to be seven for the socks. Brushing his teeth, scrubbing his face, mopping, mopping, mopping the floor. Had to be clean. Had to be just right. And then for fun he'd challenge himself to hack into computer systems.

IOI

Cliffy had never done more with computers than play video games. But in his dreams, he was a hacking wizard. Lines of code, code, code. Writing, deleting. All night long, the tedium went on and on. He'd wake up, change positions, rearrange the pillow and the same dream would begin again.

Sometimes, he'd dream he was a heroin addict desperate for a fix. In these dreams, he burgled houses and mugged strangers like an insatiable hungry ghost never satisfied, never able to get the sweet release of oblivion. He'd wake and mash the pillow again.

The dreams that bothered him the most were the Nathan dreams, also in first-person. Nathan sat and rocked and talked to himself. Nathan had the mental processes of paranoid Jell-O pudding. Nathan talked to stuffed animals, a unicorn, a dragon and a teddy bear. As he rocked, he moaned and cried, "Don't let them get me. Don't let them get me. Nathan doesn't want to get caught. Nathan won't sit in the big electric chair. No Old Sparky."

Where did these dreams come from? They were so unlike his usual dreams where he was in the driver's seat, he made the decisions, he got others to do his bidding. He was always powerful and manipulative. In the dreams he was obsessed and desperate.

He woke each morning feeling tired and irritable with nothing to whatsoever to look forward to.

Damn these dreams, he'd mutter, punching the pillow.

FIVE

Gracie was handing out menus to a group of nurses just settling into a booth as Zap walked back to his seat at the bar. The nurses were chatting all at once, venting about the difficult patients on their shift. The matriarch was an attractive woman in her forties whose mouth seemed to be tugged downward by gravity.

"I am dead on my feet," she said, leaning her head back against the booth.

"I thought that shift would never end," said a tall stringy-haired nurse.

"That old guy who looks like the Crypt Keeper put his hand up my leg!" complained another with short curly hair. "I just wanna ---*Rrrrrr!*" she said, hands out, pretending to strangle someone.

"Yeah, well, I had a bedpan throw at me!" said the loudest and most charismatic of the bunch. Gesturing with her hands, she almost hit Zap in the stomach. Their conversation stopped as they noticed him.

"Sorry!" she gasped, apologizing with embarrassment.

"No worries," he said, smiling at them.

He passed their booth. Behind him, he heard their explosion of laughter "nice move!" and comments about "Jennifer assaulting the bar hunk."

Zap was amused to be referred to as the "bar hunk". He was too exhausted to feel even remotely sexy.

The low ceiling, low lighting, heavy beams and old brick walls made him feel like he was stepping back in time to a pub in the United Kingdom. He paused to run a hand along a thick beam just overhead.

Gracie's voice behind him said, "It's really something, isn't it?"

He turned to see her carrying a tray of used glasses.

"Would you believe this building was shipped over from Ireland back the late 1800's? Every brick and beam…"

"Really?" he asked.

"Yup. Back when they used to build things to last. Oh, and lookit," she gestured with an elbow, "didja see my collection of classic horror figurines? I just love the Bela Lugosi one where he's strangling Renfield."

Zap hadn't noticed the curio cabinet despite the spotlight on it. The sides of the cabinet were shaped like coffins and varnished with a dark stain, almost black. Each shelf was full of monsters in action poses: The Creature from the Black Lagoon, Frankenstein, the Wolfman, Dr. Jekyll and Mr. Hyde. The top shelf was all Dracula figurines.

"That's quite a collection," Zap said, turning to Gracie. But she was gone.

Funny Little Stories

The long weekend was winding to a close, our first family reunion in ages gathered at the old homestead house in a hollow in the Tennessee hills outside of Lynchburg. The main event had been the previous evening—Saturday supper at a lovely old restaurant owned by a distant cousin. We had the whole place to ourselves. It was unfortunate that Aunt Wanetta wasn't able to come. She'd remained behind with a hired caregiver. Over dinner and endless posed photos, I caught up with relatives I'd not seen in decades and met cousins removed for the first, probably last, time.

In my child and teen years, my family had lived just a few blocks away and this house had seemed an extension of our own. But jobs and marriage had moved me farther and farther from Lynchburg, Tennessee and then even the United States, so that I'd not seen the extended family in almost three decades. Calls and cards had tapered slowly until I had almost lost touch altogether.

The reunion had been an exhausting and wistful success. While it was grand to catch up, I was well aware of what a stranger I'd become. Too many births, graduations, marriages, divorces and deaths to log in my head. By the end of the day my face hurt from smiling and nodding politely.

The weather could not have been better. We'd enjoyed a picture-perfect spring day replete with sunshine, gentle breezes and chirping songbirds. Back at the homestead, the adults sat on the porch drinking spiked lemonade and watched the children playing tag and frisbee on the lawn.

But that welcoming warm weather, like most of the relatives, had gone by morning. A last gasp of winter had blown in and settled a dusting of frost on the fields and dejection on my heart. I should have left the previous evening with the majority of the relatives. But I'd been gone for so long and was so tired. It felt perfectly normal to stay the night with family. And I'd wanted some time to visit with Aunt Wanetta. Now that I was back in this second home, I was aware of how much I'd missed her.

A few straggler, out-of-town aunts and cousins had stayed the night as well. We'd had a huge brunch together—quite the spread—bacon and biscuits, grits and eggs, hash browns and pastries and Jimmy's sausage. There was always Jimmy's sausage in the house. Between the gloomy weather and all that food making me sleepy, I'd not been in a hurry to leave.

Feeling tremendously guilty for my neglect to my family in general and favorite aunt in particular, I said I'd be happy to go up and sit with Aunt Wanetta. Since she was bedridden, she'd missed most of the festivities. Now that it was less hectic, I was eager for some quiet catch-up time.

"She'd love that, hon. She's missed you," her daughter, Olive said.

There was a hint of mischief in her eyes that took me back to our childhood. I never felt entirely at ease with Olive. We got along fine and played together all the time. But one never knew when she'd slip a frog between the sheets or hide all your underwear. We had once been close, but truth be told, it was more by circumstance than friendship. I recalled playing with dolls, playing tag in the yard and sleepovers in tents made from sheets thrown over furniture. Huddling in front of the mirror scaring ourselves silly chanting, "Bloody Mary please come out, Bloody Mary please come out!" I would be too frightened and run out before Bloody Mary could manifest in the mirror. Olive swore she saw ethereal fingers reaching out of the glass toward my retreating neck.

We'd grown so far apart…different interests, different lives.

"Perhaps I could read to her," I said, with another guilt pang.

"She'd love that, bless her heart. Just know that… she's… well, she's not always lucid. Sometimes she's rational and sometimes she babbles gibberish. Don't let her upset you, hon."

More guilt. Aunt Wanetta used to be truly gay—no, not in the modern sense, I mean in the old-fashioned sense: full of life and joy and love; a delight to be around, the one everyone gravitated to for her humor, warmth and compassion. Now she was dotty and bedridden and not expected to live to see summer. Most of her major organs were failing, Olive had said.

When I'd walked into the room, Aunt Wanetta was awake but only vaguely aware of me. I was shocked by how shriveled she looked, her pallor waxy and gray. She looked far worse than just the day before when I popped up to see her, but she'd been asleep.

"May I open the curtains? It's so dim in here," I said, moving toward the heavy drapes. There was a strange smell and a heaviness in the air that made my stomach queasy.

"No! No, dear, the light hurts my eyes. Here… come sit here by me."

I sat in the uncomfortable rattan chair beside my aunt's bed. I reached for her hand, but she clutched the covers up to her neck. I pulled back and surveyed the room.

What struck me was how plain and drab it all was. No colorful bedspreads or crocheted afghans, no paintings, no flowers. In fact, the room was devoid of all but the essentials — bed, nightstand, visitor's chair. No dressing table, no mirrors. In the dim bedside light, it all seemed gray.

"I'm so sorry, Aunt Wanetta. I've been gone for so long. I should have called. I should have kept up. It's just — "

She suddenly turned her head toward me, filmy eyes wide.

"You shouldn't have come."

"What?" I drew back in surprise. This was the last reaction I'd expected. "But Aunt Wanetta…the reunion was so amazing. And everyone wanted to see you and each other — "

"You shouldn't have come!" She hissed. "It's not safe, not safe, not safe for you dear."

"What's not safe?" I asked with alarm. I wasn't even sure she recognized me. Did she think I was a hired nurse?

Her head thrashed side to side in a horrible anguish, face distorted as if in agony.

"Are you in pain? Should I call for Olive?"

She shut her eyes and spat out, "No! I must tell you."

"Tell me what?"

"I don't want to be like that. I don't want to be like that. And I won't go to a nursing home."

"Shh, Aunt Wanetta, no, of course not," I lied. I had no say in her care, but her abrupt distress had startled me into dropping the book on her nightstand I'd just picked up. As I reached to the floor to retrieve it, she shot a withered arm from the covers and gripped my arm with cold boney fingers. I tried to pull away to no avail. She had me in a vise-grip.

"That's how it all started!" she said with a look of such horror across her face that I worried she might be in the throes of a heart attack. She gasped a tremendous sucking sound, her mouth a gaping "O".

"Aunt Wanetta, please let go, you're hurting me," I said, prying her hand off my upper arm. Touching her boney discolored hand so much like a great dead claw, alarmed me. I jumped half out of the chair.

Her eyes focused. Her claw hand relaxed enough that I was able to break free.

I rubbed my hand over my bruised arm noting spots where her fingernails had dug in.

"You'll think I'm raving mad when I tell you, but I'll tell you. I know what I know," she said, sinking back into the pillows, her face molding into a great frown.

"Of course not," I said, "not at all," I lied. She'd always had a good head on her shoulders and seemed more grounded than most to me, but her behavior so far was unlike any I'd witnessed from her before. Perhaps she *was* lost in a senile fog.

"It was after the Great War," she began slowly.

I eased myself back down on the hard seat, relieved that she seemed to be calming down.

"My first husband had not come home from the front and I needed to support myself and the baby. I had no particular skills to offer. But then there was an ad in the paper for a job at a nursing home. Not a nursing job, more of the unpleasant grunt work: changing sheets, bedpans, sweeping, bathing—that sort of thing."

"Mm-hmm," I said, tucking her discolored and boney arm under the covers, more for myself than for her. Though I didn't want her to be cold, it distracted and unsettled me.

"It all seemed so straightforward at first. And I needed the money so desperately," she said in a tone that one might expect a priest to hear in a confessional.

"Mm-hmm."

"But back then there weren't the kind of regulations there are now…"

"How do you mean?"

"This place was clean enough, I don't mean that, but surely there were no state inspections or anything or they would have realized—"

Aunt Wanetta's eyes shifted around the room nervously. Her claw hand reemerged from under the covers to grip the edge of the sheet.

"Aunt Wanetta? Realized what?"

"That *room* at the end of the hall. It was across from the supply closet, kind of apart from the other rooms. A good thing, that. They assigned me to that room. That… *man*." A bit of spittle caught in her throat just then. She heaved and coughed violently; her face contorted in an awful grimace.

"Do you need some water?" I asked, looking around for a glass.

She waved me away, coughed a few more times and settled back, frown firm on her face.

‖‖

"Of course, I thought nothing of it at first and was just grateful for the job. It was the middle of my shift when the nurse informed me of the additional duty and led me down the hall. Her manner shifted as we got closer to that room. She'd been kind and self-assured to this point, like a proper tour guide who has given the tour hundreds of times."

I rubbed my wrist. For a frail old thing, she'd really hurt me. I tried to focus on her story. She seemed agitated and wouldn't look at me. In fact, Aunt Wanetta was staring at a spot in the corner. She must have been reliving her memory, seeing the nursing home in her mind.

"The closer we got, the edgier she got" she continued. Her voice took on a nervous tone. "I assumed this must be a very difficult angry patient that no one else wanted to deal with and steeled myself. I would be calm and steadfast. The nurse paused before opening the door as if bracing herself and that shook me. I mean, if a seasoned nurse was hesitant…but what's more, I felt fearful before I even knew why, you know how you can just sense things sometimes." She turned her murky eyes to me and studied my face a moment. The kind old eyes I used to love were hard to find in her face. These eyes were strange to me.

I nodded, sensing keenly that I wasn't going to like this story.

"She opened the door and flipped the light switch—the oddness of this didn't occur to me until later—the dim light revealed a withered old man, a *very* old man in the bed, eyes closed, face shrunken."

She moved her mouth as if thirsty but shook me off when I offered to get her some water. She continued, "His cheekbones protruded like mountain peaks from the valleys of his eyes and cheeks. He was the oldest, most shriveled living person I'd ever seen. Like a living apple-doll — do you know what I mean? Do you remember apple dolls?"

I nodded. Apple dolls had frightened me as a child. I thought they were grotesque, horrid things made by darkly twisted people.

Her claw hand reached for her throat, crossing her chest as if warding off something.

"It was the smell that got me first," Aunt Wanetta said, her nose scrunching as if she could still smell it. "Like the homeless — soiled and earthy, but something else... something like compost but worse..." She eyes searched the room as if looking for the words, "like rancid meat."

I recoiled. My spine ground into that uncomfortable chair back. As if by the power of suggestion, I could imagine the smell she described as if I were there in the room with us. I kneaded my stomach absently with a vague notion to sooth that queasy feeling.

"The nurse explained that I was to sponge-bathe him, change him, and change the bedding. But there were peculiar rules... I was only to enter the room mid-day between mid-morning and mid-day. I was not to attempt to speak with him as it was explained he was in a coma, nor attempt to feed him, just to tidy the room and clean his body."

"But how did he get water or food?" I asked. I was aware that I had covered my nose with my hands and was taking shallow breaths. Did I really smell that or was it just apprehension and imagination?

Her claw hand shot out and held mine. "That was the horror of it."

I pulled away again. "What was?" I asked, fairly sure I didn't really want to know the answer.

"I was naïve… so naïve… I tried to do as I was told and not ask too many questions," she continued, evading my question. "The nurse watched me while I worked as though I'd never done any of it before. I fetched a basin of warm water and pulled the bedsheet down. Not much to wash, the body was so small and frail. I washed the head and face, noting peculiar ears, large and pointed and oddly hairy. I worked quickly as that smell was enough to gag a rhinoceros. The funny thing was, I couldn't figure out quite where it was coming from. Pulling off his pajama pants, I fully expected to find an awful mess, but no, he was surprisingly clean, just shriveled all over like a dried date. Kind of tones of that brownish color, too, like one of those mummies in a museum. The nurse supervised as I bathed him. That smell. Ugh! It was as if he exuded the stench from his pores. I had to assume that he was close to death and full of sickness. I told myself this as I turned him from side to side, changing the sheets and all. Even the clean smell of the fresh sheets was overpowered by that stench. But his toenails…" She coughed violently.

"Perhaps you should rest," I suggested, worried anew that she'd have an attack that would launch her to the great beyond, but also wanting to cut short this unpleasant story.

She shook her head and recovered. "I would like some water," she croaked.

Flooded with relief, I leapt up and walked briskly to the bathroom where I found a small glass sitting on a porcelain glass and toothbrush holder. I wanted some water too, but there was only the one glass. I could wait. I wouldn't stay long. I was sure that Aunt Wanetta would tire quickly. I'd leave then.

Setting the glass under the tap, waiting for the glass to fill, I felt the closeness of the small bathroom like a claustrophobe. This familial house I'd always loved and felt welcomed in, this house I'd been eager to return to, now felt confining and cloying. I caught a glimpse of my face in the mirror. It seemed that all traces of makeup and lipstick were gone. I looked ashen and worn, years older than my true age.

You can do this. Let her finish this yarn, then tuck her in and say your goodbyes. She's just a disturbed and lonely old woman. Don't let her get to you. I gripped the sink. *You can do this. You owe her this.*

I forced myself to count to ten then returned to the bedside, handing over the glass of water. I'd expected Aunt Wanetta to take delicate sips but to my surprise, she clutched the glass and drank greedily, even dribbling a bit on her nightgown. There was something almost animalistic about her that again was unfamiliar and discomforting. She thrust the nearly empty glass back.

"It took me a while to realize that the room was different from the others," she continued with determination, a renewed strength to her voice. "It was smaller, much smaller, more like the supply closet than the other rooms, and it had no windows."

"No windows? How awful!"

"And the lighting...the lighting in the room was so dim...there was only one overhead bulb and it seemed to have no more power than a night light. I have diseased eyes now and can tell you that working in that room so dark, one felt half-blind. When I asked the nurse if we could have more light, she said, 'No, no, it is this way on purpose. You see, Mr. Endgate has a very rare skin disorder…a sensitivity to natural light. When we are not in the room, we turn the light off. He's in a coma, it does not matter to him, I promise you."

"Sounds like a tomb," I said without thinking, the image of the vampire from *Nosferatu* coming to mind. I think now that she had somehow put that image in my head, because what she said next sent a frosty icepick right up my spine.

"The nurse stood well away from us. Of course, at first, I assumed it was to give me room and observe… then I thought because of the smell… and then while rolling Mr. Endgate, his foot got caught up in a bit of sheet and that's when I saw, really saw the toenails… then of course, the fingernails."

Aunt Wanetta's eyes roamed the room again as if looking for an escape hatch. They found my face. She focused and leaned toward me, those bulging eyes boring into mine.

"His nails were long and hard like talons, fat and round, not like normal nails at all. And despite the fact that it was hard to see clearly in the dim light with his body and covers and all, there was no mistaking the nails. Not like anything on a human, more like a bird of prey--they were a greenish-black with a brown crustiness at the tips. One toenail had snagged enough to prevent me from rolling him easily. The sight of those nails scared me. I jumped back, releasing him unintentionally. He fell like a sack of potatoes onto his back. His thin lips parted and jagged little teeth… I saw jagged little brown teeth like daggers…"

I was torn between utter fright and pity. I realized my hands were clenching my arms much the same way she had gripped me earlier. I tried to relax my grip but was held fast by sheer terror. Had this really happened or was poor Aunt Wanetta delusional?

116

Had she been on some medication perhaps that brought on this vivid break from reality? Or had she been recruited to care for some kind of monster? Absurd.

"But you said... you said the man had some rare disorder. Perhaps he was just deformed in other ways as well... sensitive to skin, some abnormal nail growth, poor dentition..." I heard myself saying all this but didn't believe it much as I wanted to.

She laughed in a sharp, mocking way that sounded like the shriek of a wild animal. She shook her head violently again. "No! You see, they wanted me to stay and I needed the money. They assured me that while unpleasant, by caring for him, I would be rewarded handsomely. I rationalized that I was really only needed in that room for a matter of moments. I forced myself to stay on until...until..."

Aunt Wanetta gestured for the water glass. I passed it to her. Again, she gulped down the last bit with a disturbing urgency.

"Until that final day..." She shut her eyes tight then. The wisps of white eyebrows bunched and all the wrinkles in her face scrunched tight.

I shivered and hugged myself. "You are upsetting yourself. Perhaps—"

Her eyes opened and glared at me, cutting off the thought. She continued, "I found out that so many of my predecessors had just disappeared. Girls like me who just didn't show up to work. There were rumors. Other nurses began eyeing me funny and asking how it was working for Mr. Endgate. One day, I snuck behind the nurses' station to see his records. Surely, he was going to die at any moment, yet he never seemed to get any medical attention. I never saw a doctor near his room, but I told myself it was at the end of the hall, so I wouldn't necessarily see action down there, out of the way like it was."

"Right," I said, hoping to keep the momentum of this awful story going so we could reach the end soon.

"I realized that all the other rooms had little cubbies outside the door with clipboards — you know, notation from shift to shift of medications and meals and whatnot." Aunt Wanetta leaned forward again, her eyes wide and desperate. She near whispered, *"there wasn't a cubby for Mr. Endgate. It was like he didn't exist."*

"But there had to be…" I stammered.

She smiled a horrible wry smile. "No, dear. It took me only a week or so to put it all together. And after…that day, it all made horrid sense. You see, Mr. Endgate had no need of medical attention. His was a very special arrangement with this nursing home. He *owned* it! He controlled everything and everyone. A vampire in plain sight, hiding in a backwater nursing home. Patient and staff turnover was brisk…all hushed up and swept under the rug." She made a sudden sweeping gesture over her chest with a skeletal hand.

The sudden motion made me jump two inches straight up. I'd heard her say vampire so matter-of-factly. She'd described it so thoroughly, but this had to be a delusion. Olive had said she faded in and out of reality. This was her imagination, it must be. Yet I found no comfort in this thought. My fight or flight response was screaming at me to run out of the room.

"Oh, yes," Aunt Wanetta continued, her wild eyes holding mine. "He looked like a dying old man, but there was no file on him behind the nurses' desk. Why? Because he was not really a patient. He was free to roam the halls in the dark of night, to come and go as he pleased, to feed on whoever…"

I shrieked. "Stop! Oh, please. This is preposterous. You saw this as a late-night movie, or you are subject to some wild hallucinations brought on by medications—"

"In the beginning he went out to hunt. Then as the condition persisted and he became weak, he just let the food come to him. So easy, so perfect."

The corner of her mouth trembled towards a weak smile. "The perfect set up for a dying vampire. Self-service, do you see? And I was offered up on a plate, so to speak."

I pictured the grotesque creature supposedly so weak he needed basic care reaching up and grabbing one unsuspecting nurse after another as they hovered over his bed.

"Aunt Wanetta, you are imagining things and upsetting yourself. Upsetting me. There are no such things as vampires, and you know it."

"You *think*?" She asked fiercely, thrusting her boney arm out and catching my wrist again. This time, her nails dug in like cat claws. "You think I'm making all this up, do you?"

I shrieked again. "Please let me go—"

"Then what's THIS?" she asked, releasing my wrist and yanking down the neckline of her nightgown enough to reveal a deep and jagged scar just above her collarbone, a discolored blot with four deep puncture marks in the center. While there might have been another explanation, the mark looked exactly like the outline of a mouth and fang marks.

"And THIS?" she hissed, flipping her wrists around side to side to show deep marks, marks as if she'd been held tight by some creature with strong claws.

I must have screamed though I'm sure I don't know how. My brain was paralyzed with shock and horror.

"Now it's happening to me," she continued feverishly. "It's not like in books or movies, no, no, it's like a disease. I wasn't even sure for a long time. I felt almost normal. Then I got hungry and did some unfortunate things I now regret. It makes you feel invincible and you assume you're immortal. Do you remember? I always loved to have family around me. Close. Well…" She looked away with another tenuous and trembling hint of a smile."

What was she saying about family? Yes, she had always wanted family around her. What did she mean? Had she—

I heard a keening sound as I pressed my hands to my temples. I felt the vibration in my hands and realized that the sound was coming from my own mouth.

"Some do live much longer than normal," she continued, "but most get old like everyone else. I'm old. I can control myself most of the time. But the others. The disease is just setting in for them, they're hungry and desperate like crack addicts. It's not their fault, don't blame them… but I can't protect you. I can't even protect myself. They'll come for me, too. You see," she said turning to me with a look of pity, "this reunion was a terrible trap, my dear. You aren't even safe from me. Get out while you can. Go! I'm so hungry!"

"Amah!!! Aaah!!! Aaaahh!!!" My keening was louder and stronger like a child straining to make a recognizable word for the first time.

That's when we heard the footfalls and voices coming toward the door. Aunt Wanetta fell back to her pillows, her face softened as if she were sleeping soundly. She'd suddenly gone from a highly animated termagant to a meek, frail, old woman. Why was she was faking? As a pack of relatives rushed in, I sat mutely staring at the figure in the bed.

"What happened?" they asked.

My mouth fell open, but I was mute. Realizing that my wrist felt like I'd grazed it over a hot burner, I looked down to see that I was rubbing the areas where Aunt Wanetta had grabbed me. Four thin bands. Warm to the touch. Angry red bracelets the shape of finger brands.

This home, these people suddenly seemed foreign and menacing. My mind raced. What had I just seen? And if…if sweet Aunt Wanetta was actually a…vampire… I could hardly bring myself to believe it, but I struggled desperately to make sense of what I'd just heard and seen. If Aunt Wanetta had been bitten so long ago, who else in this family was a secret monster? I had been told that she was likely to die soon, but she'd gripped my arm with the strength of a young man. And those marks. I'd not imagined those fearful marks on her neck.

I looked to my family members, my mouth hanging open, speechless. I looked at the figure in the bed. My mind raced through the last few moments—her eyes, those claws and oh, yes! The teeth! Had I not seen pointy little dagger teeth when she hissed at me, "And THIS?"

"Has she been telling you her funny little stories?" Olive asked with a gleam in her eye.

With Herculean effort, I forced my body to move, swallowed my dread, said gracious thanks mumbled something like 'Oh, gracious, look at the time, I must be on my way' and promised the usual keep-in-touch claptrap. Even as I moved toward the door, they seemed to close in on me.

"Don't y'all wanna stay for supper?" Olive asked, reaching out a hand to catch mine. "Sylvia and Mark are stayin'."

"No, no, you must let me go back to my family," I all but bleated. I would not panic. I would not run. I fought to keep breathing and focused as I hastened back to my room and gripped my bag in front of me. Get out the door. Get away. Act normal. Steady. Breathe. Keep moving. Olive, her husband, Jerome, and Wanetta's sister, Grace followed me like Border collies working a sheep.

I looked at Sylvia and Mark who followed behind them looking concerned but not predatory. They were oblivious. Or was I going mad? How could I tell them the horrible truth? How could I save them? We were like sacrificial animals. I kept edging toward the stairs. As a unit they followed me down the stairs, entreating me to stay. I felt the predatory energy as if I were being stalked by a pack of wolves.

"Please stay for dinner."

"It'll be right dark soon. You could leave in the mornin'."

"We'd be happy to have you," Grace said.

"Yeah, we're staying," Sylvia said, with a quick glance at Mark. "It'll be fun. Come on, we can all leave tomorrow."

Mark nodded half-heartedly. Did he sense something wrong?

Olive and my uncle Jerome smiled at this. "You see? Stay. It'll be jus' like ol' times."

"My children…" I stammered, "My husband will have had his hands full; he'll be so relieved when I get home," I said. "The boys'll have run him ragged."

Perhaps saying this saved me. I feel sure that had I been alone, I would never have made it to the door. For whatever reason, they allowed me to go.

You are cordially invited to the

Ravensfield

family

Reunion

Come back to the roost...

We're just dying to see you...

WHEN: Saturday
WHERE: Ravensfield house

RSVP: 615- 666- 0000

This was some years ago. I don't know if Aunt Wanetta is still alive, or what happened to Sylvia and Mark. I've severed all ties with the family. I've even legally changed my name and moved three times so they can't find me.

Driving by a nursing home, I often wonder what became of Mr. Endgate. Is he still out there somewhere in a dark room at the end of the hall waiting for that new unsuspecting nurse to come check on him? I hoped he was dead. From what Wanetta said, they were not immortal. They thrived at first, then got weak and died just like humans, thank goodness.

I've started a pill jar, just in case. I don't want to end my days in a nursing home wondering who or what is living just down the hall.

I often wonder why Aunt Wanetta revealed herself to me. I want to believe that she still cared for me enough to warn me. I think of her every time I put on the wide metal bracelets that hides the permanent marks on my wrists.

Blood relatives indeed!

BW&S

SIX

*B*ar hunk, eh? Zap thought as he got back to his bar stool. He grinned and shook his head. "I probably look more like a zombie."

He finished his fries and sipped his stout, glancing over to check on the bearded man's progress with the fish platter.

The bearded man was gone, his place cleared.

Out of the corner of his eye, Zap noticed something red moving. He turned to watch a bottle of ketchup on the bar to Zap's left shook itself free from the wire cage that kept it huddled up with a container of mustard, a bottle of hot sauce and glass salt and pepper shakers. It wiggled up and up until it broke free, hovering above its fellow prisoners.

"What the heck?" Zap asked, half-rising from his seat.

The bottle tipped one way then the other as if debating about which direction to take. Gracie came around from behind Zap. The bottle seemed to quiver in fear as she snatched it out of the air and pushed it back down into the cage.

"I told you," she laughed, "the poltergeist has been acting up tonight. Don't worry, he's just messin' with you."

Zap blinked.

A mini Zenith television on the counter opposite them flashed on.

"Oh, here we go. Showing off are we now?" Gracie asked the air with an authoritative voice.

Zap rose off the bar stool, but Gracie put a hand on his back.

"He's like a little kid wanting attention," she shook her head.

Zap swallowed. "Who is?"

Zap hadn't seen a television that small in decades. His mother used to watch her soaps in the kitchen with a Zenith just like that.

"My brother, Paul. He died when he was seventeen, poor dumb kid. He'd just gotten his driver's license and was out joyriding. Got into a wreck. Been buggin' me ever since."

Images flashed as the channel knob click-clicked. Zap eased back down on his barstool and stared in fascination. This had to be some trick, but if it was, it was a good one. The knob on a television of that vintage was hard to turn and wouldn't respond to a remote. And the floating ketchup bottle...he couldn't explain that either.

The clicking stopped and the picture came into focus. It was a re-run of the show Bewitched. Agnes Morehead as the mother was teasing Samantha about her husband.

"Our mother *loved* that show. She looked a bit like Kim Novac and was over the moon when she got her autograph on the *Bell Book and Candle* poster. Did you see it?"

Zap swiveled around following Gracie's finger pointed to the space above an empty book where Kim Novak, dressed in black and holding a cat stood off to the left of a bright red background. "The movie was the inspiration for Bewitched, you know." My mom had a thing for witches. Good ones, of course."

"Oh. Never saw it. Not much of a movie guy."

"Oh, that's a pity. It's a classic. We watched it every year before Halloween. Mom would put on her witch hat and make a huge bowl of popcorn all drizzly with butter for us." She sighed. "Such good times."

Nothing Like A Strong Pot of Tea

Part 1 Road Trip

Tossing her purse into the passenger seat, Gwen wiped a tear from her cheek and slammed the door shut. She jammed the key into the ignition. Her parents' old, two-tone, dirt-on-cream Volvo sedan roared to life. More tears blurred her vision as she shifted into reverse.

"Asshole! That lying, cheating asshole! How could he?" she yelled.

She shifted into first gear and fumbled with the seat belt. She slowed at the stop sign then floored it in a hasty left turn ahead of an oncoming toxic-toad-green Gremlin. The driver of the Gremlin honked the horn and flipped a middle finger out the window.

Gwen snarled back, "Up your nose with a rubber hose!" and sped up. Fresh sobs erupted; tears dotted her T-shirt. With no idea where she was going, she headed out through the campus gates and turned up the radio. She laughed maniacally as she realized the song was Chicago's "If You Leave Me Now."

"You'll take nothing from me, you jerk" she snuffled. She sang along, if it can be called singing to sob, yell the words and

129

pound the steering wheel. Passing through the gates, she smacked the roof of her car to pick up her guardian angel, a school tradition.

"Sorry, angel, I'm not good company right now," she blubbered. "I'm kind of a mess. You have your work cut out for you."

As if to mirror her mood and as often happened on the Cumberland Plateau, clouds had gathered in the midst of a perfect September afternoon. A light rain began even though the sun was still shining. Steamy wisps rose like baby ghosts off the hot pavement ahead of her. She flipped her wipers on.

Gwen intermittently sang and sniffled to keep back snot. Did she have any tissues? She felt around in her purse and bellowed, mangling the words, "you'll regret the things you did, you son of a lying, cheating bitch!"

A sign for a road called Scalding Skillet Lane caught her attention. She slowed, signaled and careened onto the new road. The Volvo shot past barns, pastures, old farms and little brick houses. A sign warned of a harsh turn ahead. She slowed into the tight turn.

Roads off the plateau were steep and wild with switchbacks. She gripped the steering wheel as the Volvo rocked left then right then left. The road was barely two lanes wide with enormous elephant ear leaves on either side. Gwen slowed further, well aware that an encounter with a vehicle coming up the mountain could be catastrophic.

She was the only one on the road. She sniffed and wiped at her face as anger traded places with devastation in her mind. The road levelled out. A new song started up. She didn't recognize it at first, but her blubbering began anew as Carol King's voice hit the chorus of "It's Too Late."

A signpost leaned as if wanting to catch her attention. Gwen squinted and laughed "Wildheart Pass!" She swerved and shifted. The Volvo bounced onto a dirt road and splashed through mud puddles. She had to slow down.

A farmhouse on the left had more outbuildings and stuff in the yard than she'd ever seen: old cars, farm machinery, roosters in individual pens, ducks, goats, piles of tires and a mountain of Pabst Blue Ribbon beer cans near a fire pit. She slowed further, taking it all in. There were even tacky little statues scattered about; gnomes and girls with flower baskets half hidden by high grass and car parts.

She passed a sagging barn with a faded sign for BUDDY'S GARAGE. Buddy had not seen business for at least a decade.

Wildheart Pass ended at Billy Ought Road. Gwen slowed to a full stop with no idea where she was. The rain had stopped; the road was dry here. The sun was shining as if it had been all along. She flipped her wipers off.

"Billy Ought," she mused aloud. "What a strange name for a road! What ought Billy to do? Well, Billy *ought* not cheat on his girlfriend, for one."

A left turn would go back up the mountain or continue to meander who knew where, possibly south to Alabama. A right turn would take her down the mountain. This was the more likely bet that, sooner or later, she'd find a town she recognized, like Winchester. Gwen turned right and shifted gears.

Billy Ought Road, like Wildheart, was not quite two lanes wide but was mostly a straight shot down the remainder of the mountain. She pushed her foot down on the accelerator but regretted it almost immediately. She tensed and steered the Volvo to the right, keeping it from going off the road as a Caldwell's Septic Services truck rumbled past.

"See? It's just a shitty day!" she yelled with another maniacal laugh. She was relieved to have the road to herself again.

A new song was starting up, a slow electronic riff. She'd really liked this one and remembered it from Casey Kasem's Top Forty Countdown. Another sob song of lost love, this one by Paul Davis, "I Go Crazy" described the agony of running into an old girlfriend the singer had never really gotten over.

Her lip trembled as she imagined running into Kevin on campus. Or worse, Kevin with *Evie*.

The slow, sad song rambled on; Gwen snuffled and wiped at her nose.

Gwen was lost in a revenge fantasy when she blew past a cheery rustic sign in high weeds: Pottery for sale.

She got a quick glimpse of a driveway curling toward a charming old farmhouse, rocking chairs, a bench swing, a little table with a checkered tablecloth, a vase with fresh flowers. Her head swiveled back as she shot past the driveway. Snapping her eyes forward, she slowed and looked for a place to do a U-turn.

This was the quintessential, idyllic country house. She *had* to stop in. Maybe get directions. She eased the Volvo along the rutted driveway between two half-buried wagon wheels. A pink floral wreath hung on the house door. All about the porch hung angels, bird houses, windchimes and sparkling colored-glass mobiles. An old Labrador retriever came around a massive azalea bush, tail wagging.

"This is so cute," Gwen marveled, looking for a place to park. A concrete frog holding a welcome sign grinned up at her from the bottom of the porch steps as she continued past the porch. The driveway meandered around the house to a barn, a chicken coop and a structure she guessed was an old icehouse with whiskey barrel planters on either side full of bright red geraniums. The yellow door was open. A fortyish woman with long hair and overalls appeared in the doorway and waved.

Gwen parked. She caught a glimpse of herself in the rearview mirror and winced. Her mascara was smeared, her eyes were puffy and red. She dabbed at the worst spots around her eyes and gave up.

"Hi there," the woman said, approaching the window.

Gwen got out and shut the door. "Hi, hope I'm not bothering you." She caught herself nervously flapping her hands and shoved them into the back pockets of her jeans. "I saw the pottery for sale sign and thought I'd stop. Is this a bad time?"

The Labrador wagged its way up to her and hopped on its front paws.

"No jumping, Loki," the woman admonished as Gwen patted the dog's head. "Not at all sweetheart, I needed a break. Come on in. Have a look around."

"I love your house!" Gwen blurted. There was something so peaceful and comforting about this property, it was as if she'd never breathed truly fresh air before, as if she'd found an old home she forgotten about. As if she was being welcomed back by a favorite aunt. She turned from the house to the studio realizing that it was built into the side of a hill.

"Was this an icehouse or some sort of bunker?" she asked.

Loki trotted along beside her, wagging.

"An icehouse, yes. My grandfather had a small ice delivery business back in the twenties and thirties."

"Wow. This is so amazing. You must love it here."

"Yes, I do. It was my parents' house. I'm trying to decide whether I should sell it or move in."

"Oh?"

"Mom stayed on after my dad died. But now she's passed on too. I live over near Cowan. I was renting it out, but that didn't go so well."

"Oh, I'm so sorry."

The woman gestured to go inside. Gwen stepped through the doorway. Loki followed.

"Mother taught me when I was little. When she got sick, I'd come over and keep her company in the studio. It helped her keep busy. Now I come on weekends to practice."

The studio had a comforting smell of clay and soothing nature sounds of water, birds chirping, wind caressing tree branches. The thick stone walls kept the room pleasantly cool. Sunlight streaked in through dusty windows to a concrete floor, wooden work benches with bins of tools and damp clay wrapped in plastic. On one side of the room were racks and racks of colorful pottery.

Gwen put a hand to her heart. "This is amazing! What a cool space. Makes me wish I could do pottery."

The woman smiled. "One can always learn, dear."

"Yeah," Gwen said in a wistful voice, moving toward the racks.

Blue and purple bowls, deep purple serving trays, swirling tones of blue on coffee mugs. The earthenware objects were organized by size, color and type. Green bowls. Rich brown flower vases.

"Some are mom's, some are mine."

"Right on," Gwen said, nodding. She took her time admiring the pieces, sometimes touching them or picking them up. She worked her way to a dustier set of shelves at the back. "Oh, far out!" she exclaimed, having discovered a shelf of whimsical mugs and teapots with funny faces.

"Glad you think so, dear" said a voice so close Gwen startled. She looked around in confusion. Besides Loki, contorted on the floor chewing his tail, she was alone. Loki struggled to stand up, flipped his ears out and cocked his head.

"You heard it too, then," Gwen said to Loki.

His tail half-wagged as if he hadn't really understood the question but wanted to please.

Gwen was puzzled. It had been a female's voice, but it didn't sound like the potter's voice. She was sure she hadn't imagined it. Loki bumped her hand with his nose distracting her. She shrugged and patted his head dismissing the uncanny voice. Perhaps it was a weird acoustic thing with the walls being so thick.

The woman, rearranging something across the room called out, "Sorry dear, did you say something?"

"N-no. Just talking to the dog."

Gwen's eyes rested on a small sign that read **MISFITS**. There were more mugs and teapots with funny faces. There was something about one teapot that drew Gwen's attention. It was glossy brown and somewhat misshapen with the face of a serene woman whose eyes were closed. Her mouth suggested either that she was bemused and possibly had a secret.

"I like this one," Gwen said, picking it up. She turned it around. The pot had some heft to it. That was good, less likely to break. She liked the way if felt in her hands.

The woman walked over, joining her in the aisle. "Oh, that's the misfit shelf… stuff my mom did before she passed. I'm afraid she wasn't quite herself then. The things on that shelf all have flaws like the glaze didn't completely cover it or the shape wasn't quite right. Her eyesight wasn't the best at the end. She wanted to keep making things but, well, some of them are just… off. I know I should just chuck them. No one would want them, but it's hard." She paused and rubbed the back of her neck. "She put so much love into her work, it seems disrespectful somehow. I've been putting it off."

"I like misfit things," Gwen said, cradling the pot. "I feel like a misfit most of the time."

"Oh, sweetheart, everyone feels that sometimes. You're young and beautiful. You've got your whole life ahead of you."

"Yeah," Gwen said without conviction.

"Where didja come from, sweetheart? I mean, you're not from around here, I can tell."

"No, I'm going to the University… I was just having a shitty day and started driving. I'm not even sure where I am right now. I just started turning down country roads…"

"I wasn't going to say anything," the woman said, approaching her, "but I could tell you were upset. Listen. Would you have time for a cup of tea? I think I have a box of cookies here somewhere. We've always kept cookies in the shop."

Loki popped up and wagged recognizing the word "cookies."

Gwen nodded.

The woman took the teapot from Gwen's hands, guided her to a stool and said, "I won't be a minute." She disappeared around a partition and Gwen heard familiar sounds of a kettle being set on a burner, spoons clinking, and what was likely rummaging in a cupboard for teabags. The music switched to Japanese flutes and gongs.

137

"My name is Solstice, by the way. What's yours, dear?" the woman called.

"Gwendolyn. Gwen."

"Ahh. A Welsh name then. Lovely. It means blessed ring, I believe."

"Does it? I never knew that." Gwen said.

Solstice arrived with a tray with two teapots, two mugs, honey, a plate of cookies and a pitcher of cream. She set Gwen's teapot down in front of her. "I thought you should get to know each other properly," she said with a peculiar smile.

And for the next thirty minutes, Gwen felt like she was talking with a best friend, therapist and long-lost relative all in one. The herbal tea, homemade cookies and girl talk calmed her mind and soothed her soul.

"So, I just go down the road to Buggy Top and turn right and that puts me into Cowan?" Gwen asked.

"That's right, dear. You can't miss it."

"And you're sure I can't pay you for this teapot?"

"I'm sure. It's a gift, sweetie. Mom would have wanted you to have it, I just know."

They were standing outside the doorway by the geraniums. Gwen reached out a hand and touched the lustrous red flowers. They're so gorgeous. Don't you just love geraniums?" She leaned in. "I love that *smell.*"

Solstice ran a hand down the length of her ponytail and pulled it across her face as if savoring the smell of her conditioner. The gesture made Gwen think of a cat flipping its tail. It was a peculiar yet playful and seductive movement. Gwen wondered if Solstice was a witch. If she was, she was a good one. A powerful one.

What a peculiar thought, Gwen thought. *Where did that come from?* She blinked and shook it off.

Solstice said, "Yes. A good earthy smell. Grounding. Balances your energies. Have a safe trip back, dear. Come back anytime."

Gwen made her way back to campus in a contented fog. She hardly thought about Kevin or Evie. When the Fleetwood Mac song, "Tell Me Lies" came on the radio, Gwen sang along with amusement. The previous hurt, anger and desire for revenge were gone, replaced by a feeling of freedom and peace. Kevin could just go tell his lies to Evie. She was free of him. On to someone better.

In her contented reverie, she didn't notice the humming voice from the back seat wasn't coming from the speakers.

Part 2 Tia

Gwen's moods vacillated over the next few days from self-righteous to angry to tender to hopeful that someone better would come along. Her friends rallied around her telling her that she would find someone far better than Kevin, someone who would truly appreciate her.

Just back from breakfast at the dining hall, she walked into her dorm room to find her roommate Sheila searching for something on Gwen's desk.

"What're you looking for?" Gwen asked.

Looking guilty, Sheila began edging back to her own desk. "I was um, out of staples, so I was going to borrow your stapler. I couldn't find it. It's no biggie; I'll figure something out later and buy some next time I'm at the supply store."

"It's right here," Gwen said, picking up her stapler.

"Oh, *duh*. How'd I miss that, right? Never mind, I have to get to biology," Sheila said, scooping up a pile of books, her phone and room key. She flounced past Gwen who was still holding the stapler. At the door Sheila turned back, "Um, I was hoping that Brandon and I could have some privacy here Saturday night. You don't mind, do you? You can stay over with Kevin or whatever his name is, right?"

"We broke up. I told you." Gwen said, in disbelief. "And yeah, I mind. Where am I supposed to go? This is my room too you know."

"Whatever," Sheila said. She turned and skulked away.

Gwen scowled and closed the door. She sat down at her desk. She and Sheila were not friends. They'd been assigned to each other based on the freshman roommate questionnaire that had asked questions like "Are you a smoker?" and "Are you a morning person?" It hadn't covered questions like "Are you a callous, selfish person with no regard for others?" If it had, Gwen felt sure Sheila would have checked the box for yes. It was only a few weeks into the first semester. The tension between the two had been escalating.

She surveyed her desk. *What was Sheila really looking for? Was anything missing?* She opened her drawers and did a quick inventory.

"I'd change roommates, if you can, dear. That girl is trouble," a voice said.

Gwen jumped and looked around. The door was still closed, there was no one else in the room. The voice had been so close. *Where?*

"Sorry, if I frightened you dear. Come sit back down," the voice said.

Gwen leapt back from the desk and leaned against the door, ready to bolt. The voice had come from her desk, from… the *teapot*?

Gwen stared at it. There was a bit of glare on the surface of the desk that reflected the face of the mug upside-down.

"Please, honey, I promise there's nothing to be afraid of."

Gwen covered her mouth to keep from screaming. She'd seen it this time. While the face on the teapot remained calm and serene, the upside-down face had moved.

"She was looking for money," the upside-down face said.

I'm seeing things. This can't be happening. Gwen reached for the door handle.

"Sweetie, come on. Sit back down. Let's talk, shall we, while we've got the chance? Come on. Girl talk."

Gwen stared in disbelief as the teapot reflection-face crossed its eyes in an impatient, clownish way.

"Would you be a dear? Get me some water? It drains my energy to be empty. Water helps."

Gwen's hand clung to the door handle. She blinked several times. "This can't be happening. I'm dreaming. It's stress. Yup, that's it, a hallucination brought on by stress. They say freshmen put on weight. They don't say they hallucinate but maybe—"

"Please? Just a little water."

"I'm having a conversation with a teapot," Gwen said, exhaling. "Far out." She grabbed the door handle and ran down the hall to the communal bathroom. She washed her face with cold water and stared at herself in the mirror. "You're cracking up. You've got to get a grip."

Two other students entered the bathroom in the midst of a conversation. One went into a stall while the other kept talking. Gwen took a deep breath and walked out. She stood in the hallway, staring at the open door to her room. She'd go in, get her keys and wallet and go for a drive. But as she waited for her fear to subside and her resolve to kick in, Courtney, one of Sheila's friends came down the hall.

"Hey. Sheila in?"

"No, she went to a class."

"Dammit. She owes me some money. Told me to come by this morning."

Gwen shrugged.

Courtney made a face, her shoulders slumped in defeat. "Well, if you see her, tell her I came by." She turned around and walked away.

"Will do."

Money. I did toss a twenty-dollar bill in my drawer the other day, but I removed it. Was that what Sheila was looking for?

Gwen eased back into her room and closed the door behind her. The teapot was in the same place with the same serene expression.

"Was she looking for money in my desk?" Gwen asked.

The eyes of the reflection face opened. The mouth opened and stretched in a face that could only mean, "Well, duh! It's about time you caught on!"

"If... if I pick you up, you won't hurt me, will you?" Gwen asked. She imagined the teapot chomping down on her fingers somehow. She pictured herself as a heroine in a bad horror movie, dancing around helplessly with a teapot biting through her hand to the bone.

The reflection face rolled its eyes and went even more cross-eyed with obvious exasperation. Gwen laughed with relief. She reached out and picked the teapot up. Nothing happened. The teapot was solid and unmoving, the face, eyes closed, perpetually serene. Gwen carried it down the hall to the bathroom and filled it with tap water. Back in the room with the door closed behind her, she set the teapot down and backed away.

"That's better, dear. Thank you. Now, where were we? That roommate of yours is no friend. Don't trust her. She talks trash about you when you aren't here. And that boyfriend of hers *Brandon,* "she emphasized his name with disdain, "is a bad influence. He's getting her hooked on drugs. I don't know what you have to do, but the sooner you get away from them, the better."

Gwen knew in her gut that this was true. She had met Brandon only a few times. He was almost handsome — she could see why Sheila liked him, but there was something slimy about him that gave her the willies. He had the kind of false smile that made her want to scrub herself down with a loofah sponge to get the ick off. She didn't like him invading her living space.

"I'll go talk to the Residential Life office," Gwen said. "They might not be able to do anything — "

"You have to think positively, dear. Have a little faith. Meanwhile, lock up or hide anything valuable."

"You really think she'd steal stuff from me?"

"Don't you?"

"Yeah..." Gwen conceded. "This still feels so weird, but okay, I've got a teapot that can talk. What should I call you? Do you have a name?"

"You know, I was wondering about that. While my creator put a lot of energy into me, she neglected to give me a name. Since I'm a teapot, why not call me Tia?"

"Far out! Tia. I like it."

And for the remainder of her free period, she found peculiar hiding places for her nice jewelry, her purse and other personal belongings she didn't want stolen.

And so began the peculiar relationship between Gwen and the talking teapot.

That afternoon, Gwen went to the Residential Life office and inquired about a different roommate situation, citing only that the relationship was escalating in hostility and she was unhappy.

"I know you probably don't have anything, but I thought I'd ask."

"Hmm. Well let's see," the clerk said, pulling a file from the file cabinet. "You're right. Once the semester begins, we don't have much. But it just so happens..." Her eyes followed her finger down a spreadsheet. "Yes. I thought so. We have a student who has dropped out. I'll warn you, it's a small room on the third floor. It's a bit of a walk from campus, but it's a single room out in Montmoor. You'll have to share a bathroom. As I recall it has a clawfoot tub with an attachable shower nozzle, so if you prefer a standup shower, you're out of luck."

"No, the tub's fine," Gwen said, not believing her luck.

"We don't usually offer freshmen single rooms but this one, well, let's just say, I can make an exception because of its size."

Gwen's face lit up. "I have a friend in Montmoor. That'd be great."

"Of course. Want to look at it before you commit?"

"Yes, I mean, no, not if someone else might get it. I'm sure it'll be fine. I'll take it. I never dreamed I could get a single. That's perfect."

"Hmm. Well, let me pull up a few papers to sign and it's yours."

Gwen's friend Abby Gail helped her move in. Setting up the record player and speakers was the first priority. Once that was situated, Anne studied the record collection in the crates under the player. "Ooh! This is what we need!" she exclaimed, pulling out the Saturday Night Fever album. She pulled out the first record and set it on the player. "I'm so glad you'll be out here with me! This is going to be groovy to the max!"

Gwen glanced around her tiny room reminding herself that this was what she had asked for, a room of her own. It felt like a broom closet with windows. Worse, it had a weird, unhappy vibe to it. She hoped it would be better once she got it decorated. She'd get used to the size.

"Yeah, groovy," she said, without conviction.

The Bee Gees began singing "Staying Alive". Abby Gail sang along, surveying the piles of stuff trying to figure out how to help. Noting Gwen's sullenness, she asked, "What's wrong?"

"Oh, nothing. I just hate moving," Gwen said, mustering a half-hearted smile for Anne. She wasn't sure where to start.

"Oh, it'll be great! You'll see. I know it's small, but you'll cheer the place up in no time," Abby Gail prattled on. "Once you get some posters up, maybe some small plants on the windowsill..."

"Yeah, I guess," Gwen answered, resting her hand on the back of an overstuffed chair upholstered in a patchwork of brown tones. "Where should I put the Archie Bunker chair?"

Her friend laughed, "No offense, but *that*" she pointed, "is some *ugly*. Where did you get that?"

"It was my dad's. It's ugly, but really comfortable. How about here by the window?"

Abby Gail shrugged. "Yeah, that works. "As Gwen pushed the chair into place, Abby Gail grabbed a pile of clothes off Gwen's new bed and heading for the small closet. "I'll just hang them up — I don't know how you want them arranged."

"That's fine." Gwen said over her shoulder. She sat down in the chair and put her feet up on the radiator. "Yeah. I like it. I'll cover it with a throw, so it won't be so... *brown*." She stood up and considered the bare wall opposite. "The ceiling's so high, I feel like I'm in a fish tank. Ugh! Gotta put something on that wall!"

She rooted around and found her stack of framed artwork. Soon she was on her desk, holding up her new A Star is Born poster. "Iv viff too high?" she asked, with a nail in her mouth.

Abby Gail sighed, "Nope, it's fine. Oh, that movie was so romantic. I went to see it *twice*. Kris Kristofferson is such a fox!"

Gwen tapped a nail into the wooden rail that ran around the room over the concrete for the purpose of hanging artwork. She hung the print and centered it. "Totally. Is it straight?"

"Yeah, looks great!" Abby Gail said, picking up another armload of clothes. In two steps she was back to the closet. "This is a small room."

"Yeah, I know. I feel like I'm in a shoe box."

"But it's *your* shoe box. No Sheila, no Brandon." Hoping to get Gwen to lighten up, Abby Gail imitated the iconic John Travolta dance, pointing her index finger in the air then down while wiggling her hips.

Gwen cracked a smile and pulled out another poster.

"What's that one?" Abby Gail asked.

"Andy Gibb. *He* goes over the *bed.*"

Some time later, Abby Gail sat back on her heels and surveyed the room with satisfaction. "Your fish tank is looking pretty homey!"

"It is, isn't it?" Gwen agreed.

"I've gotta do a load of laundry before dinner. See ya later, alligator."

"Right. Well, thanks so much for all your help. I'll come down to visit in a little while," Gwen said. She needed some time to adjust to her shoe box. It looked a *lot* better, she had to admit and yet there was still a draggy downer feeling about it. Like she was in an old folk's home.

"Okay. No problem. Just come on down. We can go to dinner together."

"Right. Catch you on the flip side," Gwen said, watching her leave.

When Abby Gail got to the door she paused, "I'm really glad you're going to be here at Montmoor. It gets kind of film noir dark here at night. I feel better knowing I can call you and you're just down the hall."

"It'll be great," Gwen said with a forced smile. "We'll have fun."

She found the box marked DESK STUFF and began unpacking it. Organizer bins, pens, notebooks, liquid paper…She dug down to a padded ball, pulled it out and unwrapped it. She took the teapot to the sink in her airplane-compartment-sized bathroom and filled it with water. She set it down in the middle of the desk.

This desk had a dull surface. She wondered if the teapot could talk without the reflection.

"Well, here we are, the new digs," Gwen said with a disheartened voice.

"Oh," said the teapot with the kind of tone used when one bites into a rotten tomato. "Ohhh," Tia repeated, this time with the tone of distaste one gets watching a cockroach crawl under the toaster.

"Small, huh?"

"Oh."

"It's all ours."

"Oh, dear."

There was something in the voice of the teapot that caught Gwen's attention. She wasn't just reacting to the size of the room. There was something else.

"What?"

"Listen dear, will you trust me? There's something I want you to do."

"Oh?"

"Get out some paper and a pencil."

"What? What for?"

"Do as I say, please. I'll explain."

"Do we have to do this now, I kind of wanted to —"

"It's important. Trust me."

"O-kay," Gwen said with whiny teen unwillingness. She dug in a box for a notebook and pencil. "Okay."

"First draw a circle."

"Yeah."

"Now put the pencil in the center of the circle. In one continuous line, draw four fan-blade-like flower petals—right, up, left then down for the four directions."

"What is this?"

"A witch's knot—it should look like a fancy cross when you're done."

"Like this?" Gwen asked, showing Tia the paper.

"Exactly. Well done. Do it again."

"What's this for?"

"Listen to me very carefully. As you are probably aware, with a building this old, there are bound to be some, uh, weird energies in this building, some residual energies, unhappy spirits. Most are harmless. Some are just confused, but some are strong and not anything you want to tangle with, trust me."

"What?" Gwen asked, dropping the pencil. "Are you saying the ghost stories about Montmoor are true?"

"I don't know the stories, dear, I'm just telling you what I'm sensing. Focus now. It is important that for everything I tell you to do. Do it with intention. You must concentrate or it won't work.

"Okay," Gwen said, doodling another cross.

"Good. Now, repeat after me, with conviction, please:
Dear Divine Universe, bless this pencil to my hand
That it will seal this room with my command
Bless-ed spirits welcome you are,
Dark, troubled spirits, stay away far
Protected by Light, may I be
Troubled spirits seek me not
I lock you out.
Blessed Be. Blessed Be. Blessed Be. Three times three."

Gwen held the pencil in front of her and recited the poem as the teacup fed it to her line by line. At the end she said, "The last part doesn't rhyme very well. I mean not and out don't rhyme and the meter is off."

"Don't worry about it. It's the intention. Now hurry. I want you to put that witch's knot over each window and the doorway — write it small, so it's not noticeable, on either side, left and right. Keep repeating the poem as you write."

"I feel silly doing this."

"Imagine the worst nightmare you've ever had."

"*Eww.* I used to have dreams that I was in quicksand."

"Fine. Imagine that these symbols would have protected you from those nightmares. Do it now. With intention. Come on, 'Dear Divine Universe...'"

And for the next half hour, Gwen dragged a chair around the room and drew small witch's knots to the teapot's specifications. When the last one was finished, Gwen climbed down from the chair.

"Now can I sort my clothes?"

"Not yet. The next thing is, you need to create a sigil. "S-i-g-i-l. Begin with a shape that you like and add letters or pictograms. Like with the witch's knot, you're going to write lots of them, so keep it simple."

"But I'm not really artistic."

"Sweetie, it doesn't matter. You can do an x in a circle, just as long as while you make it, you concentrate on keeping evil away."

"You're beginning to scare me. Am I in danger here?"

"Not if you do as I say."

And while Gwen had planned to organize her belongings and do homework, she found herself doodling various designs and rejecting them.

"Whatever you connect with, what comes from your heart. That's all the matters."

"Can I use angel wings?"

"Of course you can."

In the end, she made a collage of elements she felt a kinship with—the wings of Michael the Archangel; the Japanese characters for the elements, earth, wind, fire and water; her first initial G; the Eye of Horus. She set these in a web design around the letter P for protection. After practicing the design a few times, she could copy it in a few minutes. She penciled it along the baseboards, the windows, her closet. She wrote it on scraps of paper she stuck in cracks in the floor.

It was getting late. She'd missed dinner and was too tired to begin homework. She slumped into the Archie chair with a granola bar and a bag of chips.

Andy Gibb smiled down at her. Unlike her previous dorm where it seemed like a perpetual party was going on in the hall, here it was quiet. And so dark outside. She finished her granola bar and sighed. She still hadn't gotten sheets on the bed.

"What is it, dear?" Tia asked.

"Nothing. Just tired. This place is so... *quiet.*"

"Hmm," Tia said in a tone that implied polite disagreement.

Gwen hauled herself up, hunted for her bedding and made her new bed. She selected a simple outfit to wear the next day and set it out for easy access and found her pajamas.

Having washed her face and brushed her teeth, she fell into bed exhausted. Clicking off the light by her bed, the room went surprisingly dark. Deep closet dark. She guessed it was a new moon. Gwen lay on her back waiting for her eyes to adjust. She felt uneasy, like she was being watched. Had it not been for the feather-light pressure against the window, she would have missed it. But there *was* a movement outside. Just outside her window on the *third* floor. Something even darker than the darkness in the room hovered just outside the window. She sat up and fumbled for the light.

"What is it, dear?" Tia asked.

"There was a weird shadow outside my window. It felt like it was looking in at me. That's silly, right? Maybe it was just the trees casting a shadow."

Tia didn't say anything. Gwen got out of bed, found her favorite purple marker and sketched out her new sigil on the open edge of her pillowcase.

"What are you doing, dear? You should get some sleep. You've had a busy day."

"I just got this idea that I should put my sigil on the pillowcase, too."

"You *are* a quick study," Tia said, sounding pleased, "good girl."

Gwen finished her sigil and returned the purple pen to her desk. Taking a few steps back the bed, she paused, turned and rooted around in a box. She pulled out a large jewelry box and pawed through a drawer. She found an antique rosary that had belonged to her grandmother. The beads felt cool and comforting in her hand. She set it down in the center of the windowsill, turned the light out and turned her body away from the window.

"Good night, Gwennie."

"Good night, Tia."

Montmoor 1947 prior to restoration

Part 3 Montmoor

Gwen slept uneasily that first night, dreaming of dark hallways and a stern-faced woman yelling "Go back to your room!" Disembodied children's voices echoed. Some singing, some laughing, others crying. Upon waking in the pre-dawn light, she snapped on the light with an uneasy feeling that it would be best not to look either at the window or in the mirror.

The room seemed even smaller than the day before.

As Gwen brushed her hair in haste, she thought of a frightening story she'd heard somewhere about a room that got incrementally smaller each day until it crushed its occupant.

The knock at the door surprised her.

"Gwennie? You there?"

Gwen unlocked the door to find Abby Gail looking relieved.

"Oh, good, you're here. I thought you were going to come get me and we'd go to dinner last night. I thought maybe you forgot so I went by myself thinking I'd see you there. "

"Sorry, I got caught up in unpacking," Gwen said stepping back to show the mess that was her room. Half-opened boxes covered the floor. "I lost track of time, I guess. I'm ready to go." She grabbed her keys and her bookbag and made sure she locked her door behind them.

"What do you know about Montmoor?" Gwen asked as they walked downstairs.

"I heard it was once a home for 'lost women', you know, a euphemism for women who got knocked up out of wedlock. They were sent here to have their babies."

"I must have heard that before. I had weird dreams last night. There were children's voices and dark hallways. Gave me the crawlies. I've heard there are ghost stories. Do you know any of them?" Gwen asked opening the front door.

"Nah, I don't pay much attention to stuff like that. Oh! Gee whiz! I forgot my riding bag. Mind if I run back to get it?"

"I'll come with you, I'm in no hurry."

"Great!"

They fast-walked back to the stairwell and trotted up the steps then turned left and fast-walked to the last door on the left. Abby Gail fumbled for her keys and opened the door. Gwen followed her in.

"Hey, you changed the room around since I was here last."

"Yeah. Pippi's idea. Like it?" Abby Gail asked, grabbing her gym bag off the floor.

Gwen considered the previous arrangement of furnishings noting that now there were dark curtains on the windows and the bunk bed had been moved to the other side of the room.

"I guess. It's so dark. Seems kind of strange." She couldn't define it, but the new configuration felt awkward somehow.

"Yeah. Pippi says she doesn't want to sleep near the window."

"Oh?"

Abby Gail shrugged. "Says it bothers her to be overlooking a graveyard. Let's go."

"I didn't know there was a graveyard here."

"It's just a walled-in patch of weeds," she said grabbing her bag. "*She* says it was a graveyard. I dunno." She looked at her riding bag. "I'm riding a new horse this afternoon. Bruno. He's huge. I'm kind of nervous. Riding Bruno is a big deal."

"Cool beans, I guess," Gwen said not really paying attention. Her mind was stuck on the patch of weeds below the window.

That evening, as the dining hall crowd was thinning, Gwen spotted Pippi at the end of a long table with her boyfriend, Joey.

"Hey, guys," Gwen said approaching them, "What's up?"

"Hey, Gwen. Abby Gail said you moved in to Montmoor yesterday. Scored a single room, didja? Sweet!" Pippi said, adding, "though I'm not sure I'd want a single room in Montmoor."

"Yeah? Why not?"

Joe and Pippi exchanged glances.

Joe asked, "Do you believe in ghosts?"

Not long ago, Gwen would have said no, but now that she was roommates with a possessed teapot, she faltered. "I'm not sure."

"You probably will now. Montmoor is full of 'em."

"Oh?" Gwen asked.

"Shadows walk the halls...children cry at night... footsteps when there's nobody there and a clock chiming... except there is no clock."

"Get out."

"Nope," Pippi said, "Serious as a heart attack."

"There was a provost back at the turn of the last century," Joey began, "who was married to a kind Danish woman named Sophie Madsen. She came from a wealthy family and took pity on young unwed mothers who were cast out of society as sinners. She built this place to house and support the mothers and their children. 'Moor' means mother in Danish, so the place is called 'mother mountain'. All was well for a while, but at some point in the thirties, a nurse named Millicent Sharpe was hired."

"How do you know all this?" Gwen asked.

Joe and Pippi exchanged looks again. Pippi looked at her napkin and began twisting it in her fingers.

"After Pippi told me some of the weird things she's seen, I chatted up my dorm matron, Mrs. Sweedums. She's Dean Chattsworth's mother-in-law. Been here since the dinosaurs. A historian and fiendish chess player. Sometimes I'll visit with her. She plies me with brandy cordials and cleans the floor with me in chess."

"And?" Gwen prompted, not sure she was ready to hear the answer.

Joe continued, "Nurse Sharpe was hired because she had excellent credentials. She took the job because she had to. She wasn't married. She moved in with her brother who worked at the school as a janitor and handyman. Mrs. Madsen's health went into decline and as she became less and less involved with Montmoor, Sharpe insinuated herself into the staff hierarchy until she was practically running the place. But she was no Mrs. Madsen. Nurse Sharpe treated the women and children horribly, believing that the women were fallen; the children were bastards at best and children of Satan at worst. It is unknown exactly how many women and infants 'died'" – Joey made quotation marks with his forefingers – " in childbirth."

Pippi looked up then, her face grave. "Can you believe that? Instead of helping the women to deliver the babies, she was *killing* them."

Gwen wrapped her arms tight across my chest. "Here? Oh, how awful. That gives me the creeps. How did she get away with it?"

Joey shrugged.

Pippi looked Gwen in the eye. "My room?" she said as if it was a question, "I mean, Abby Gail's and my room? It's Sharpe's old apartment. Well, part of it. They put partitions in and split it into three dorm rooms. We're in her old office. I've seen her sitting at my desk writing late at night. I've seen her walk through the wall from the next room as if she's pacing the floor."

"Whoa!" Gwen said. "Has Abby Gail seen her?"

"No. She doesn't believe me, but she let me move the room around. It hasn't really helped."

"I've seen things at my window," Gwen said. "Shadows and faces. And I've heard footsteps in the hallway, but I'm the only one there."

Joey nodded, "Yup."

Gwen asked, "So what happened to Sharpe? Did she get caught?"

Their eyes met Gwen's with apprehension. "Yes, finally. She was being investigated," Joey continued. "It seems that when the investigation got too intense, she killed herself. Lethal injection of something."

Gwen shuddered.

"I have a question for you, Gwen," Pippi asked. "Does Abby Gail seem…different to you recently?"

"I haven't seen that much of her…I just figured she was busy with homework and stuff."

Pippi nodded.

"Why do you ask?"

Joey spoke up. "At first, I thought she didn't like me or something. But we've both noticed that sometimes she's just not herself."

Gwen raised an eyebrow.

"She can be so snippy. And she has gaps in her memory," Pippi said.

"Sometimes she stays out until late at night," Joey said, nodding to Pippi.

"Yeah, like last night. She was gone until like three in the morning and when she came in, I don't know, I can't quite describe it, she just seemed like someone else. Like she was angry. Not at all like Abby Gail."

"I was supposed to go to dinner with her, but I…I was busy unpacking." Gwen said. "It got late. I skipped dinner."

"She didn't show up at dinner either."

"That's odd. She told me she went," Gwen said, recalling the conversation.

They both nodded. "See?"

"I saw her in that creepy garden late at night about a week ago. I swear it had to have been her. She was sneaking around and moaning."

"Whaat?" Gwen asked in disbelief.

"I'm telling you, it's bizarre. When she came in, she smelled like dirt. She thought I was asleep. I watched her undress — she wadded everything up and stuffed it under her dresser, not in her hamper. But this morning, she was normal again."

"Has anything happened that she's upset about?" Gwen asked.

They shrugged. "She hasn't said anything."

Gwen hugged herself. What was going on? It was all too strange. "Well, thanks guys. See you around." She turned to leave.

"Oh, hey Gwen," Pippi called after her, "it's Mork and Mindy night tonight. Common room at 8 P.M. Be there or be a parallelogram."

Part 4 Comparing Notes

Gwen sat on the floor in the crowded common room watching Robin Williams' antics as Mork. Much as she enjoyed the communion of fellow students gathered together in close quarters enjoying a moment of amusement, she couldn't concentrate on the storyline. Instead, she kept stealing glances at Abby Gail. This was one of her favorites shows, she knew, and yet Abby Gail regarded the screen with a sour face. In the episode, Mork, an alien visiting earth, had regressed himself to a three-year old.

Freddie, an animated, extroverted senior sitting on the couch behind Gwen, guffawed with gusto as Mork threw a tantrum. This incited laughter from the onlookers who laughed at the program and at Freddie. Abby Gail scowled. When the commercial break began, Gwen looked around to see that Abby Gail had left the common room.

When the show ended, Gwen tagged along with Pippi and Joey going back to Pippi's room.

"Did you see the look on her face?" Gwen asked.

"Yeah. Weird, huh? She *loves* that show. And that was hilarious. How could she keep a straight face?"

When they got to Pippi and Abby Gail's room, the door was locked.

"Hey, Abby Gail, it's me," Pippi called out, unlocking the door.

They walked in to find Abby Gail at her desk, doing homework.

"You missed the end! That Robin Williams was so funny," Joey said.

Abby Gail looked up. "I had homework."

"Oh," Gwen said, "We just wanted to make sure you were okay. You seemed upset. I'll go. I've got some history to read tonight."

"I'm fine. Mind your own potatoes."

"My po*ta*toes?" Pippi laughed. "What?"

"Abby Gail looked up, her face dark. "Fussy babies, always crying and wailing—drives me nuts, can't get a *thing* done." She looked back down at her textbook, her eyes began moved back and forth.

"What?" Pippi asked.

Gwen was stunned by how rude and weird Abby Gail was being. This wasn't like her. Previously, Abby Gail had said she'd made quite a lot of money that summer babysitting. She'd told funny stories about her "girls".

"Uh, okay, then, I'll, uh, see you tomorrow, I guess," Gwen said backing out of the room.

Abby Gail looked up and asked, "What?" This time the darkness was gone. She looked surprised to see the three of them standing there. "Oh, hey, Gwen. Didn't see you."

"Well, catch you on the flip side," Gwen said. She waved to Joey and Pippi with -what-the-heck-was-that eyes and left. She half-ran back to her room, hurriedly opening the door and securing it behind her.

"Tia, we need to talk," she said.

"Yes, dear. Why don't we have a nice soothing cup of tea? It'll help us both. Oh, you don't have any lavender do you...I'll have to get you a list of herbs... have you got any chamomile?"

"Yeah, I think so," Gwen answered. She was anxious and flustered, not at all interested in making tea, but she complied while telling Tia about her conversation with Pippi and Joey and Abby Gail's odd behavior.

Once the water was boiling in the hot pot, she poured it over the teabag in Tia.

"Mmmm," Tia cooed with pleasure. "That's lovely. Don't be in a rush, let it steep a little. You can add some honey now if you like."

Gwen got some milk from her mini-fridge and poured some in her favorite mug. "It's like Abby Gail is possessed or something, she's not herself."

"That's exactly what it is, dear. I'm sorry this has come up so fast. I haven't had time to teach you. There's so much —"

"Wait, you're *serious*? She is possessed?"

"Something trying to work through her, yes. I've sensed something around her, a female entity."

"A ghost? A demon? What does it want?"

"I don't sense that it's demonic, just dark and very unhappy. Pour your tea, dear."

Gwen made a face and said sarcastically, "*Unhappy?* Well, maybe we should throw it a party."

Tia rolled her eyes. "Not funny. If you are going to be like that, then I'll say good night."

Gwen sighed. "Wait, no. It's just that all this is so scary, and I don't understand. I want your help. I need you." She touched Tia gently. "Tell me."

"I think we need to go out to that garden."

Gwen looked lost. "And do what?"

"I don't know. It could be anything...something important to the entity. Something that binds the spirit here perhaps. A memento of some kind."

Gwen made another face but poured tea into her mug and stirred in some honey.

"Gently dear, with care. With appreciation. *Intention.* You aren't mixing concrete, you're making the perfect cup of tea, releasing the power of the herbs."

"Power of the herbs," Gwen repeated with stoicism. "Right."

Tia sighed. "You know, it's a pity that Americans have never really understood tea the way the Brits do... tea can be so *settling.*"

"Yeah, right, " Gwen rolled her eyes, "can we talk about my friend who is going crazy, please? What is going on? How do I help her?"

"We'll need to get Pippi and Joey to help, but of course, they mustn't know about me. Is Pippi a sensitive? She must be if she knows about the graveyard."

"But there's no graves."

"Aren't any, dear."

"AREN'T any," Gwen repeated with annoyance. "Can we skip the grammar lesson? There are no gravestones out there."

"Have you been out there?"

"Well, no. I didn't even know about it until I found out Pippi rearranged the room."

"I want you to go there tomorrow. Maybe we could go together. Yes, that would be best. Hide me in a backpack and take a journal or something. If anyone sees you, you are just memorizing a poem, not talking to a teapot."

"Right. We can go before dinner. But why?"

"Perhaps we can find what she's looking for. I need to get a sense of the place. I hope we'll learn something useful."

"From what? A patch of weeds?"

"You'll see, dear. Have patience. Drink your tea."

Part 5 The Garden

Gwen stumbled through her Calculus homework then tried to concentrate on her English Lit poems, but Edmund Spenser's "The Fairie Queene" seemed like tedious blah-blah-blah and would have put her to sleep had she not been hankering to get out into the garden with Tia. She tried reading it aloud. That helped, marginally. She was in a section about a lush garden "adorne[d] with all variete" and was about to slam the book shut when she got to stanza sixty.

60

"In the midst of all, a fountaine stood,
Of richest substance, that on earth might bee,
So pure and shiny, that the silver flood
Through every channel running one might see;
Most goodly it with curious imageree
Was over-wrought, and, and shapes of naked boyes,
Of which some seemd with lively jollitee,
To fly about, playing their wanton toyes,
Whilst others did them selves embay in liquid joyes."

She dropped the book. "Tia, this sounds naughty. Are they doing what I think they're doing?"

"What? No! You've got a filthy mind! They're just splashing in the fountain! We should go. It's dark outside. I had hoped to go earlier, but of course your studies come first."

"Yeah, well, enough of this," Gwen said, closing the book. I'm getting dressed in stealth black and we're going to explore *our* mysterious garden!"

"You need to do that protection spell I taught you before we go. No telling what kind of energies are out there waiting for us."

Gwen, pulling on dark jeans, froze. "You really think it's going to be bad, don't you."

"I'm afraid so, dear. At the very least, stick burrs and thorns. No flowers, no fountains, no frolicking cherubs and no golden cup in this garden, I assure you. More like restless wraiths. Finish dressing."

Gwen crept down the hall and down the stairs feeling like an inept cat burglar. Her sneakers made too much noise and the backpack bumped against her back. She made her way to the back of the dorm only turning on her pocket flashlight when she was close to the garden door. She turned the handle and pushed. It was locked.

"Shit!" Gwen stamped her foot and tried again. The door wouldn't budge. She was about to admit defeat when it occurred to her there must be another door. "She gets in somehow, right?"

She moved farther down the wall running her right hand along the wall just in case there was a secret door. Just before the end of the wall, there was a narrow ornate gate, just wide enough for one person, a slim person to get through. She found the latch and pushed. It gave.

"Yes!" she whispered.

Keeping the flashlight beam low, she moved forward with caution. As Tia had predicted, the weeds were high. Thorny tendrils tugged at her pant legs. But there was a faint path where the weeds had been tamped down. She followed the trail.

Gwen had never been especially intrepid, unlike her brother who seemed to have no fears at all. She doubted she'd get in trouble if she did get caught, but she was a good girl who feared the judgement of others. But far outweighing the possibility of getting reprimanded, it sure was dark and creepy here. Like the shadows had shadows. Like *nothing* had lived in here in centuries except the weeds. The air felt stagnant. And there was a strange lack of sounds—no crickets, frogs, owls. Nothing but silence, the backpack bumping and her steps.

She reached the center where the weeds had given way to ancient pavers in a circle. In the center of the circle, was a round stone slab about six inches thick.

Gwen turned slowly to be sure she was alone then sat down and unpacked the backpack. She unwrapped Tia and set her on the slab.

"Oh, no, please, not here." Tia said. "Get me off this. You too."

"Why? What is it?" Gwen asked.

"Death. So much death here...this was a well once. The slab covered it over. When the well went dry, it was used to dispose of... bodies. I feel so much death here. So much sadness and loss. Chant that protection I taught you. Quietly but with intention."

Gwen obeyed.

"Gwen! Shh! Someone's coming!' Tia hissed.

Gwen looked around and flipped off the flashlight.

"Move away, closer to a wall," Tia ordered.

Gwen stood up and began walking.

"Hel-*lo*, you forgot me!" Tia hissed.

Sounds of footsteps approaching in the grass made Gwen freeze. She could see the dark shape of someone coming closer. The person walked briskly and without a flashlight. It was Abby Gail, and she was sobbing.

Gwen took exaggerated steps, picking her feet up high so they wouldn't brush through the grass. There was no time to rescue Tia.

Shit-shit-shit! What if she sees Tia? Gwen's mind raced. *It's dark. She won't. How can she see? What the hell is she doing? Why is she crying? Should I say something?*

Abby Gail prostrated herself before the well cover, "I'm so bad, so bad, so bad," she wailed as she writhed about. Somewhere in her rolling and reaching, she touched something unfamiliar. Her writhing stopped. She cradled the object and felt its contours.

What should I do? What should I do? Gwen wondered in a panic. Tia had said to hide. Should she stay hidden or confront Abby Gail and get Tia back?

She tried to force her body into action but remained rooted in place. And then to her horror, she saw Abby Gail raise her hand high in the air. There was a great whacking sound and a groan.

What the hell was the girl doing?

Whack. Moan. Whack. Moan.

Gwen recognized the sound of a riding whip. Abby Gail was whipping herself again and again.

"I'm so ba-aaaa-ad."

Whack.

"*Owwwooh.*"

Gwen's paralysis broke as the flight instinct propelled her forward. She bolted through the grass sprinting for the narrow gate. She sped past Abby Gail and heard a moan and a mumble behind her. She almost ran into the wall by the gate. She pushed herself off, turned sideways and was through and gone.

Once back in her dorm room with her door locked, Gwen paced the floor and fretted. That had gone horribly wrong and was too bizarre. Was there any other possible explanation for what she'd seen? Had she imagined that Abby Gail was beating herself? No, she had not.

She pulled off her stealth clothes and threw them in her laundry basket. She wished she could peel off the past few hours as well; wished she could as easily peel off the fearful feelings in her mind and body.

Get a hold of yourself. Be strong. Focus.

A hot bath would help. A hot bath and a strong cup of tea. Yes.

Gwen found her pajamas and a bathrobe and slipped next door to the shared bathroom. She locked the door and turned the hot water on in the clawfoot tub.

This was one of the perks to Montmoor, this bathtub. Deep and long, a soak in this tub was pure heaven. The hot water heater wherever it was in the bowels of the building never seemed to run out of hot water.

She poured in some aromatic bubble bath and paced while the tub filled.

She had to get Tia back, but how? Why had Abby Gail taken her and what was she going to do with her?

Gwen caught a look at herself in the mirror, surprised that she looked a lot better than she felt. She looked almost normal, almost pretty, but her eyes had a trapped animal wildness about them.

Though she didn't really need it, Gwen reached for the face mask tube. The cool paste on her face, the minty smell would be soothing while she soaked. She spread green mask evenly over her cheeks and around her eyes.

If only the mask could take the impurities out of my mind as well as out of my skin, she thought.

The bathroom was unusually spacious for a dormitory bathroom. In addition to the antique tub, there was a hefty wooden armoire painted pale yellow and ornamented with tiny ribbons of roses. The three girls who shared the bathroom had claimed drawers and cubbies to keep their belongings. Gwen pulled a few rose scented candles out of her little cubby and lit them. She placed a couple on the windowsill and set the others on top of the armoire.

When the tub was full, Gwen flipped off the overhead light and eased down through the foam of bubbles. She lay against the sloped back of the tub as the hot water enveloped her.
She closed her eyes.

Neck rolls. Ankle rolls. Relax the shoulders. She focused on the sensations: the slippery water, the floral soapy smell mixed with the mint, the gentle sounds of water swirling.

Nothing I can do tonight. Homework. Get some sleep. Come up with a plan tomorrow.

Gwen crossed an ankle over her knee and began working a washcloth between her toes.

"Where's my mommy?" a thin child's voice, very close to Gwen's head asked.

Her eyes flew open as she righted herself with a great slosh of water, fully expecting to find herself eye to eye with a child. Wisps of steam rose off her arms and torso as gooseflesh formed on her forearms. The temperature in the room was frigid.

Old buildings, she thought with distraction as her eyes darted around the dark room, finding no child.

Why is it so cold in here? she wondered with a shiver.

Confused but relieved, she ducked back into the bubbles and the comfort of the warm water. Hadn't it been hot just a moment before?

Wait, I can see my breath! she realized with a jolt. *So much for a relaxing bath!* She scrubbed herself quickly with the washcloth noting that the water in the washcloth was now barely warm, now tepid. Gwen's teeth began chattering as she pulled the drain plug and stood up.

172

Somewhere in all the sounds of stepping out of the tub with the water gurgling, knee bumping the tub, joints in her feet popping as she stepped onto the fuzzy mat, reaching for the towel on the rack, there was a sound that didn't quite fit in with her motions. A tumbling, rolling sound. She wrapped the towel around herself as she danced to keep her blood flowing. The mirror wasn't even steamy, it was clear. She could fog the mirror with her cold breath! She was too cold to put on her pajamas, and reached for her thick bathrobe, pulling it on hurriedly.

The candle flames on the votives on the windowsill were leaping and dancing as if fighting a great draft or ceiling fan. But the window was tight enough, there was no fan running, nor air conditioner or heater. So, what then?

She glanced up to the top of the armoire and froze with fear far worse than the cold. That's when the strange noise came back to her mind. The bumping, rolling sound that hadn't correlated with her motions. The bumping and rolling that must have been the child's building blocks appearing from nowhere to bump into being between her votive candles. Antique child blocks that she knew were not in this bathroom, nevertheless, here they were. Spelling out HELP ME.

Gwen screamed into her hands and backed up to the locked door. She swung around and fumbled with the lock. The door opened, she swung it wide and ran to her room, locking herself in.

She stood shaking, staring at her door, half expecting a cold vapor to seep through the door and grab her.

"Gwen? Are you okay?" a familiar voice asked, followed by a knock at the door. "It's me, Zora."

Gwen had tensed, about to leap out of her skin. She relaxed.

Zora lived across the hall and was one of the girls with whom she shared the bathroom.

"Yeah," she answered. She absolutely wasn't okay. She was freaked out. Despite the heat in her room she still shivered from cold and jangled nerves. *Damn.* She'd left her pajamas in the bathroom. She wasn't about to go back in there. But she hard hardening face mask on too. *Double damn.*

"Gwen?"

"Yes," Gwen called, pulling her bathrobe close and opening the door.

"You okay? I thought I heard you scream."

"You didn't put building—no, of course you didn't. Do me a favor, Zora. Go look at the armoire in the bathroom and tell me what you see."

"Why? What's going on? What did you see? It's not a giant spider, is it? You're on your own if it's a spider."

"Not a spider, I promise," Gwen said with a laugh. *I could handle a big spider, easy.*

Gwen stayed in her doorway as Zora went around the corner.

"Candles?" she asked. "What am I supposed to be seeing?"

174

"You don't see anything else?" Gwen asked, tip-toeing closer.

"No. It's kind of cold in here," Zora said, reappearing. She was rubbing her arms. "That's funny, it's much warmer out here in the hallway."

"Yeah," Gwen said, peering into the bathroom. On the armoire were the three votive candles close together. The flames were steady streams of light. No dancing despite possible hallway drafts. The candle on the windowsill had blown out.

And there were no alphabet blocks.

"Must have been my imagination," Gwen said. "Guess I'm seeing things. Stay right there, do you mind?"

Zora shook her head and leaned against the door jamb.

Gwen dashed in, blew out the candles and hurriedly rinsed her face. She grabbed her pajamas and scooted back out to the hallway. "Thanks."

"You sure you're okay?" Zora asked.

"Scared myself, I guess. I'm fine," Gwen lied. "Thanks again."

Gwen attempted to catch up on her reading assignment for religion class. The book of Jeremiah. Babylon. Smiting the wicked. The Lord is seriously pissed off ..."and I will bring them down like lambs to the slaughter"... "shame hath covered our faces: for strangers are come into the sanctuaries of the Lord's house..."

She fell asleep with the Bible in her lap. She dreamed of a child running down the hall screaming. A severe woman with mannish shoes, squeaky shoes was following the child and the words "lambs to the slaughter" looped again and again as the child ran down a hallway into darkness.

Part 6 Small Surprise

There was a sharp *knock-knock* at her door as she was dressing to go to breakfast. She opened it to see Abby Gail standing there looking stiff and tired.

"Oh!" Gwen said. "Uh, hi."

"Going to breakfast?" Abby Gail asked. "I'll go with you."

"Yeah, uh, sure."

Gwen's mind raced. Abby Gail looked mostly normal, but she seemed like a husk of her usual perky self. How could she ask about Tia? She imagined phrasing the question, "So could I have my talking teapot back? The one you took while you were whipping yourself in the haunted garden?

"Did you hear the news about Pippi?" Abby Gail asked in a nasty, juicy-gossip tone.

"No, what?"

"You won't believe it."

"What?"

"Pippi killed the rabbit."

Gwen's face contorted, "What rabbit?"

"As in, the rabbit died. The little slut went and got herself pregnant."

Gwen had been brushing her hair. She spun to face Abby Gail and dropped the hairbrush. "*What?* No way, Jose!"

"Yup. *Stupid* girl. How's she going to finish school with a *baby*?"

Gwen shrugged. "Well, it's not great timing, that's for sure, but... does Joey know?"

"Joey. Pppppptt." Abby Gail said, making a disgusted face.

"What? I like Joey. He seems like a good guy. I think he loves Pippi."

"Love. Ppppt. He'll drop her like soiled underwear."

"Abby Gail!"

"*What?* It's true. She's throwing her life away."

"You don't know that. What's gotten into you? You're like a different person lately." Gwen said. She hadn't intended to be confrontational but the attack on Pippi was too much.

"Am *not*," Abby Gail answered.

Gwen frowned. "You are. You're pissy and judgmental all of a sudden."

"Well, *excuuuuse* me!" Abby Gail replied, putting her hands on her hips. "Are you ready or what?"

Gwen pulled on her shoes and grabbed her keys and phone. She moved towards Abby Gail and stopped short. Abby Gail was standing in the doorway with the white hallway behind her. There was something about the early morning light in the room and the hallway—Gwen could see colors around Abby Gail's head and shoulders: swirls of sea-green and charcoal with balls of black just over her head like a jagged crown.

"*What?*"

"Nothing," Gwen said. She wasn't sure what she was seeing but it couldn't be good. She'd never been a good liar, she knew she didn't sound convincing, but she was now motivated to get this dark energy version of Abby Gail out of her room. "I'm good. Let's boogie." Walking forward, Abby Gail had to back out of the room. Gwen turned and locked it behind her.

They began to walk toward the stairs. She noted that Abby Gail was walking with discomfort. She didn't know how to ask, "So does the flagellation hurt much?"

Abby Gail seemed to read her thoughts and volunteered, "I'm kind of sore this morning. I fell off my horse yesterday."

Yeah, that's one way to put it, thought Gwen.

As they walked, Gwen recited protection prayers in her mind and kept a bit more space between herself and Abby Gail than usual.

"Cooler weather coming," Gwen said with artificial enthusiasm. "I love it when it's chilly. You know, sweater and hot cocoa weather. Or *tea.*" She eyed Abby Gail. "I'm getting into drinking TEA lately."

"I'm a coffee person. You know that."

"But you must like tea too, right? Didn't I see a cute teapot in your room?" Gwen asked.

"No. Pippi might have one. Don't think so."

Gwen studied Abby Gail's face for any hint of deception but saw none. She hadn't really expected Abby Gail to come out and say, "Oh, I found a teapot. Would you like it?" But this stone face was weird. She had seen Abby Gail picking Tia up in the garden that night, hadn't she?

She let it go. She'd have to sneak into Abby Gail's room and hunt for Tia. She tried another tack.

"Hey, have you ever been around back of the dorm? You know, to that garden that Pippi thinks is sinister?"

"Why would I do that?" Abby Gail asked, turning to look at her like she was nuts.

"I don't know. I went there just to poke around. There's some weird thing in the center like where there might have been a fountain or something. Only it has a big cover on it."

Abby Gail shrugged and changed the subject. "I'm really liking my Intro to Religion class."

The most popular band on campus, Oedipus Complex, was playing at the favorite pub, Shenanigans, that Friday night. Dinner in the cafeteria had been unidentifiable. Gwen had gone back to her dorm intending to catch up on her assignments, but the lure of fried mushrooms and the social scene was strong. She set aside the poetry and grabbed her keys.

Shenanigans was bustling but not packed. Yet. Oedipus Complex was doing a soundcheck as she ordered her food. She put some change in the tip jar and moved away. Focusing on zipping her wallet, she bumped into someone.

"Sorry," she said, looking up.

The lights in Evie's eyes disappeared. Her mouth became a thin line. "Excuse me," she said, moving to the counter.

And Kevin was right behind Evie. His eyes hardened. He followed Evie passing Gwen as if she were a stranger.

Gwen's mouth fell open and she dropped her wallet. Adrenaline surged through her body like a lava flow, momentarily paralyzing her in a hot cocoon of emotion.

What to do? Play it cool. Play it cool. Ignore them.

Someone bumped her shoulder and stepped on her wallet.

"Oh, shit!" she said, and breaking free from her stasis, stooped to pick up her wallet as her stomach did a backflip. Shame and anger swirled in her head. She wished she had a gorgeous boyfriend to show off. Instead she was here alone. She felt vulnerable and alone.

Don't be a spaz, she chided herself. *Chill out.*

She prayed neither Kevin nor Evie had seen her drop her wallet like an idiot. Forcing herself not to look in their direction, she straightened, looking at the bulletin board. A postcard-sized flyer caught her eye. It had her favorite colors: clouds of pink, raspberry, blue and purple.

CENTERED SOUL

Crystals books incense candles
Angel cards pendulums gemstones
readings classes
Magick in Murfreesboro

There was a phone number, an address and a thumbnail map. This seemed like a sign. She'd been meant to see this card. This was exactly what she needed — maybe she could talk to someone about the weird goings on at her dorm. Maybe get some books on magick. Yes. Tomorrow, she'd road trip to Murfreesboro. She'd get up early, go straight there and back.

She could be back by early afternoon and work on her studies all weekend.

She tucked the card into her wallet with a feeling of purpose.

"Order for Gwen!"

The band began "Queen of Chaos" as Gwen found a bar stool in the corner. She'd listen to the set, enjoy her food then go back and study. She forgot all about Kevin and Evie. Her thoughts were on the delicious mushrooms, the tasty Shenaniwich and her trip the next morning.

Part 7 Centered Soul

"Can I help you?" a handsome man with fluffy brown hair asked. He looked a lot like Greg Evigan on that new show *B.J. and the Bear*.

The shop smelled of patchouli. Gentle harp music played from small speakers. Sunlight played in hanging crystal light catchers casting rainbow beams on the walls and shelves. It was a lot to take in.

"I hope so…" Gwen began, distracted by a dazzling display of amethyst geodes. "I'm afraid you're going to think I'm crazy, but I suspect I have a friend who is getting possessed by a bad spirit."

"Oh," he said, cheerful smile fading. "Tell me about it. What's been happening."

Gwen's plan to keep her story simple vanished. She found it easy to talk to this man with the fluffy hair and the interested eyes. He listened and nodded as she described Abby Gail's mood swings and nighttime jaunts to the derelict "garden."

"What do you know about the place?" he asked, guiding Gwen towards a selection of used books.

She told him what she'd heard about Mrs. Sharpe and the rumors of how she disposed of orphaned babies.

"Horrible," he said, running his fingers over book spines. "This one, yes. This may help, too," he said, pulling books out. "Are you a psychic or sensitive?"

"I don't know. I...I, um, have a friend who has been teaching me some stuff. And that's part of the problem. She's not able to help me just now. I kind of lost her."

"Oh, had a falling out, did you?"

"Not exactly," Gwen hedged, no longer able to meet his eye. Her eyes roamed over a shelf of decorative spray bottles with labels like LOVE FOCUS DREAMS HEALING ATTRACTING BANISHING. She picked up a black BANISHING bottle.

"I was going to suggest that. That's very powerful. It's got rosemary, white sage, hot peppers and garlic."

"How does it work?"

"You can spray it around your doors and windows. You can spray it over your friend too, just be sure you avoid the eyes. If you can spray the top of her head and around her body. Palms of her hands. Her heart. Spray in the center of her chest."

"Here. You'll want this book of runes, too. Do you know about thurisaz, the thorn rune?"

"No."

"Here." He pulled the book back from her and flipped pages. "This rune has many meanings and uses, among them giant and strength. You can remember it as strong like Thor. It can bind and fetter, destroy your enemy." He flipped pages. "This one, nyd, is a good one too. Read up on this one. You can remember it because it looks like two sticks rubbing together to start a fire. Very powerful."

"Okay."

"Do you know about sigils?"

"Yes."

More page flipping. "Use this too. Here, I'll mark the page." He moved toward the register and grabbed a store bookmark. He marked the page and handed her the book. "What else? Candles. Here, let's put these down for now." He took her books and spray bottle and set them on the counter. "Let's look at candles."

"Okay," Gwen complied. She followed him like a puppy glad that he hadn't laughed at her. He seemed to be giving her the tools she was looking for. Or was he? The suspicious part of her mind wondered if he weren't just loading her up with stuff she "needed" –easy target, right? Somewhere in her mind she heard Tia's voice whisper "truuusst."

As the shopkeeper prattled on about candles, she closed her eyes. Yes. This is what she came for. She felt like her feet were grounded and her mind was vast and open.

"Did you want to get your friend back or is that relationship over?" the man was asking.

Gwen opened her eyes. "Oh, very much. I want to get her back."

"This pink one for attraction then… and black ones for protection against the entity."

As Gwen signed the credit card charge, the man said, "I'll put an extra store card in your bag. If you have any questions, don't hesitate to call. Good luck."

Gwen thanked him and carried the hefty bag hugging it to her chest.

As the Volvo passed through the gates of the campus, Gwen slapped the roof to release her angel. A new song started on the radio. She laughed out loud when she realized it was Donovan's "Season of the Witch."

The next week flew by in a blur. Gwen attended her classes and chipped away at her assignments, but whenever possible, she was holed up in her tiny room engrossed in her new books.

Her sleep was fitful. In her dreams she walked down dark hallways with shifting shadows and distorted voices like records played at the wrong speed.

In one vivid dream, it was late at night. The dorm was quiet. She had to pee. She got up and shambled into the bathroom. The light in the bathroom seemed to be on a dimmer switch, dimmed by an unseen hand. She had to pee a lot and it sounded loud in the otherwise still night. She hurried, sure that the sound was attracting some dark thing that had been loitering in the hallway like a lost drunk staggering outside of a closed bar.

"Hurry, hurry, come on," she whispered.

Relieved to be relieved as it were, she flushed the toilet and winced. More noise. *Damn. That had been stupid. She should have put the lid down and flushed it in the morning.*

Glancing in the mirror while washing her hands, she didn't see her own reflection, instead she saw an older woman with dark hair pulled back into a bun at the base of her neck. She scowled at Gwen and rasped, "Get back to bed!"

Gwen woke with a start. She leaned back against the wall and pulled the covers up around her neck. She listened. The room was dark. The dorm was quiet. She held her breath, heart pounding.

Out in the hall by the bathroom she heard the faint sound of retreating footsteps heading towards the stairs.

Part 8 Coming to Terms

Gwen was a wreck. She missed Tia, friend and calm voice of reason. She was frightened by Abby Gail's irritability and meanness; stressed by the upcoming midterms. She was behind in her reading assignments and had a ten-page paper due in anthropology in a week with only a hazy notion of a topic. It had all been intriguing to read about banishing evil spirits, but doing it alone was a whole nother matter. Her senses told her there was a quickening coming soon. She had to be prepared.

Gwen was ready to leave for breakfast when Abby Gail knocked on her door.

"Good morning, Abby Gail."

"Good morning, Gwendolyn."

Gwen bristled. Only her mother called her Gwendolyn when she was in trouble. "What's with the formality?" she asked, hoping to sound playful.

Abby Gail's hair was pulled back with a hairband. Wearing a thin gray sweater with gray slacks, she looked like an exam proctor. She ignored the question and asked her own. "Are you coming to my jumping show this weekend? I'm riding Bruno. I've been working hard. I'd like you to come."

They arrived at the stairs and Abby Gail held onto the rail. She took the steps with care.

"Sure. What time?"

"Saturday. The event starts at one o'clock. I'll probably be on about two-thirty or so."

"Okay, sure. Are you alright?"

"Yes, just stiff."

They passed through the food line and took their trays to their usual table. As Gwen was about to eat her cereal, Abby Gail said, "I think we should say grace."

"What?"

"It's not proper to eat before saying grace," Abby Gail said.

Gwen lowered her spoon. "What? Since when?"

The conversation of friends farther down the table tapered as Abby Gail's voice became harsh.

"Gwendolyn. Say grace."

Gwen frowned. "Look, you can if you want to, but I don't. Okay?"

"We must be pleasing in the eyes of the Lord."

"*What?*"

Someone down the table emitted a nervous laugh.

And then Abby Gail blinked. Her eyes refocused and her face relaxed. She was Abby Gail again. "Well, don't have a cow, Jeez. What are you staring at?"

"You told me to say grace," Gwen said.

"Don't be a dork, Gwennie." Abby Gail said with a laugh. "I'd never say something like *that*. Jeez, don't harsh my mellow," she said, playfully punching Gwen on the shoulder.

"You did!"

"Yeah, right!"

Gwen was in the library looking through microfiche for an article on cultural violence when she heard a familiar voice behind her.

"*Hola, chica.*"

She turned to see Joey leaning over the carrell smiling at her.

"Hey, Joey," she said, pushing back from the viewer.

"Got a minute? I wanted to ask you about something."

"Yeah, sure."

Joey looked around nervously. He waited as a student eased behind him with a large backpack and wandered out of hearing range. "I wondered...um, see, the thing is..." He shuffled about and ran a hand through his hair. "It's about Abby Gail. She's been really weird lately and seems to be hostile lately towards Pippi." He blushed, hesitated and began again, "Do you know about...?"

He moved a hand in front of his stomach.

"Yeah, I do."

Joey relaxed a little. "Good. I mean, well, not good, but yeah, okay. Abby Gail has been bullying her. It's so weird. She was never like this."

"I know. I've noticed it too."

"Right?" Joey said with a simpatico hand gesture indicating shared ideas. "Pippi's already on edge about it. I mean, of course, we're gonna have it, but she's stressing about it. Her parents aren't real happy with us."

Gwen nodded wondering where this was all going. She couldn't tell him she suspected that Abby Gail was possessed by some dark spirit, could she?

"Could Pippi crash with you for a while? I know your room is kind of small... but she can't stay with me, dorm rules, you know, but she can't take it much more."

Normally, Gwen would have been evasive. She hated getting involved in other people's problems. Even though Tia wasn't there, crap, she didn't know where Tia was, though she was pretty sure Tia was safe. She'd feel it if something had happened to her. She felt Tia's energy within her, Tia's strength moving up her spine. Tia's surety as she said, "Tell Pippi yes, she can come. We'll find room somehow. I need to talk to her."

Joey looked surprised and relieved. "Oh, far out! You rock!"

Abby Gail's stinging comment "He'll drop her like dirty underwear" came back to her mind. "Are you guys okay?" Gwen asked.

"Yeah, we're cool," he said with a hint of a smile.

"Good," Gwen said.

Joey nodded. "See ya on the flip."

Gwen leaned into the viewer. The words swam in front of her. What had she just agreed to? Where was she going to put Pippi? What would Abby Gail do when she found out?

She had to find Tia. Maybe Pippi could help.

Gwen grumbled as she retyped page two of her paper. She'd gotten distracted and typed in the bottom margin. She'd tried to fix it with the white correction-fluid brush, but it looked sloppy. She had to pay attention. The paper wasn't finished, she needed to do some more research and come to some conclusion, but she felt secure enough about the introduction to type it. It made her feel she was making progress.

There was a knock at her door. "Gwen? Can I come in?"

Shit, shit, shit. She really needed to get this done. "Yeah," she called out still pecking at keys.

The door swung open. She turned at the sound of sniffling. Pippi stood there with tear tracks down her cheeks, hugging a pillow with one arm and carrying an overnight bag with the other.

"Oh, hey, what's up?" Gwen asked, moving toward her to give her a hug.

As Pippi relaxed into the hug, she dropped the bag. "I just can't take it anymore. She's so--"

"Shh. It's gonna be okay."

Pippi sobbed; Gwen pushed the door closed with her foot.

She led Pippi over to the bed and sat her down.

"It's so weird. It's like she's possessed or something. She doesn't sound like herself. Have you noticed that lately she's been wearing a cross necklace? She's spouting scripture at me and telling me I'm going to go to hell. I thought she was an atheist. She told me she hated going to church as a kid and got groped by her Sunday school teacher. Now she's all high and mighty…She's gone mental. I've wondered if I should tell the Dean or what. She'd hate me forever."

"Pippi…I've seen it too. You might think I'm crazy, but I think she *is* possessed. There's something about this dorm and that garden. I felt it my first night here. I think, I really hope I can do something about it, but I'll need your help."

Pippi sniffed and her eyes widened as they met Gwen's eyes. "You really think she's possessed?"

Gwen nodded.

"Well, she's not the Abby Gail that I started the semester with, that's for sure."

Gwen thought, *Whew, glad she doesn't think I'm crazy about that. Now how do I tell her about Tia? I'm friends with a witch who happens to be in a teapot? Well, here goes…* "Um, Abby Gail stole something from me, and I really need to get it back. See, I had it with me when I went out to that walled up garden and she came out. I had to hide so she wouldn't see me. She took my teapot. I couldn't believe it!"

Pippi's face scrunched up in confusion. "A teapot? What were you doing in the garden with a teapot?"

Gwen winced. "Um, well, I was doing a Wiccan ritual…the teapot was a part of it…"

"A *what?*"

Gwen squirmed. "Wiccan. It's like a nature thing," she said, her hands flitted about like nervous butterflies, "finding balance, harmony with nature, kind of like Celtic or Native American stuff."

"A teapot?"

"She's… I mean, it's smallish with a woman's face. It's brown. She took her. I need her back. Have you seen her, uh, it?"

"No. Why would she steal it?"

"Why is she spouting scripture?" Gwen countered.

Pippi sniffed and nodded. "Right? None of it makes sense. I bet she's stuffed it into her desk drawer or hidden it in her closet. That's another thing. She's thrown out some stuff she used to love. Her desk has almost nothing on it anymore. She gave away her Scooby Doo cookie jar, can you believe it? That was one of her favorite things. She makes her bed every morning like she's got to pass inspection. She makes mine too and tells me I'm a…I'm a whore." Pippi covered her face with her hands.

"You're not a whore, you know that. Listen. We need a plan. Tomorrow morning when she leaves for breakfast, we can search for Tia. I mean, the teapot. I've named her Tia."

"Okay." Pippi nodded.

"Look. I've GOT to work on this paper. I'll get you a clean set of sheets—do you mind making the bed?"

"I can't take your bed!"

"Well, it's either the bed or the chair, and I'm fine with the chair, really. Fall asleep in it all the time. You get some rest. I'll be fine."

Later, Pippi settled into the bed with her history book and Gwen pecked away at the typewriter.

"What do we do if she comes looking for me?" Pippi asked.

"We don't answer the door," Gwen said.

Late that night, Gwen pulled the history book away from Pippi's lap and set it aside. She stood with her hands hovering over Pippi and whispered blessings for protection.

> "Great Goddess of the day and night.
> Protect us with all your might.
> Shield us from evil power,
> keep us safe hour to hour."

She paused then not sure how to continue. She'd been watching Abby Gail's perky upbeat self slowly slough away replaced by...by what? Or who? She'd been observing the transformation with concern and growing fear, yet she'd done nothing. Should she have tried to contact Abby Gail's mother? Talked to a psychologist? Or a priest? She'd put blinders on, wishing that the situation would resolve itself, that it was just her imagination. She'd pulled away from Abby Gail, clueless about how to help her. She felt guilty. Could she have done something? What? She was so out of her depth here. Pippi was being victimized by her friend and she'd just watched from afar. She couldn't keep her head in the sand anymore. She had to act. But do what? *Tia, where are you? what do I do?*

> "Bring Tia back to me
> That we can send away

This dark entity
To rescue our friend Abby Gail."

Pippi moaned in her sleep and shifted her position. Gwen felt another wave of guilt wash over her. There was a tiny baby to protect now too.

"Please Divine Spirits,
We cannot fail.
Protect us all,
Guide us, help us.
Save Abby Gail.
Blessed Be."

The following morning, a loud knocking at the door startled the two women.

"Gwendolyn!" Abby Gail's shrill voice called. "You coming?"

Gwen gestured to Pippi to hide in the closet. "Coming," she called.

She slumped her shoulders and relaxed her face, pulling her robe close over her clothes. She opened the door a crack and leaned against the wall as if weak. "Sorry, not today. I feel like shit. Didn't sleep well. You go on. I'm going back to bed. Skipping Biology so I can work on my Anthro paper."

Abby Gail frowned. "Oh. Sorry to hear you're poorly. Want me to get you anything? Chicken soup or something? Garlic's good too. You should eat something with garlic."

"Mm-mm. Maybe later. Not hungry. You go on. Don't want to get you sick."

Abby Gail pursed her lips. "Right. Okay. I will pray for you. Take care."

Gwen was closing the door about to lean against it with relief when it pushed against her.

"You haven't seen Pippi, have you?" Abby Gail asked. "Haven't seen her since yesterday. Don't know where she slept, the hussy. Probably with her no-good boyfriend."

"No, I haven't seen her," Gwen answered in a raspy voice. "Hope she's okay."

"*Hmmpf.*"

The pressure against the door released. Gwen closed it and locked it as Pippi came out of the closet.

"We'll give her ten minutes to make sure she's really gone, then we'll go to your room." Gwen said.

Pippi nodded.

Part 9 Rescue

With a last glance down the hallway, Pippi opened the door and let Gwen in.

"Whoa!" Gwen exclaimed.

"Yeah, I know."

It had been a little while since Gwen had seen the room. This time, Abby Gail's side was austere. Gone were the colorful pillows and stuffed animals on her bed. Gone the clutter on her desk, the David Cassidy picture taped to her mirror.

There was a Bible in the center of Abby Gail's desk.

"She got rid of a lot of stuff," Pippi said.

"Oh, no," Gwen moaned. "Can I look in her desk?"

"Sure. I'll look in the closet."

Gwen opened the two large drawers to find notebooks and school supplies. Nothing under the desk. "Any luck?" she called.

"Not so far. Try under the bed."

Gwen got on her hands and knees and looked under the bed. A fat suitcase! She pulled it out and opened it. "Ah!" She found the David Cassidy photo—this was a good sign that she hadn't thrown out the things she'd taken down.

"Oh, thank God!" Tia whispered. "Get me out of here!"

Gwen pulled out more items she recognized from Abby Gail's desk before she spotted a familiar-shaped bundle wrapped in paper. Holding up the bundle, she exclaimed, "Got her!"

"Great!" Pippi answered from the closet.

Just then the door opened. Abby Gail walked in and roared, "What are you doing in my suitcase!"

Gwen's mouth fell open.

Pippi stepped out of the closet. "Oh, shit!"

"What are you two doing?"

"I—I—" Gwen floundered as her hand wrapped around a familiar form covered in tissue paper. She set it behind her back and closed the suitcase.

"I forgot my Walkman," Abby Gail said, "What are you *doing*?"

Pippi composed her face and said calmly, "Gwen started her period. She didn't have any supplies. I thought I did, but I'm out too. We thought maybe you had some."

Brilliant! Gwen thought, *but I don't think she's going to buy it.*

Abby Gail turned to face Pippi, "No, I bet *you* don't."

"Abby Gail, don't!" Gwen said, pushing the suitcase back under the bed.

"Get away from that!" Abby Gail snarled, pushing Gwen aside. She pulled the suitcase out, opened it, appeared to be satisfied that nothing was missing, secured the latches and wrestled it back under the bed.

Gwen felt a strange vibration in her hand and heard an unfamiliar hum.

"We didn't mean any harm," Pippi said.

Abby Gail stood up and blinked. "Oh yeah, my Walkman. Sorry, I can't help you." She grabbed her Walkman and left.

Gwen and Pippi stared at each other.

"Whew!" said Pippi.

"Way to go with the cover story!" Gwen said.

"That was so weird."

"We've got to do something. This is too crazy. Tonight's a full moon. I think we need to try dealing with this tonight," Gwen said. "Can you get Joey to join us?"

"You bet!" Pippi said.

"I'll just put Tia in my room, and we can go to breakfast. Meet you on the stairs," Gwen said, getting up.

"Sure."

Gwen left, cradling Tia. She trotted down the hall, popped into her room and closed the door.

"Well done!" Tia said, her voice thin.

"So glad you're back. Tonight. Banishment with the full moon, right?" She began to collect her schoolwork.

"Yes. Could I have some water please, dear?"

"Oh, shiznits, yeah!" Gwen dropped her books and took Tia to the bathroom to fill her with water. She dashed back to her room and set her down on the desk. "Okay. Gotta go. We'll come up with the plan when I get back."

"Yes. Oh, find some black candles if you can. And lots of salt."

Gwen paused at the door, "Got black. Salt? Easy."

"You have black candles?" Tia asked, sounding impressed.

"Yup. I've been studying."

"Well done, Gwen. And thank you for rescuing me."

Part 10 And Now, In the Center Ring

Joey and Pippi were in Gwen's room late Saturday morning planning the evening's event.

"Um, how does this work, exactly?" Joey asked, regarding the pile of supplies on the floor. "Do we slap a cross on her forehead, yell, 'evil demon come out' or what?"

Pippi rolled her eyes.

"Not exactly," answered Gwen. "We get the garden ready, then lure her out there. Your job, Joey, is holding her down while we spray her with the banishing oil."

"In the circle, right?" Pippi asked.

"Yes. We have to make a protective circle with the candles and the salt. A pentagram. We stand inside it. You hold her, we chant, I spray her and…and we hope it works." Gwen said, eyeing them both with apprehension.

She heard the faintest "psst" coming from her desk and looked over to see where it was coming from. Tia was sitting next to a box of tea. In her mind she heard Tia chastising her about her tea making skills. "Not like mixing concrete. With *intention*." And hadn't the Greg Evigan lookalike/fluffy-haired guy said that intention was everything?

"We have to believe in what we're doing," Gwen said, feigning conviction. "We have to have *intention*. That's the key."

Somehow, she knew Tia must be smiling in agreement.

"She'll be so pissed if we miss her riding thing," Pippi said, making a face. "Even though she hates me half the time, she told me I should be there."

"I know. I think you and I have to go. Joey can prep the garden with the salt and stage things while we're gone. We can't really do anything serious until after dusk. We'll meet in the garden and get it all prepared, then you can lure her down there," Gwen said.

"Lure her down…" Pippi repeated.

"I have a plan," Gwen said, biting her lip.

Forty-five minutes later, Pippi got into the Volvo and closed the door. "How many miles are on this thing, anyway?"

"Too many," Gwen winced. "But she's been reliable so far."

Gwen drove them out to the stable. They dutifully watched the riding competition and waited for Abby Gail's turn to show off.

Gwen's mind was split in three directions—tension while awaiting Abby Gail's performance, guilt that she was behind in her studies and unease over the plans for banishment that night. What if it didn't work? What if the entity was stronger than she was?

Finally, Abby Gail led her horse into the ring. Bruno was massive! Pippi and Gwen both gasped.

"Look at the size of him!" Pippi exclaimed.

"Good Lord, he's huge," Gwen said. "Oh, I hope nothing goes wrong. If she falls—"

"She'll do great," Pippi said, clenching her fists in her lap.

They watched as Bruno lapped the ring, jumping the hurdles with ease. Abby Gail's posture was straight and relaxed.

"I knew she was pretty good, but *wow*," Pippi said.

The crowd roared when they finished. Pippi and Gwen jumped to their feet and clapped.

Abby Gail and Bruno aced their jumping event and won first place.

Pippi and Gwen descended from the bleachers and hung around to congratulate her.

"Thanks so much for coming," Abby Gail beamed and hugged them. They chit-chatted a bit until Abby Gail excused herself, "I'm supposed to go to this banquet ceremony thing... I'll see you guys later. Thanks again for coming." She waved and moved away to join other riders.

"It's so weird. She seemed normal just now, "Pippi said as they headed to the parking lot. "Is she the same person who appears over me at night whispering weird things like 'May the Lord forgive you your sins' and 'May the spawn of Satan be driven away?'"

"Maybe it's stronger closer to Montmoor," Gwen suggested.

Pippi pondered this. "Oh!" she exclaimed, "Did Joey tell you about the photos he got from Mrs. Sweedum?"

"Huh-unh,"Gwen shook her head and backed up the car.

"He got an album about Montmoor with pictures of Sophie Madsen and Millicent Sharpe and some of the orphans."

"Great! Can't wait to see them!"

"Mrs. Sharpe looks like she's straight out of a horror film," Pippi said, making a face. "She's all pinched and severe looking. Not someone who should be around infants or moody pregnant women. She hardly looks like an agent of comfort and support."

"Somehow, that doesn't surprise me."

Part 11 And Now, In the Center Ring II

Gwen drank two cups of a ginseng blend while strategizing with Tia about the banishment for Abby Gail.

"It'll help you focus and give you energy," Tia had said. "Plus, it helps me too."

"How do we get her to the garden? Couldn't we just do it in her room?" Gwen asked.

"You could, but we aren't sure how she's going to react. You don't want to attract attention. If she fights you, you'll have the whole dorm down your neck. But more important, there is something about that garden that the spirit wants or needs. I think the key is in the garden. Don't forget, get her in the circle, spray the holy water over her head, grind the garlic into her palms."

"Got it. Joey and I will be there already, Pippi will tell her she needs to see what she found in the garden. When they show up, we get her in the salt and incense circle..."

"Yes. I suspect that the spirit will be strong in the garden. Address her directly. Ask her who she is and ask what she wants. If I can, I'll talk for you in your voice, but if it doesn't work, you'll need to stay calm and ask her to leave, like we talked about."

Gwen nodded. "But what if it doesn't work? What if Abby Gail just freaks out? What if —"

"Shh, dear. Finish your tea. No point in the what-if game."

201

It was just after dark when Gwen met Joey in the garden. He had a sheepish expression indicating that he wasn't sure he knew what he was doing. "I salted a circle around this thing," Joey said, gesturing to the raised circular slab, "then I salted another circle like six feet out from that. I kinda got thin toward the end there, hope that's okay." He looked at Gwen and back at his wobbly salt circles.

"Yeah," Gwen said, not sure. Nothing they could do about it now. Pippi was supposed to bring Abby Gail any minute.

"Let's light the incense sticks," Gwen said, handing a bundle of Dragon's blood sticks to Joey with a packet of matches. "Around your outer salt circle. I'll do the frankincense around the inner circle. Unless, maybe I should alternate them in the two circles?" She shrugged.

"You're asking me?" Joey asked with a clueless expression.

"Nah, you're right. Let's keep it simple."

They placed the sticks in relatively even intervals around the circle. Soon, the air was thick with frankincense and Dragon's blood.

Joey coughed. "I think you got enough incense, anyway."

Gwen bit her lip. "Where are they? I feel like we've been waiting for an hour."

"It hasn't been that long."

"What if something went wrong?"

"Want me to go check?"

"Not yet. Let's give it a few minutes."

Joey coughed again, more fervently this time. When he had recovered, he laughed, "Well, if I had any evil spirits in me, they're coming out."

Gwen rolled her eyes. She walked clockwise around the circular cover. The cover had a sinister air to it. *You'd want something heavy to prevent anyone from falling in*, she thought, *but still. This is overkill.* She lit her last stick and watched the smoke rise in a wiggly pattern. Without wanting to, she felt compelled to look at the cover again and the horrible thought struck her. *What if the cover is to keep something from coming out?* She looked away and spotted the backpack. "Almost forgot the candles!"

She walked to the backpack and crouched down. She pulled the box of tealight candles out of the backpack and whispered, "I'm so nervous," to Tia. She thought she heard a response, "Patience."

Gwen tried to stay positive while setting out the candles. She reviewed all the things Tia had told her. But the bad feeling that something went wrong persisted along with the sinister suspicions about the cover. She wanted to get away from it; out of the garden. She was getting cold. This was supposed to be over by now. Pippi should have managed to get Abby Gail down here long ago. Where were they?

She looked up at the dreary back windows of Montmoor and thought the room with the heavy curtain must be Abby Gail's room. What was going on up there?

As she approached her backpack, where Tia was nestled out of sight, she wished Tia could advise her. Maybe she could hint for a signal. She pretended to be thinking out loud. "Should we stay..."she paused and listened. From the bag came a faint clipped, "yes."

The temperature was dropping. Gwen hugged herself and kept walking to keep warm. Joey sat cross-legged poking the ground with a stick.

"Did you see that?" Gwen asked, pointing to a dark shadowy area where the wall met the back of the building.

Joey looked up. "No. What'd you see?"

"I'm not sure. I thought I saw someone walking."

They froze, listening. They heard nothing.

"Shadows moving in the night breeze," Joey said, scraping the stick across the circle he'd made.

"Joey, there is no breeze. It's still as the grave out here and just as dreary . Oh, shit, what was that? Did you hear it?"

They froze again, straining to hear.

"I hear it," Joey said, dropping the stick and jumping away from the circular slab. "It's like a baby crying in a well, isn't it?"

Gwen nodded, her mouth agape, eyes wide.

The sound grew louder. The fussing baby cries grew more desperate turning to long wails but with a distortion as if coming through a tube from deep in the earth.

"What the hell is that?" Joey whispered.

Somehow Gwen knew it was the cry of a long dead baby coming up from the pit. The agonizing sound wormed into her head and gripped her heart. Terror gripped her as adrenaline sent electric fingers down her spine and over her arms. "I can't--" Gwen couldn't finish her thought. She began to run for the opening in the gate. The coin was flipped in her fight-or- flight mind. The answer was flight.

"Well, I'm not staying here alone," Joey said, joining her in a sprint to the gate. Joey had had enough sense to turn on a small flashlight. Unfortunately, the battery seemed to be dying; the light was a fuzzy orange. It was better than total darkness.

Gwen turned sideways and stepped through the gap. Joey had to work at squeezing through the narrow opening. As he shifted and mumbled, the gate responded with a metallic groan. Gwen was launching into a sprint again when she almost ran straight into Pippi. She jumped and squealed.

"Oh, it's you!" Pippi exclaimed. "You scared the crap out of me."

Gwen's posture collapsed, "Ditto!" She pointed behind her, "we got scared—there were horrible cries coming from that old well thing."

"She never showed up. I looked for her, but she didn't come back to the dorm. I came to tell you."

"Oh?" Gwen frowned. "That thing at the stable is over, isn't it?"

"I thought so," Pippi said.

"Oh, well," Joey said. "Hey, you know, we ought to go back and get the stuff we left."

Gwen remembered Tia. She'd lost her once, how could she leave her behind again? She'd just panicked. "Yeah. Pippi, come with us, will you?"

"Do I have to?"

"Please?" Gwen begged.

The three crept back to the gate.

No one wanted to go first.

"It's so dark out here," Pippi said. "And cold. Why am I so cold all of a sudden? I'm getting the serious creeps."

"Wait until you hear what we heard," Gwen said hesitating. She forced herself to slip through the opening.

Pippi followed. Then Joey, making a lot of noise with heavy breathing, foot shuffling and grunting.

"Shh," Gwen said.

"Sorry, I can't help it," Joey whispered.

They stood just inside the entrance, listening.

"I don't hear it," Gwen whispered.

"Why is it so quiet in here?" Pippi asked. There are no bugs, no owls, no breeze…what's up with that?"

"Let's just get our stuff and get out of here," Gwen said.

Joey held the flashlight guiding them forward. The small circle of tea lights looked spectral in the darkness but gave them a focal point to head toward.

"Maybe I should just blow out the candles and come get them in the morning. They'll be too hot to put in the backpack," Gwen said, thinking out loud. They had just reached the center of the garden when the fussing baby sound began again, low and tentative.

"What is that?" Pippi asked with alarm.

"Oh, let's hurry!" Gwen said.

"I'm outta here," Pippi said, turning to run back.

"Wait for me a sec!" Joey hissed, picking up his backpack and shining the light at Pippi. That's when he noticed motion by the gate. It was a leg stepping through the gap. "Look! Someone's coming!" He aimed the weak light toward the gate.

They could barely see her in the darkness, but the rest of the body emerged. It was Abby Gail.

The tinny baby began to cry louder in full plaintive sobs.

Abby Gail advanced toward them effectively blocking their exit. Well, Abby Gail's body was moving; the gait and the expression were not Abby Gail's. Not even close. Her face had taken on a strange layer, like a thin latex mask. An older woman's face reflecting a lifetime of disappointment and despair. Two tracks of tears ran down her face. Her walk was that of a middle-aged woman used to perambulating with a certain amount of bulk. Weight in the ankles. It was not Abby Gail's athletic walk.

"You are not authorized to be here," Abby Gail said in a matronly voice looking each of them in the eye. "You must leave."

"We're sorry, Mrs. Sharpe," Gwen said with hesitation. "We heard the baby crying."

"The baby..." Abby Gail said, her voice cracking with emotion. She was almost in the outermost circle.

Aha! She is Mrs. Sharpe! Gwen thought, her mind racing. *Protection. Intention. What should I do next? Oh yes, move her into the circle.* "Yes, here, the baby here," she said, pointed to the cover.

"The baby..." Abby Gail said again, moving forward. "You saw the baby?"

"Yes," Gwen lied. "Don't you hear it?"

Abby Gail stepped closer. Pippi and Joey circled slowly behind her. Pippi whispered,

"Divine Energies of All Directions,
North South East and West
We ask for your protection
May Abby Gail be safe and blessed
Freed from this unhappy spirit—"

"What are you doing here?" Abby Gail asked, glaring at Pippi. "You are unclean!"

Gwen darted to the backpack and reached for the spray bottle with the banishing solution. *Just keep her engaged*, she thought, *keep her in the circle.*

Joey asked, "What right do you have to be so judgmental?"

"What right? What right?" Abby Gail asked, as Gwen moved around behind her.

The baby made sounds as if it was choking. Abby Gail's authoritative voice waivered as she tipped her head, looking toward the heavy well cover. "What authority?" she asked again and dropped to her knees. "My baby! Where are you? Why can't I see you?"

"Your baby?" Gwen asked in shock.

Pippi was chanting again,

"We ask for your protection
May Abby Gail be safe and blessed
Freed from this unhappy spirit
May she find peace and rest
Depart from this place
Depart from our friend Abby Gail--"

Joey said, "Oh I get it! Millicent Sharpe had to give up a baby here — she was a patient long before she became a nurse. She must have hated coming back here, but remember, she came because of her husband's job?"

"She was tormented by having to take other women's babies when they'd taken hers…"

"Poor woman," Pippi said.

Gwen spritzed the banishing spray over Abby Gail's head. "Unhappy spirit be gone from this place."

Abby Gail lowered to her knees. "My baby. They took her."

Pippi added, "May God forgive you your sins."

The baby wailed.

Abby Gail sobbed, now a crumpled heap at the edge of the well cover. "I'm so sorry. I had no choice."

"Abby Gail, come back," Joey said in a gruff voice.

"Dear Divine Universe, bless the baby," Gwen added, spritzing Abby Gail again, "Millicent Sharpe, may you be reunited with your lost child."

"So much wickedness," Abby Gail said in Mrs. Sharpe's voice. "I had no choice."

As if in response, the flames of the tea candles around them swayed all in the same direction in perfect synchronicity. Gwen, Joey and Pippi looked at each other in amazement.

"Whoa," Joey said. "That's not…natural."

Gwen was shivering with cold and emotion. She reached down and put her hands on Abby Gail's shoulders.

"Millicent Sharpe. You must leave this body, this place. You are surrounded in divine white light. Go to the light. Find your baby. Be in the light. Leave Abby Gail." She shook her for emphasis.

Abby Gail let out an animal growl that rose in pitch into a wrenching wail. She turned her head to look at Gwen, Joey and finally Pippi. The anguish on her face was heart-breaking. She whispered to Pippi. "Why do you get to keep your child when I lost mine?"

Pippi continued the prayer:

"We ask for your protection

May Abby Gail be safe and blessed

Freed from this unhappy spirit

209

> May she be reunited with her baby
> From her torments saved be
> May she find peace and rest
> Depart from this place
> Depart from our friend Abby Gail--"

Gwen sprayed her again with the banishing mist. And then to their relief and surprise, the baby's cries faded away and Abby Gail's body relaxed. The latex mask of Millicent Sharpe faded. She wiped her face. *Her* face! The mask face of Millicent Sharpe was gone.

"What just happened?" she asked. "Where are we? What are you guys doing? What's with the candles?"

Pippi and Gwen hugged Abby Gail and helped her stand up.

"Let's get out of here," Joey said.

"I'm turning into a Sno-Cone," Gwen said with a shudder.

They blew out the candles, collected the backpacks and headed toward the narrow gate.

As Joey struggled through the opening once again, he dropped his backpack.

"Smooth move, Ex-lax!" said Abby Gail with a smirk.

The others laughed, glad to have Abby Gail back.

Part 12 Take Care of Her

"I'm so proud of you!" Tia exclaimed when she and Gwen were finally alone again. "It was a bit rough, but you all did great!"

"Thanks," Gwen said, putting on her warmest pajamas. "That was far out. Did you know about Mrs. Sharpe giving up her baby?"

"I knew there was something, some reason she was connected with that cover, but no, I didn't know what. Poor tortured soul."

"Yeah, women had it hard back in the day," Gwen said.

"The struggle isn't over, my dear. It's still a man's world out there, but every day and every way, we make it better and better, right?"

"I guess," Gwen said.

"You did a great thing tonight, honey. But starting tomorrow, you've got to get back to the books. Don't you have a paper to finish? Aren't your mid-terms coming up?"

"Yeah," Gwen buried her head in her pillow.

It was a struggle, but Gwen managed to pull her grades up by the end of that semester. She and Tia guided several lost souls of Montmoor into the light. The following semester she was just shy of the honor roll and she began dating a cute anthropology major who made her laugh. She graduated toward the top of her class.

Tia remained her secret friend, confidante and mentor in life and magick.

Two decades later, on a sunny day in August, Rhiannon closed the door to her bedroom with a sigh and went downstairs.

"All set, sweetie?" Her mother Gwen asked from the kitchen doorway.

"I guess," Rhiannon answered, sweeping her long blonde hair behind her back in a way that reminded Gwen of Cher back in the Sonny days.

"Oh, I've got something for you."

"Yeah?" Rhiannon said, raising an eyebrow. She followed her mom into the kitchen.

Gwen handed her a summery plaid gift bag with green tissue paper.

"What is it?" Rhiannon asked, excitement in her face.

"Open it."

She pushed aside the paper and pulled out a square box. She tugged the box lid open and pulled out a brown teapot.

"A teapot? That's nice, mom, but… I'm not really a tea drinker. Coffee girl, remember? We just bought me all the pods for my machine?"

"I want you to take this teapot to college with you. Trust me. Think of her as a good luck charm."

"But… this is yours. You've had it up on the shelf for like ever. Why don't you keep it."

"I want you to have it. But you must promise to take good care of her. Don't lose her or drop her or break her or anything."

"Yeah, okay." Rhiannon did a quick eye roll and put the teapot back in the box. "Sure, mom."

Seeing Rhiannon's disappointment, she said, "Oh, sweetie, I think you're going to love her. Like I do."

"Sure. Okay."

"Call me when you get there and tell me everything," Gwen said, pulling her daughter in for a fierce hug. She kissed the top of her head.

"I will Mom."

"I love you."

"Love you too."

They separated. Gwen followed her out to the driveway where the Mazda Millenia sat stuffed to the gills.

"Drive safely."

"Yeah, mom, jeez." Rhiannon said.

"Take good care of her," Gwen said as Rhiannon tucked the box into some bedding on the passenger seat.

"I will Mom. Love you. Bye."

Gwen eyes filled with tears. It was hard to see her little bird fly free from the nest. So much ahead of her. A rush of nostalgia for her college days washed over Gwen. But after a moment a knowing smile widened across her face.

Rhiannon thought I was talking to her.

Tia would take good care of Rhiannon, she knew.

BW&S

SEVEN

"**A**nother beer?" Gracie asked, taking Zap's empty plate.

"No, I need to get home. Thank you, though, just the check."

Gracie looked disappointed but nodded and moved away.

Zap wished he didn't have to drive, but he was feeling better now that he'd gotten some food. Still, if he could teleport to his bed, he'd be there in a flash. Second best would be a taxi. His mind drifted in a fantasy about giving a driver his address, climbing in the back seat and falling asleep.

Saturday the 14th

I'd wanted to surprise my wife Jeannie for our twenty-fifth wedding anniversary. Her mother had died from cancer earlier that year. It'd hit her hard; they'd been close. Simultaneously, our son had gotten into some trouble at school and we'd had multiple frustrating meetings with a rigid principal determined to expel him. Then our faithful Labrador had died from some mysterious stomach thing.

We were all stressed and grieving, but I was worried about Jeannie. I often caught her staring out the window with a vacant expression. She wasn't sleeping well. When was the last time I'd seen her really laugh or seen the joyful sparkle dance in her eyes? That sparkle had been replaced by worry lines and a pitiful look of resignation.

I'd gotten a raise and wanted to splurge on a weekend trip that might recharge us. I'll confess, that over the years, I'd forgotten our anniversary more times than I'd remembered it, and it was usually Jeannie who reminded me. But this year was a big anniversary and we'd been in survival mode for so long, I couldn't remember the last time we'd just gone away for fun. When I spotted bargain flights to New York City, I snagged them. *Turandot* was on at The Met — not my thing really, but Jeannie had a minor in voice in college and loved Puccini. First balcony center seats — she'd be elated. There was a blessing of the animals at St. John the Divine on Sunday. We both loved animals, and this would not just be dogs and cats. I found out that New Yorkers have all kinds of pets that they bring for blessings--iguanas, ferrets, pot-belly pigs, exotic birds. And once, when the Ringling Brothers was in town, they say an elephant was presented and blessed! Wouldn't that be something.

I spent a couple weeks secretly creating our long weekend itinerary: museum exhibit, carriage ride through Central Park, *Lion King* on Broadway. We'd stay in a plush, historic, Italianate villa turned bed and breakfast called The Viennese.

We'd arrived mid-day on Thursday. So far, it had been even better than our honeymoon. At first, Jeannie'd resisted. "What about Jack and school?"

"My mom is coming to house sit and stay with Jack. All arranged."

"I had a dental appointment that Friday — "

"You can reschedule a dental appointment."

Resistance yielded to excitement. "Where are we going? What should I pack?"

When we got to the airport, I handed her an envelope with a formal invitation to join me for a weekend in New York City with the itinerary of planned and optional events. Her face went through a panoply of emotions from stunned disbelief to delight.

"Oh, George! Really? Really! And you came up with all this by yourself?"

She bounced, hugged me and kissed me. The vibrant Jeannie I had fallen in love with was coming back to life.

Saturday night: all had gone swimmingly so far. The weather had been perfect—gorgeous autumnal foliage in the park, perfect temperatures during the day with the crisp, chilly evenings. We'd spent the day at the Museum of Natural History, had dinner at a fantastic Thai restaurant then off to the Metropolitan Opera.

"I can't believe we're out so late," she said with an impish giggle as I pulled her close. "It's way past my bedtime."

We stood outside of a coffee shop pulling up our coat collars against the night air. We could see our breath.

"How are we going to get back?" Jeannie asked. "They say you shouldn't take the subway at night."

"It's fine. We'll get a cab."

"This has been such an amazing day, George," she said in a sleepy voice, leaning against my chest. "The museum, and Turandot! Spectacular! You really outdid yourself. Did you know that Franco Zeffirelli did the set design? Incredible. That was so over the top! And then this charming place, the coffee and that killer chocolate cake. I feel like a spoiled princess."

"That was the idea," I said, kissing the top of her head. "I hope you won't get all Princess Turandot on me and have my head chopped off."

"Not a chance, honey, you're a keeper!" She answered, snuggling into me.

"I'm relieved. Let's wander up that way. That looks like a main street. Should be able to flag down a cab."

They say that New York is the city that never sleeps, but that's not entirely true. After the opera, we'd hopped into a cab and headed to the Village to wander around. Not the best idea; it wasn't quite what we'd expected. I'd pictured more music clubs, restaurants and quaint shops open late. Most had closed. There were some streets that looked boarded up for a hurricane; no lights, no people, not even a trash bin.

The happy glow of the day was wearing off as I realized how tired I was, and that I'd lost my bearings. We passed a few gaudy shops with mannequins dressed in leather and chain bras with black leather knee boots, surrounded by sex toys.

"Oh my!" Jeannie said, huddling closer to me. We were passed by a bevy of beautiful women dressed like hookers, but their voices were distinctly male.

"Wow, I wonder how they can walk in those heels… my feet are killing me and I'm in pumps," Jeannie said.

"Ah, here we go. Sixth Street," I said with relief. The full day of activity and the sugary cake caught up with me all at once. I was exhausted and ready to be back to our B&B.

"I'm *freezing*," Jeannie said, shivering. "Sure hope this doesn't take long. The wind! It was fine on the side streets, but it's cutting right through my coat."

I had the uneasy feeling that we were being watched. In danger. I glanced around — there were no people near us on Sixth Street. I looked behind us. There were two men in dark clothing moving toward us, keeping to the shadows. Bums? I didn't think so. They stopped and huddled together when they knew I'd spotted them. I turned to face them and squared my shoulders, putting myself in front of Jeannie. I'd heard that direct eye contact was a deterrent to muggers as they preferred a blind ambush. But there were two of them.

Jeannie said, "Here comes one!" She stuck her arm up and waved.

I turned to look. A shabby cab with a dim in-service light was two blocks away. It changed lanes without signaling and whooshed toward us.

"Here we go," I said, my voice unnaturally loud to tell our would-be muggers we were saved.

"Oh, great!" Jeannie said as it lurched to a stop.

Great indeed. I hoped Jeannie hadn't seen the menacing men behind us. I glanced back to see them moving back the way they'd come.

"Oh, I swear, the temperature just dropped another ten degrees!" Jeannie said. "Hurry! The door!"

It was an old Checker cab with fogged up windows. The driver's face was a strange fleshy blur through the windshield.

Why did I hesitate? I couldn't explain it. We were cold, needed to get back and here was a cab. Perfect, right? And yet I had a visceral reaction when I touched the door handle, I pulled my hand away as if pulling it away from an attack dog or a hot skillet.

"George, hurry!"

"Yes, I'm sorry." I forced myself to touch the door handle again and pull open the door.

Jeannie scooched in and over gushing to the driver "Thanks so much. It's getting so cold tonight. But, ooh, it's chilly in here too. Could you turn the heat up a bit?"

"Where to?" the driver asked, looking up into the rearview mirror at me.

He was an unremarkable middle-aged man, balding and with the kind of course dark beard that even when shaved you can see the dark dots of hairs just waiting to sprout out again. I glanced at his identification card above the meter. It was worn and faded in a deep water-stain brown. Joseph Campanero or something approximating that. It was difficult to read.

"We're going to Bedford-Stuyvesant. I pulled the card from the Viennese out of my pocket and handed it to him. "Here. Do you know it?"

He grunted, nodded and flipped the meter on.

I closed my door and the cab lurched away from the curb.

I leaned back into the seat and pulled Jeannie to me.

"Why is it so cold in here?" she whispered.

"You believe in déjà vu?" Our driver asked suddenly with a heavy New York accent. There was something eerie in the way that he asked the question. A flatness. And the question itself was so peculiar.

"I dunno," I said.

"That's a funny thing to ask," Jeannie said with a nervous titter.

"Saturday the fourteenth. You know, most people are superstitious about Friday the thirteenth. Not me. I get nervous about Saturday the fourteenth."

This is not what you want to hear from your cab driver late at night while zooming along mostly empty roads.

"Well, it's so late, perhaps it's already Sunday the fifteenth," Jeannie said, "so nothing to worry about." There was a lilt in her voice that belied her light tone. I could tell she was a bit edgy, as I was.

"Superstitious hogwash," I said. "Thirteen is a *lucky* number in some cultures. We got married on the fourteenth. We're celebrating our twenty-fifth anniversary this weekend."

"Oh?" Our driver said without enthusiasm. I had expected a congratulations or "Wow, that's great" but was disappointed.

"The heat? Could you bump it up *please*?" Jeannie pleaded.

We'd flown through a series of green lights and were coming up to the Williamsburg Bridge. I imagined that we'd have a head-on collision and go flying off the bridge to our deaths, or Joseph would turn the wheel and aim for the rail. We'd crash through and be airborne in a moment. We'd have to wait until we sank to the bottom before trying to get out. In the dark. Windows were harder to break than one thought. What could we use? My mind raced along this irrational track as we rose higher over the East River.

Joseph hadn't responded to Jeannie's request for heat. I suspected the heater was broken. Joseph must have been hot-blooded, as it seemed he was just wearing a windbreaker. Well, no matter. If we survived the bridge, our destination wasn't far.

"Funny you requested this address," Joseph continued in his disconnected voice. "I've got family in this neighborhood. We go way back."

Jeannie has always enjoyed being chatty with strangers. She volleyed with, "Oh, that's interesting. Where are you-- " but was cut off.

"I remember one night—it was a Saturday the fourteenth. It seemed like all my fares were lousy. It was an awful night. First fare was a bunch of drunk guys, and one of them vomited all over the back seat. I had to stop and clean that up at a car wash. What a mess that was."

"Oh, yuck!" Jeannie said. She craned her neck around to look at me with an eye roll toward the driver and an I-can't-believe-this-guy expression.

I shrugged and whispered, "Almost there."

"The next fare was this mafioso guy—white shirt, black pants, dark sunglasses and a Rolex. He had this package with him. It smelled funny. Like a dead animal."

Where was this story going? I didn't want to know and the dispassionate way he spoke was getting to me. But we were over the bridge now, thank God. I breathed a sigh of relief. Jeannie caught my eye again, with a look of desperation.

"Sounds awful," she said, a little too loudly, "but I imagine you've had all sorts of fares. Say, uh, have you ever driven anyone famous?"

"And then I had a fare in Bedford-Stuy…" he continued as if he hadn't heard her. "Near here, in fact."

"Someone like Al Pacino or Johnny Depp? Cher? That would be so cool. But I guess they all have drivers, right? They probably never take cabs."

We shot passed a brightly lit bank, a colorful flower shop, an enormous furniture store.

"I was to pick up someone from an old house in this neighborhood…" he said, flipping on a turn signal.

We turned right passing a bakery advertising "Scrumptious vegan treats". I'd have to remember that place. Jeannie loved indie places like that.

Jeannie had been delighted and impressed that I'd found The Viennese, the impressive villa from the mid 1800's. It offered only six guest rooms each with a king-sized bed and deluxe bath; luxury in a homey atmosphere with a long sunny porch, a private garden, personal service and all modern conveniences. Less hustle and bustle, an easy affordable getaway from the city. But now, I regretted picking a place this far out. If I'd gone with a hotel in mid-town, we'd be getting into bed already. Just a few more minutes.

"When I got there, this scrawny greaser got in. He was so young and skinny, I didn't think much of it. Thought he was playing tough. I'm not usually afraid of anything, but there was just something about this kid…" his voice trailed away following the memory.

Greaser? I thought. Well, there's a word you don't hear anymore.

He turned again, this time onto Malcolm X Boulevard. Just a few blocks to go. I realized I was holding my breath and exhaled.

We came to an abrupt stop at the next stop sign. Jeannie and I were thrown forward into the seat back.

"Oh!" she cried out, bracing herself.

"What the—" I blurted, then "Ow!" My ankle had twisted funny.

"George?" Jeannie said pawing at my arm. "Where's our driver?"

I wiggled back onto the seat, rubbing my ankle. "What do you mean?" I asked with annoyance.

The taxi was stopped at the stop sign. The engine was running. But Joseph was not in the front seat. I leaned forward to be sure he hadn't slumped down. No, there was no one.

Jeannie clutched my arm. "George?"

"He couldn't have gotten out—" I said.

"No, we'd have heard—"

"No way—"

It had been frosty in the cab all along. I can't say for sure if it was our imagination or what, but it was now unbearable. Meat locker cold. And I will swear I saw tiny bits of frost forming on Jeannie's face. It was colder in the cab than it was outside, I was sure. Jeannie screamed and pulled away from me, reaching for her door handle. Her scream broke my paralysis; I launched myself out of my door and ran blindly until I heard her voice and her steps just behind me.

"George!" She pulled at my arm. George, look!"

I'm ashamed to admit that I was overcome by a dread I've only felt one time before when I went through a Horror Nights haunted house when I'd stepped into a room made up like a morgue. It had stopped me cold. When something moved under the sheet on a gurney, I was overwhelmed with terror. Truly, blind terror. I ran on instinct not even looking where I was going. I smacked into a wall and gashed my forehead. This was *that* kind of terror. No thoughts at all just the urgency to run.

"George, look!" She said again. I glanced back to where Jeannie was pointing. An empty street. There was no checkered cab.

"But—where--" I stammered.

"What's that?" Jeannie asked, pointing at the ground.

"What?" I asked, but then I saw it, a white leaf falling right where the cab had been. No, it wasn't a leaf. It was the wrong shape and size.

Jeannie pulled away from me and took a few tentative steps toward it. "It looks like—" she said, striding over, bending down, "yes, it is… it's the card you gave him. For the Viennese." She picked it up and trotted back to me to show me. There was no doubt. This was the card I had given to our cab driver. The man who disappeared. In the taxi that vanished into thin air, as they say.

"Let's…go," I said, removing the card from her hand to an inner jacket pocket, then holding her hand firmly, I began walking.

"It's like the cab just, just—"

"Disappeared," I said, finishing Jeannie's sentence. "Yes, come on." She was holding back. I felt like I was pulling a rowboat to shore.

"But—"

"Come on. Let's get out of here. I think the Viennese is just up the road that way a couple blocks."

She relented and picked up the pace, glancing back a few times. "It's just not possible. He couldn't have driven away—"

"No," I agreed.

"Surely, if there was some mistake, he'd come back—"

"No."

"We didn't pay the fare," she said with another glance behind her.

"No." I would have won a speed-walking contest had I not had Jeannie in tow. "Come on. You're cold."

"Did that just happen? Did we just see a *ghost*?" she asked, brow all scrunched in confusion. "But…okay, I didn't really believe in ghosts. But the taxi…George, we got here in a taxicab."

"Yes."

225

"That disappeared."

"Yes, so it seems."

"How is that possible?"

"I've no idea."

The whole thing was too uncomfortable for words. I wanted to put it out of my mind. It couldn't have happened, but it did. There was no explanation that made any sense at all. I was ready for a hot shower and a nightcap. A double Scotch. The grand façade of the Viennese appeared through a patch of trees. "Ah, here we are."

"Why did it stop just there?"

"I don't know," I said, fishing for the gate key.

"He was telling that awful story, and then we came to the abrupt stop."

"Apparently," I said, securing the gate behind us. "Could I trouble you to change the subject?"

"Yes, it's just that—"

"I need a drink," I said, and punched the combination code into the front door lock.

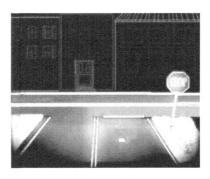

We slept in and arrived downstairs on the porch for breakfast with just enough time to spare that our hostess Benedetta was not yet antsy to clear the buffet offerings. It seemed the other guests had been and gone.

"Have you enjoyed your stay in New York?" Benedetta asked as she poured our coffee. She was an attractive woman in her forties, I guessed, with large eyes and wildly curly dark hair in a mane that cascaded down her back.

"Oh, yes, wonderful!" cooed Jeannie. "We've been everywhere." She gave the *Reader's Digest* version of our trip so far.

"You came in late, yes?" Benedetta asked. "No problems with passcode?" Her English was clear but retained a bit of Italian accent and cadence.

"No problem," Jeannie said with a smile for Benedetta but a wary glance in my direction.

"We uh—" I began, not sure if I should proceed. "Had a strange experience on the way home."

"Oh, yes?" she asked, filling our water glasses.

"Well, it will seem crazy… impossible. I don't know how to explain it. We were out late and hailed a taxi. It was an older one, a Checker cab—"

At this Benedetta's eyebrows rose. "Ah, yes?"

"The driver picked us up in the Village. I'm not sure where we were exactly, we kind of got lost—"

"A checker cab, you say?" Benedetta asked, setting down the water pitcher. She had the strangest expression on her face and, not paying attention to the pitcher, bumped the edge of the table with it, making a startling noise and splashing a bit of water on the table.

"Yes," I continued, wiping the water with my napkin. "I was relieved because right before the cab showed up, there were two

227

men coming up behind us. I was afraid they might attempt to mug us."

"What darling?" asked Jeannie setting down her coffee cup. "You didn't say anything."

"I didn't want to frighten you."

"Go on," said Benedetta. She seemed very interested in the story.

"It was getting quite cold, so we were relieved when the cab came," Jeannie said, "only the heater in the cab didn't work. It actually seemed colder in the cab than outside. And the driver was—"

"Was what?" Benedetta interrupted.

"Well, he was kind of... odd," I said, groping for the right word. "Distant. Stuck in the past. Jeannie tried to be cheerful and keep the conversation flowing, but he kept talking about how he had a bad feeling about Saturday the fourteenth."

"Yes," Benedetta said, nodding.

"You know him?" Jeannie asked.

"What else did he say?" Benedetta asked.

I eyed the food on my plate, rather sorry we'd gotten into this conversation. I was hungry and the bacon and biscuit were calling to me, but I didn't want to be rude.

Jeannie regarded me as if wondering what to share. She looked back at Benedetta and offered, "He said his family was from this neighborhood."

Benedetta must have seen the wistful way I was eyeing my biscuit. "Oh, please, eat, don't worry, I don't mind. Please, go ahead."

I began buttering the biscuit.

Jeannie hovered her fork over her omelet. "He seemed far away and sad...but he drove like he was in the Indy 500!"

Benedetta laughed then, but there was melancholy in her eyes as if she was recalling an old memory. "Did he drop you off here?"

The delicious biscuit caught in my throat. The way she had asked the question was as if she knew what had happened.

"No—" Jeannie said, shooting a nervous look at me. "That was the weirdest part. He was telling us about bad cab fares. Then we were coming up to the stop sign just a few blocks from here. He slammed on the breaks—we got thrown forward...but you know, I didn't see anything other than the stop sign. We were thrown forward and—"

"And then he was gone?" Benedetta finished.

Jeannie nodded.

"Yes," I said, feeling the goosebumps rise on my forearms. "You've heard this before?"

"We thought we were in *The Twilight Zone*," Jeannie said. "Because first the driver was gone. Then when we got out, the whole taxi disappeared."

"Yes," Benedetta said nodding. "I know this story. But your food is getting cold. Please eat. We can talk later. You enjoy your breakfast."

"You can leave us hanging like that," I said. "Tell us."

She sighed. "The driver was my grandfather. He was a cab driver until his death in 1964 when he was murdered by a passenger at that intersection. He was shot in the head and died almost instantly."

"That's horrible!" Jeannie exclaimed.

"But...but how..." I stammered, "how is it possible that we were in that cab? We got from the Village to here in a solid vehicle."

"Yes, and then it disappears. I know. I can't explain it. It happens on the anniversary of his death...it's like he wants to finish the ride and never does."

Jeannie and I stared at each other. Her face had gone pale.

"The name on the ID was Joseph Campanero or something like that," I said.

"Yes, that's right. That was my grandpa Joe. Did you look at the photographs in the living room?"

I confess, we were in the living room for cordials on Friday night, but I hadn't paid particular attention to the pictures on the wall. There were so many," I said.

"Um, just a minute. Please eat. I'll be right back."

It was hard to enjoy our food after a shock like that, but we picked at our plates. Benedetta returned with two framed pictures. She presented them.

"That's him!" We said in unison, pointing.

The first picture was a black and white photograph of a wedding couple. The man was a much younger version of the man we'd seen the previous night. The second was the same man, a bit older with a small paunch now, smiling back at the camera. He stood proudly next to a Checker taxi with his arm draped over the partially-opened driver door.

"I was young when it happened," our hostess said. "He was a wonderful man. Looked out for his parents, his family, his neighbors. If anyone was sick, he'd take them to the doctor. If they were in trouble, he'd help them, if they were—"

I remembered how the cab had showed up almost out of nowhere just after I'd noticed those suspicious men. "He did come at the perfect time," I said.

"He was like that," she said with a sigh before leaving to return the photographs to the wall. She returned once more and asked, "What have you got planned for today?"

"We've got to get all the way uptown to St. John the Divine for an eleven o'clock service—the blessing of the animals," Jeannie said. Her voice was back to sounding chipper and her pallor was improving.

"In fact," I said, reaching for the mini subway map I'd stuck in my back pocket, "could you show us how we can get there?"

She smiled, "I can call you a taxi, if you like but it will be cheaper to go by subway."

"Please," I said, "no more taxis after last night."

She smiled and pointed to the map. "You are here... you go back to that intersection... the subway entrance is just there on the corner."

While I didn't relish going back there, at least we'd be there in the daytime this time.

We made our subway connections and got to St. John the Divine in plenty of time. The rest of our weekend and flight back home were relatively uneventful.

I've never paid much attention to Halloween. If it weren't for our son, I'd probably miss it without a thought. To me, October thirty-first is just another square on the calendar.

But now I get a particular shudder those years when the thirteenth lands on a Friday because that means that Saturday is the fourteenth. And when I see that, I'll invariably hear Grandpa Joe's flat voice in my head saying, "You know, most people are superstitious about Friday the thirteenth. Not me. I get nervous about Saturday the fourteenth."

EIGHT

Zap wanted desperately to be home, but he was so tired, so terribly achy and tired. He had paid the check and was slumped in the barstool, mustering the energy to go outside in the rain again.

"Hey Sugar, you look beat," Gracie said, patting his arm. "Why don't you crash out for a little while in one of the booths back there? I can call your wife for you and tell her you're alright if you want."

"No, I can go, I just need a moment."

Gracie was suddenly next to him, not opposite the bar. "Come on, Sugar, you need a lie down. It's alright, let Gracie take care of you. You can go home in the morning."

"No, I... my wife..."

"That's it dear," Gracie said. "Come with me, just a few steps to this comfy little booth."

Zap let her lead him like a trusting child. He just needed a few hours of sleep and he'd be right as rain. He obeyed Gracie and let her guide him to a booth. Zap fumbled for his phone before collapsing in the booth seat. He stared at the phone. He felt like he was already asleep. It was so hard to concentrate. He pushed the button for the home phone. "Pammie, it's me. Honey, I'm so sorry it's so late. I'm going to sleep a while then come home. I just wanted to let you know I was okay and not to worry. I love you."

In no time, he had his boots off and had his legs up and he was snoring.

Above him, on the wall was a framed article about a man who was struck by lightning seven times. The last time, it killed him.

"I'm sorry for your loss, Mrs. Powers, he was one of the best," Daniel Bruder said, patting her shoulder. Daniel was Zap's boss and friend. "Freak thing. I should have gone up the pole, but Zap said he had it. We were packing it in. It should have been a routine thing. I'm so very sorry."

Pamela Powers nodded, sniffing back tears. "Thanks, Dan."

"I'm so sorry," Brad said, his voice cracking, "he was like a mentor to me. Taught me everything."

"I know," Pamela said, clutching his hand. "He thought of you like a brother, Brad."

"It's just so inconceivable," the reverend said, "but the Lord works in mysterious ways. Rest assured, he's at peace."

"Yes," Pamela sniffed, "but to be *electrocuted* again. Of all things. I just, I just…" Her face crumpled then as the tears fell and the sobs insisted on being heard. The reverend put an arm around her and pulled her in a side hug. "It was his profession, Pamela, hazards of the profession, not the wrath of God, I assure you."

They stood clustered outside the little church. The black funeral vehicles were lined up, a funeral director was handing out the magnetic signs for mourners to put on the hoods of their cars to indicate that they were part of the procession to the cemetery. Pamela hugged little Zachary to her as they walked to their designated limousine behind the hearse.

"It's bothering me, Reverend. I got a phone call the night he died. It was from his phone, but when I answered it, there was just static and the sound of rain. But the call came *after* the ambulance picked him up. He was already…gone."

The reverend patted her shoulder, not sure what to say.

Dan walking just behind them said, "Sounds just like Zap. He loved you. I'm sure he wanted to say goodbye."

"It's the weirdest thing, though," Pamela said, "they never did find his cell phone. But I begged the police to check his phone records. There was a call… it's not possible, I know but the phone records show an attempted call from some small town called Fleeting."

"*Fleeting*?" Brad said, frowning. "How'd his phone get there? I know where that is. It's a tiny little town. Not much there but a post office and Seven Eleven."

"I know," Pamela said, "it's between our house and where the…the accident happened."

Brad smiled. "There *used* to be a cool bar there, a long time ago. My dad took me in there once when I was a kid, just cause of the way it was decorated. The whole place was done up in Halloween decorations. Nice lady that ran it too. She kept running it even after her husband died. But it went out of business *ages* ago. I think she had a stroke or something. I still have a little, oh, whatcha call it, figurine. Yeah, a Dracula figurine the lady gave me 'cause my dad told her I was crazy about Dracula."

"Do you remember what the place was called?" Pamela asked.

"Something basic. Oh, what was it? Oh yes, The Beer Wine and Spirits Pub."

A Fleeting Idea

"I don't know Frankie, I know you have this crazy nostalgia, but I'm telling you, this'll never work. No one is going to come out here to the middle of nowhere to visit this place." Stewart said, shaking his head. "I mean, I get it your nostalgia, but, *puh!*"

"I'll make it happen," Frank said, wrestling the key in the rusty lock. "You'll see."

"Wow, Frankie, it's just like I pictured it when you described it," said his girlfriend Stardust getting out of the back seat of the van.

"Well, the place sure looks like it should be haunted anyway," Leon said, standing back and looking along the roof line. "Sure gonna take some work to get it up to code."

"Yeah, yeah," Frankie said, "Ha! Here we go!"

The padlock released with a clunk as it struck the massive wooden door. Frankie tugged it free of the catch and pushed the door open. It resisted at first, but then swung open with a groan. The three men entered followed by Stardust, the team's psychic empath. The men gravitated to the dark, imposing bar while Star hung back, entering slowly with her hands extended, fingers splayed out wide.

"Oh," she said with a sharp intake of breath and a look of surprise.

"It's great, isn't it?" Frankie said, turning slowly in place.

"Is the power on?" Leon asked.

"Hope so," Frankie said, walking to a bank of switches by the bar. "Earle Electric was supposed to have it turned on today."

"Hooray!" Stewart said as lights came on over the bar and in sections of the restaurant. "Hey, this place hardly needs spooking up, it's naturally spooky."

Star walked to the antique cash register like a sleepwalker. She stood in front of it for a moment before running her fingers over the ornate buttons. "This is gorgeous. Your Mom loved this old thing."

"Yeah, my Dad got it for her as a present. We kind of teased her about it, but she wouldn't part with it. Said it matched the bar."

Ping!

The cash drawer slid open, hitting Star in the belly. She jumped back.

"I didn't do that!" she said, "I didn't push any of the buttons, I was just touching them, you know, to feel them. I think your Mom is here, Frank. She wanted to get my attention. I have to say, it worked."

"You're joking, right?" Leon asked. "You're just messing with us, right, Star?"

"No. She's here. I can feel her." Star answered.

Leon and Stewart exchanged skeptical looks.

"Oh, I'm sure they're all here," Frank said, "Mom, Dad, and my uncle Paul. I never met him, he died when he was seventeen, but he was always here, messing with my Mom."

"Messing? How messing?" Stewart asked.

"He loved to tease her. Move stuff around, mess with customers. Dad did too when he passed. The kitchen was his domain, he was the cook. I'm telling you, that's what so great about this bar. It's like a beacon for passing spirits and has at least three permanent ghosts. They'll be tickled to bits if I get this place up and running. And with social media these days? We'll be packing them in to see the bar, experience the ghosts and pay big bucks to spend the night in the most haunted bar in the South."

Stewart and Leon wandered slowly through the main room checking out the structure and the décor that was in remarkably good shape despite having been locked up for a few years.

"I wish I could have come back sooner," Frank said, joining them. "I was deployed when Mom went into the hospital. There was just so much going on, I couldn't deal with this place right away. But now, this is my dream come true. We don't have to be ghostbusters looking for the next gig somewhere. And the next. Always travelling. We can stay here. Business can come to us."

"You sound so confident that this place will, um… perform." Leon said.

"I bussed a lot of tables here in my teen years. I *know*."

"He's right," Star said moving towards them. "Leon, you might want to bring in your meters—"

A rattling noise over the doorway to the kitchen caught their attention. Leon and Frank walked toward the door for a better look. Star and Stewart stayed where they were. Stewart shot a questioning glance at Star.

"It's coming from the fire alarm up there," Leon said, pointing.

"He's showing off as usual," Star said.

Frank's head swiveled around to look at Star.

Stewart's eyes widened. "Stardust, what are you talking about, "as usual"? And who are you imitating? That doesn't sound like you."

Star didn't answer or look at Stewart, she was grinning and watching the fire alarm.

The fire alarm jiggled with more force then lifted up and away from the wall. The batteries flew out from behind it falling to the floor as if thrown like dice. They rolled to Stewart's feet and stopped abruptly as if someone had stepped on them with a shoe.

"Whoa!" Stewart said leaping back.

"Wow," Frank said with a chuckle.

Stewart looked at the three of them in shock. "You saw that, right? Batteries don't just do that! Why me? Why did they roll to me?"

"He's just showing off," Star said, turning to Stewart slumping her shoulders in a get-with-the-program impatient way. She put a hand on her hip. "He don't mean any harm; he's just messing with you."

"WHO is, Star?" Stewart asked, backing up.

"My uncle Paul," Frank said, and "Paul" Star said, in unison.

The fire alarm slid back in its place on the wall.

"Hi hon," Stardust said to the air around her.

"Hon?" Leon asked.

"I think she's channeling my Mom," Frankie said, his eyes tearing up. "Mom? Is that you?"

"Hey Sugar," Stardust said, walking toward Frankie. She cupped her hand and placed it on his cheek. "I'm so glad you're back."

Frank took her hand in his and held her hand to his face.

"Star?" Leon asked. "Stardust?"

"You'll help, won't you, Mom?" Frankie asked.

"Of course, Baby," Star said.

Leon had pulled out his cell phone and began videotaping Stardust and Frankie.

"No, not this, Sugar," Stardust said, turning to Leon. She touched his phone with her hand and the screen went blank.

"Hey!" Leon whined.

"Star, what are you doing?" Stewart asked, his voice rising in fear and aggravation.

"Love you, Mom," Frank said hugging Stardust.

She hugged him back.

"Okay, this is too weird for me," Stewart said. "I've been with Extreme Ghost Hunters, We B Heebee-Jeebees, and Ghouls Just Wanna Have Fun, but this…this…" He left the sentence incomplete, threw his hands up in surrender and walked toward the door.

"Hey, Stewart, come on," Leon said. "Come back. Besides, you can't go anywhere, Frank's got the van keys."

"Yeah, well, I'm done. Most gigs you bump around, say it's getting cold and, oh my, what was that noise, shake the camera, flicker the lights and it's a wrap. This? Batteries flying out of a fire alarm at me? Star here getting possessed? I didn't sign on for this weirdness. Peace out."

The front door yawned open as Stewart approached it as if an unseen butler were opening the door for him.

"No way!" He yelled. He stopped for a moment, eyes darting around for another exit, but finding none, he bolted through the open door.

The door slammed shut behind him.

Star blinked and pulled away from Frank with a confused look. She was herself again. "Your Mom really loves you."

Leon said, "I don't know if you noticed, but we just lost Stewart."

Stardust smiled, "I had a feeling he wouldn't last. Nice guy, but he's a phony. Pity. He's a talented cameraman, but we'll find someone else."

The light on Leon's phone lit up. "Hey, my phone's working again! Awesome!"

Stardust strolled around the main room touching the tables and low beams, pausing to look at the dusty movie posters, the figurine collection, and lifelike bats hanging under the wall sconces. "I wish I'd known your parents, Frank. I love all this. You know, when you first described this, I didn't get it. But I'm starting to now. This will be a paranormal Mecca. If we host overnights here on special occasions, people will hand over bags of money to stay the night."

"Yup!" Frank agreed, grinning.

"I can feel them. Can you guys?" Stardust sat down at a booth large enough for six people. "Like right here… I'm sitting next to a man… he feels really solid, like a football player… but I'm getting images of wires and… Oh!"

"What?" Frank and Leon asked. They had both reacted when Stardust jumped.

"Something to do with electricity. I just felt a huge jolt of energy pass through me."

"You sure gave me a little shock," Frank said.

Stewart pulled out his phone, punched a button and aimed it at Star.

"Hey look, Frank, do you see something there?"

Frank looked at the screen. There was his girlfriend talking to empty space... no, not exactly empty... there was something in the seat next to her like a hint of a shadow. It swayed as if caught in the faintest breeze.

"Yeah, I do."

"Man, I wish I'd thought to bring in my equipment. I never dreamed we'd have activity like this. "Stewart said. "Want me to set up?"

"Nah. Plenty of time for that." Frank said. "I just wanted you to see the place."

"Oh... yeah," Stardust said, talking to an empty seat. "You can do it. I'll help. You have to find the white light. Don't be afraid. Pamela? No, I don't know her, but I could..." She closed her eyes and stopped talking.

As Leon and Frank continued to watch Star, their eyes moved from the screen to Star to each other. An excited smile spread across Leon's face.

Frank nodded, also smiling. "You're getting it, aren't you. You see that this can and will be huge. Why, we'll kiss this sleeping town back to life better than the prince ever dreamed for Sleeping Beauty."

Leon nodded, "Yeah, man. I'm all in with you!"

Know a good cook?" Frank asked Leon. "Or a bartender or two? Once I get this place in shape, I'm gonna need reliable help."

"Yeah, actually, I might."

The two men continued talking keeping an eye on Star having an animated conversation with thin air.

"Mm-hmm. I'll tell her for you." Star said nodding. "Yes, there you go. You take care. You'll be fine. Yes, yes, I'll tell her." She leaned back in the chair and opened her eyes.

"Such a nice man. I'll have to find his wife, Pamela. He gave me a message to tell her."

"You helped him move on?" Frank asked.

"Yup. He's gone."

"Hey wait a minute," Leon said. "If you send all the ghosts to heaven or wherever, we're gonna be out the main attraction. What are you doing?"

"Relax," Frank said. "There will be plenty more. This place is like a rest stop on the great highway to the beyond. Trust me."

Stardust nodded. "I love it here. Hey Frank? How long do you think it'll take to get it fixed up?"

"Oh, I don't know. Depends on how fast I can get permits and work crews. It'll need a new roof, new kitchen equipment… next spring? Next summer?"

Stardust wiggled out of the booth and stood right in front of Frank, looking up at him, their noses almost touching. "I want to get married here. Next Halloween!"

And that was how the Spirited Away began. Frank and Stardust were married on Halloween night by a minister dressed as an undertaker. The bride and groom were dressed as Morticia and Gomez Addams. The cash register drawer dinged and flew open right after Frank said, "I do."

Guests threw dried corn as the happy couple drove away in Gracie's old truck and the wedding videos went viral on real-ghosts-captured-on-video pages on the internet as orbs danced around the room during the ceremony and there were extra heads and hands in the group photos.

Five years later, the bar was the home base for a weekly podcast about the latest paranormal activity. Bookings for special overnight stays were full ten months out. The wait time for a table was never less than thirty minutes and occasionally guests commented on the outstanding service from the flirty and efficient waitress who seemed to disappear and reappear out of thin air.

The town of Fleeting had expanded to include a bed and breakfast, a coffee shop, an antique store, and several souvenir shops with ghost mugs, coasters and T-shirts.

Stardust's belly bump was evident when the Spirited Away team shook hands with the mayor as cameras and videos captured the unveiling of the new welcome to Fleeting sign.

And if you look very closely, you can see three less-distinct people standing behind Frank: a large man, a teenager and a smiling woman.

The Hoarder House

Famous ghost-story writer, Chad Benton, the moderator, looked down the table to the last of the four panelists. " Shalynda, your turn. What's the most intense paranormal experience you've ever had? I hear you've got a doozy of a story."

Shalynda Shadow exhaled and leaned back in her seat. She ran her palms over her nose and cheeks in a washing motion. "Most intense? Well, the hoarder house was the most everything, most intense, most bizarre, most frustrating and most satisfying."

It was Friday evening, the first day of the paranormal convention and there were only thirteen people in the audience. The three other ParanormaCon panelists, a parapsychologist from Michigan a cryptozoologist from North Carolina and ghost story writer Chad Benton had each shared a story. All eyes were on Shalynda Shadow.

Brushing her long black hair over her shoulder, she said, "As a psychic medium and paranormal investigator, I get called in to investigate hauntings all over the country. Right off the bat, this case was different." She laughed. "Ooh, yeah, that's an understatement." She laughed again and shook her head. "I had no idea what I was getting into."

Some of the people in the audience shifted in their seats. Some leaned forward.

"I was contacted by family members worried about their aging mother, a famous spiritualist back in the sixties. I met with the three daughters and one son. None of them had seen her or been in the house for years, they'd only talked to her on the phone. They reported that she'd always been eccentric, but they were concerned for her health and well-being. At this point, I was puzzled; I reminded them that I was a medium, not a nurse."

There were a few chuckles from the audience.

"Oh, yes, we know, they said. We need you. We are afraid to go into the house. It's not…safe."

Shalynda paused, cocked her head, making a this-sounds-fishy face. "At this point, I'm picturing a house that needs to be condemned, right? So, I said, 'look, maybe you need a contractor –' but they cut me off again. 'No, no, the house is haunted. Very haunted. Dangerously haunted.'"

Shalynda stopped again, looking relieved. She continued, "'Oh, well, no problem, I can help', I told them. And before I could get more information, they were passing me legal documents to sign, all kinds of confidentiality agreements. My team couldn't even use video equipment if we swore not to share it. That was understandable but a pain all the same. And, oh my God, if we *had* been allowed to use video?" She swung her head and flipped her hair, "The video hits on YouTube? We could have retired fat and happy. But we weren't allowed to use any of the material." She mock-sobbed. "Crying shame."

Pausing to take a sip of water, she continued, "The first thing that struck me as odd was, the daughter kept saying she wanted us to 'catalog' what we found. I think she even used the word 'itemize'." She made a confused face. "I'd never heard of that before."

249

"That's different," noted Peter Downs, the parapsychologist.

"Yes. Most people who contact me aren't even sure they have a haunting. And if they are, they usually have one, maybe two entities. But I soon found out that this family not only knew that they had an infestation of spirits, this house had so many entities in it, they really did want me to catalog them."

"You're kidding," said Chad. "That's crazy."

"Yup." Shalynda said with a quick nod. "This house had it all--higher and lower order entities: ghosts, wraiths, shades, poltergeists, elementals, animal spirits — it was like an interactive museum of paranormal activity."

"Was the mother still living in the house?" Winslow Whatley, the cryptozoologist asked.

"Oh, yes," Shalynda said, nodding again, eyes wide in a can-you-believe-it expression. "She was central to it all. It was a symbiotic, co-dependent kind of relationship."

"But you said she was a spiritualist. She should have been able to banish the spirits," Peter said.

"Well, yes," she answered with a laugh. "Back in the sixties and even into the early seventies, she was a famous medium. Even got on Carson once. I can't use her real name, so for the sake of this story, let's call her Carol. Carol made a living writing books and clearing homes. I can only aspire to follow in her footsteps--she was amazing in her day. But then she fell madly in love with a man — you know the type, all wonderful and loving at the start, but then more and more critical and controlling. Oh, yes, he was after her money. He gaslighted Carol to make her crazy and sedated her a lot of the time. Got control of her finances and turned her against her family."

There was a sympathetic murmur in the room.

"It took a while, but the daughters and son figured out that the man was a slimeball. They had an intervention with mom and after a long ugly battle, drove him away. One daughter reported that they had the best Thanksgiving ever that year, all reunited again. Carol never mentioned his name again, he was just "That Cad". But after that, Carol fell into a depression. Stopped writing, turned away business. She became a recluse in that house."

Shalynda paused for another sip of water as the sympathetic murmur died down.

"Did a spirit help oust the guy?" Winslow asked with a chuckle.

Shalynda shook her head. "I doubt it. Carol was lonely and depressed. And here's the interesting part. You've watched that television show about hoarders, haven't you?" She looked around to see nods. "In those shows, the hoarder people were kind of normal until some traumatic event. They took comfort in collecting stuff that made them feel a certain way and then it got out of control, right? Well, in Carol's case, she didn't collect thrift store *tchotchkes* or clothes or whatever, she collected spirits."

Winslow leaned forward to look down the table at Shalynda. "Wait, wait, wait...*what?*"

"Yup. Kind of the reverse of what we normally do. Instead of sending the spirits off to the white light or banishing them, she invited them to stay with her. Like pets."

As this drew responses of amusement and incredulity, Shalynda leaned back with a smile and waited.

"That's crazy!"

"Oh my gosh!"

"No way!"

Shalynda held up a hand. "I know we don't have a lot of time, so I'll summarize *months* of work. When my team first got there, Carol's children met us in the parking lot. They got Carol to come outside to talk to us. You could tell that she was once an amazingly powerful medium and an attractive woman, but she was a husk. She walked and talked like she was in a dreamworld. Her color was awful. Her breathing was feeble. She looked and smelled like a homeless person. It was pitiful. But she seemed happy to see her children. The first day, we just talked in the driveway. She sat in the passenger seat of my car. We never even set foot in the house. The second day, we brought chairs, food and drinks. We talked again as we picnicked in the driveway. This time, she granted us permission to go in the house."

Shalynda put her palms down on the table and exhaled.

The room was silent in anticipation.

"I was the first one to go in," she said, flaring her fingers up from the table. "Wow. I've never seen anything like it. I've done a lot of investigations where there is next to no activity. We might get cold spots or strange sounds but nothing really concrete. This house…this house was unbelievable. I walked in with my partner Andrew and the front door slammed shut behind us. Poor Andrew was kind of new to our team. I shouldn't have brought him. My mistake. He did really well, all things considered."

"Uh oh," Chad said.

Shalynda raised an eyebrow. "A huge black cat shot past us and ran up a flight of stairs but vanished before it got to the top. Thumping noises came down the hall as if someone was bouncing a basketball. The light fixture in the hallway swayed. Tiny orbs floated around us." Shalynda floated her hands around indicated the swirling orbs.

"I would have run right back out the door," Chad said.

Shalynda smiled. "Oh, I thought about it, believe me! But I kept reminding myself that Carol lived here. If Carol could live here by herself, I could at least walk around for a few minutes. I called out, 'Hello, my name is Shalynda and this is Andy. We're just here to visit. Carol gave us permission to be here.' We walked toward the kitchen where a bunch of knives were sticking out of the wall as if someone had been practicing knife throwing at the county fair. A green mist hung on the ceiling. Andy noted that the temperature in the kitchen was about fifteen degrees lower than in the foyer. He commented that he felt overwhelmed by sadness. As he said it, the water faucet turned on and water poured full-force out of the tap."

"Nope, I'm outta there. And frankly, if you ever write this story, you'll put me out of business," Chad said. "You've only been talking five minutes and I'm scared to death."

"You know, the problem wasn't the scary — I mean, I'm used to ghosts, right? It was the intensity. I should mention now that the intensity of this house was so strong that after this first day, I could only stay two hours at a time. This was a small part of why the clearing took so long. The jumble of sadness, dread, loneliness, cold, angry, depression, rage and needy all moment by moment was intense. I can't begin to describe it. I would leave the house, go home and sit in a hot bath with lots of salt. I'd be wiped out for the rest of the day. Can I just say, I bought a LOT of salt during this time. Went to the stores where you can buy in bulk. Cartloads. It was crazy. Good thing salt is cheap."

"I know what you mean," Peter said. "Even moderately haunted houses are draining. I can't imagine what you went through."

253

Shalynda nodded. "Where was I? Oh yeah. We were heading toward the staircase — filmy-green ectoplasm was dripping down the banister just like how candles drip wax, you know?" She made a gesture indicating long drips. "Just then the front door opened, and Carol and her children hovered in the doorway. 'We tried to stop her, but she insists on coming in' they said. Carol teetered in very agitated. 'They're mine! They need me! Don't hurt them' she repeated."

"Oh boy," Winslow said, shaking his head.

"We didn't have much choice. She was too emotionally fragile. We relented and let her give us the house tour. Carol introduced us to Mabel, a suicide who hung out in the pantry. We met Howard, a spirit she'd brought home from the cemetery in town because he was lonely too. There was the black wraith in the basement who loved the damp and darkness and wanted his own space to haunt. Bob who was killed in an auto accident; he seemed to like tinkering about in the garage. We met Aunt Lizzy who'd been poisoned by her daughter — not Carol's Aunt Lizzy, mind you, she couldn't quite remember where Lizzy had come from, but they were old friends. Lizzy was teaching her to knit. They often sat together in the living room. There was Monty, a middle-aged man with anger management issues. He liked to break things to get Carol's attention. Fortunately, Petunia, a bright the little girl who'd fallen down a well somewhere in Iowa was more than happy to sweep up. Clyde had died in Florida from yellow fever. Once a gardener, he tended to the rose bush out back and mowed the lawn. Upstairs were Lorenzo, an immigrant taxidermist and his wife Rosalia, a couple Carol had brought home from a graveyard in upstate New York." Shalynda bit her lip and looked up. Let's see what else? Did I mention the elemental in the upstairs bathroom?"

Winslow interrupted, "Uh, some of us might not know what an elemental is. Could you explain that?"

"Oh, right," Shalynda said, nodding. "Eighty-nine percent of the entities haunting Carol's house were spirits of dead people just hanging out. They were human once. But there was an elemental upstairs. An elemental is a very primitive energy that was never human. They are usually tied to an element, earth, water, fire, air so they tend to hang out near rivers, firepits, beaches. They are difficult to get rid of because they are also like elemental emotions: anger, envy, distrust. It's hard to rationalize with them. They don't understand words, just feelings. They aren't necessarily bad," she said, making a face, "but they aren't exactly good. They have to be handled with extreme care as they are powerful. Somewhat rare and tend to avoid humanity, preferring to hang out, like I said, in bogs, woods, beaches or remote mountains and such."

"Thanks for clarifying," Winslow said.

"Sure. Where was I? Oh yeah. We walked with Carol through the entire house. The air near the elemental's bathroom was oppressively muggy, sticky-wet hot like a jungle. I caught a glance in the mirror--" Shalynda shuddered and took a minute to recompose herself. "I saw a hulking furry face and glowing eyes...a heatwave of raw evil billowed out as the mouth grinned wide in a crazy, drooling—*euhh*!" She shuddered again. "I was already pushing everyone farther down the hall when this awful belching, gurgling came from the sink and toilet as if the whole septic system was going to gush out. We ran. Carol's children were really freaked out. One of the daughters ran outside and never came in again until the house was entirely cleared. Andy stuck by me, God bless him, but I could tell when Angela bolted for the door, he wanted to bolt too. We went upstairs…the sticky ectoplasm… and oh—" Shalynda scrunched her face and hunched her shoulders. "The man with the hat." She shuddered. "The spirits in the house were active, definitely wanted our attention, but they didn't do anything to us. Well, they touched my hair, and Lorenzo pinched my butt…oh, and there was a shadowy bat thing that flew at Andy and jump-scared him silly. But they weren't really scary, until the man with the hat. He was alone in the attic sitting in an old chair."

"Wait, Hat Man?" Winslow asked, but Shalynda didn't seem to hear him.

"Did I mention that this house had forty-eight rooms, eight bathrooms and an elevator? Not to mention outbuildings—a garage, a workshop and a shed. It took a long time to walk through the whole house." Shalynda hunched again as if bracing to continue. "There was a door to the attic and normal stairs going up. When we opened the door, the smell of rot was intense. We had to cover our faces. Real rats and ghost rats ran away squeaking. The attic light had either burned out, or the man in the hat didn't want us seeing him up there. And trust me, I didn't relish seeing him either. The attic was huge but mostly empty. There were some boxes and a few pieces of furniture, but you could see end to end."

"Sorry, is this The Hat Man?" Winslow asked, eyes gleaming.

"I think so. I'd never encountered him before, but I'd heard of him." Shalynda looked out at the audience, "For those of you who aren't familiar, Hat Man is a shadow, not a human ghost. There are different species of spirits, like the elemental. The shadows are dark, malevolent entities, possibly demons, that feed on fear. They love to terrify. And trust me, they're good at it. The feeling of dread in that attic was so bad…"

"Oh, man, I wish I could have been there," Winslow said. "I've never seen one."

"Better you than me, Winslow. Once was enough. Hat Man stood up, and as he rose to his seven feet tall self, a tornadic wind whipped up. It pushed us back out the door and slammed the door so hard it cracked. Then the door kept opening and slamming, opening and slamming *wham, wham, wham* the whole time we ran downstairs. I found out later that the door yanked off its hinges and was reduced to splinters. Poor Andy — he was a wreck for a few days after that. He could barely talk coherently and I'm sure he wasn't sleeping."

"Yikes! Bet he needed to change his drawers that day!" Winslow said, laughing.

Shalynda bit her lip. "Well, I know I've taken up a lot of time. I'll wrap it up. It took a team of mediums and psychologists three months to get Carol to let go of her spooks. I cataloged them, room by room. And Carol herself, once she kind of got on board with the clearing plan, tackled the Hat Man, the wraith and a few other nasties. I kind of kick myself now. I'd love to know how she did it, but I wasn't going to go back up in the attic again. No way. Funnily enough, the scariest ones were the ones she got rid of first. She knew in her heart that they were bad and had to go."

"Huh. Kind of makes sense, but I wouldn't have guessed that." Peter said.

"I know. Surprised us too. The psychologist worked with Carol to get her to admit that she was being unfair to the spirits, keeping them like that. She should let them go on to their next adventure and not keep them. It was a battle. 'Carol, look at Mabel here hanging in the pantry. You know she's unhappy. You know it's not fair to keep her. Let her go into the light. Can you do that, Carol? Carol… let's talk about Charlie on the porch. You know he'd be better off with his wife and family. They've been waiting on him for decades and so on. It was exhausting."

"Wow. I'll bet," Peter said.

Shalynda shook her head. "And we caught her backsliding! One day we arrived and there was a shade blocking the front door. Hey wait! He wasn't here before! Who's this? She admitted that she had found him in town behind a dumpster and invited him back."

"Unbelievable," Winslow said.

"Yup. Happened a few times. Oh! Almost forgot the biggest shocker!" Shalynda said, pressing her hands to her head. "When we got Carol to release the creeper in the basement — and it was, ugh, stubborn as all get out — that took a couple ugly days — but there was still something lingering. I noticed she was being kind of squirrely and evasive. Her eyes kept straying to this ugly metal box on a shelf. You won't believe this — well, you might. I didn't think she was this vindictive, but the psychologist finally wormed it out of her. "

Shalynda surveyed her audience and paused for a sip of water. "When the Evil Cad died, she went to his funeral. She managed to lure *his* ghost back to the house. She worked some magick on him and trapped in a metal box. He'd been sitting on that shelf in the basement for ten years. When she was in a foul mood, she'd go down and shake him around, and in the wintertime, she'd alternately put him in the fireplace to 'burn his sorry ass' or, if there was snow, set him outside to freeze."

"That's hilarious," Chad said.

"Woman scorned," Peter said.

"Oh, we had a time getting her to let go of him! To be honest, we were all secretly cheering her on about that one, but we could not in good conscience let her keep tormenting him. As a consolation prize, the psychologists told her she could keep two spirits. That was tough. She wanted to keep Clyde the gardener and Petunia the sweet little girl. Clyde was so devoted to the roses and you know how hard it is to get good help. Carol was reluctant to let him go. She hated to have to hire a lawn service — strangers coming over--but she relented.

"Petunia was another struggle! The psychologists explained that yes, Petunia may be like a surrogate daughter, but somewhere in the great beyond her real mother was waiting for her and missing her terribly. In the end, with a heavy heart, Carol realized that the greatest act of love would be setting her free. Bittersweet days when she guided Clyde and Petunia to the light.

"She kept Pyewacket, the black cat. A great choice, really, since you don't have to feed a ghost cat or fool with kitty litter."

There was a ripple of laughter.

"And though we argued against it, she and Aunt Lizzie were firm that Carol would never figure out that intricate sweater pattern, so Lizzie could stay on until the spring."

This brought a burst of laughter from the audience.

"See?" Shalynda said with a smile, "all's well that ends well."

Chad said, "Wow, that was an amazing story, thank you Shalynda. Before we open it up to questions from our audience, I have one. When did this take place and like in the shows, did you ever do a follow-up visit? Did Carol turn out okay, or did she go back to hoarding again?"

259

"Great question," Shalynda said, nodding. "Glad you asked that. Yes, the initial cleansing took place two years ago, from September to almost Christmas. In fact, the children all came for Christmas and decorated. They invited us. The house was unbelievably gorgeous. Carol looked great too. Much healthier. And the house was happy and bright. Such a difference. I should mention too that Carol pulled me aside. She thanked me again and added, 'it's so nice to be able to play Christmas music. At first, when they were all gone, the quiet drove me nuts. I can hear the clocks ticking now; it used to be all chatter and moaning. A long time ago, I used to enjoy listening to the radio, but once the house got full, the spirits could never agree. I liked classical music and easy listening, but Sleazel wanted Heavy Metal, Clive wanted hip hop, Lizzy liked Frank Sinatra and Petunia wanted The Andrews Sisters. The bickering was too much. After Monty hurled the radio at the wall, I never bothered to replace it. I haven't had music in this house for decades.'"

"That's insane," Chad said, shaking his head.

Peter leaned forward, "What about now? Do you have an update?"

"Yes, I do," Shalynda said with a smile. "I was invited to her seventy-fifth birthday party — it was just a couple weeks ago. Huge party, like sixty or seventy people and the house was decorated with balloons and streamers. Very festive. I only knew the children of course. The good news is, Carol began dating last year! She has a new boyfriend. A retired librarian, I think, named Wendell. I got good vibes from him; he had true love in his eyes when he looked at Carol. I think he'll be a keeper. Had to laugh! Carol was getting compliments on the Christmas sweater she was wearing. I have to say, she did a great job, it was pretty with a red body and a complicated white neckline. I didn't see Lizzie, but I had a feeling she was there, hiding. I thought I caught a glimpse of her in the kitchen but didn't see her again. But oh!" She paused, putting a hand to her mouth suppressing a giggle. "The best was Wendell. I left the party early. You know, kind of uncomfortable around strangers. When I slipped out, I looked back. Carol and Wendell were sitting cozy together with Pyewacket perched on the arm of the couch. Wendell was petting him. I'm pretty sure Wendell didn't know Pyewacket was a ghost! Like I said, all's well that ends well."

Notes

BW&S

I am indebted to Dan South for suggesting these little vignettes to act as the grout to hold together this mosaic of stories. I designed the book cover with an English pub sign in mind but had not come up with a pub story. Thanks for the nudge, Dan.

Coral Ardisia

The seed for this inspired by true events as evidenced by the photograph of my beloved Jersey shovel. I truly believe that plants can communicate and posse up for protection.

I dedicate this story to my fifth-grade teacher, Mrs. Margaret Lopez: teacher, mentor, role model and life coach. Also, to friend and Master Gardener, Dr. Elaine Young.

Night Vision

In 2018 I discovered several Facebook pages dedicated to the classic ghost story: Classic Ghost Story Tradition, The Sheridan La Fanu Appreciation Society and the M. R. James Appreciation Society. From these pages I have been directed to articles, artwork, videos, films and more and more classic ghost story writers. I am gleefully burrowing deeper down this rabbit hole of treasures.

This story was inspired by M.R. James's story, "A View from a Hill". .

Lost Island of Unsonsy

In a shameless attempt to get Hedonistic Hound Press some notice, I held a Name-the-Beastie contest for this story. As an afterthought, I added a compose-a-few-lines-of-a-sea-chanty challenge and additionally asked for a proper Latin name.

Initially, the contest got encouraging attention and quite a few
👍*on FB. Few people actually gave it a whirl, but the responses received were all suitable.*

Langhan Edwin Turner submitted "murk lurker" as a common name and insomnichthys diabolic a "nightmare fish of the devil" for a Latin name. Elaine Young submitted Gillicks gliderunglia - based on two Old English words "grimlic" meaning fierce, voracious and "gliderung" meaning phantom, apparition. I couldn't decide so I combined the two.

Aaron Benson of Seven Hills Slingshots went above and beyond by delving into an Algonquin dictionary to come up with an Algonquin (Powhatan) name, :zhaabonigannamens babaamibibide which he says means flying needle fish. Dan South submitted the terrific ditty and Dave Tomlin is the genius behind the "fillets your mateys" limerick.

Thank you all for your wonderful contributions!

This story is 100% fiction. The islands north of Unsonsy are real. Tangier is a charming island with an uncertain future. If sea levels continue to rise as predicted, it may disappear like Unsonsy. I was privileged to know an Eastern Shore family whose livelihood was entirely dependent on oysters and soft-shell crabs.

Pillow Talk

A few years ago, I spotted a set of thick, good quality, queen-sized sheets at an estate sale for something like six dollars. The color was a peculiar, unappealing something between beige and pumpkin puree, but for six dollars, I could not pass them up. I'd been thinking about getting an extra set of sheets and here they were.

It did occur to me that sheets might fall into that no-no zone of thrifting along with undergarments and bathing suits. They looked new. Hot water and soap, good as new. Who cared about the unappealing color in the dark?

I put these sheets on my bed a few times. They felt great. But whenever I slept on the pillowcase, I had unsettling dreams or outright nightmares.

The bad dreams stopped as soon as I changed the sheets. Lesson learned. With regret, I disposed of said sheets.

Funny Little Stories

This one began as a small seed with the image of an old man in a nursing home. I'd recently had a conversation about Anne Rice novels and how much I loved the beginning of *The Witching Hour*. As the idea of the family reunion took shape, I pulled from the one family reunion my beloved great-aunt Betty Allone pulled together before she died. Though she looked so frail and withered that many said she shouldn't have been brought to the reunion, I believe it was the reason she held on. She got to see five generations of family all together. She passed not long after.

I had no idea where this story was going until Aunt Wanetta started talking.

Strong Pot of Tea

The University of the South aka "Sewanee" is the loose model for the unnamed college of this story. Located on the Cumberland Plateau about an hour northwest of Chattanooga, it is a gorgeous campus in rural surroundings. Getting up and down "The Mountain" is pretty dramatic; the side roads are rustic. I borrowed some real road names, but one would not be able to follow the directions as related in the story.

I will forever be indebted to my grandfather for convincing my parents that we needed to add Sewanee to our college shopping list. I owe everything I am now to my four years at The University of the South.

At the time of this writing, 2019/2020, Sewanee is celebrating its 50th year of coeducation. Not long ago I joined a Facebook group of Sewanee women including faculty, alumni and current students. Reading the various testimonials was eye-opening. My college experience was close to idyllic, but for many women, it was not.

The stories softened my heart.

While ruminating on the testimonials I'd read, wishing these women could have had guardian angels or gentle motherly guidance especially back when we didn't have cell phones and calling home was costly, I was hunting online for a new teapot. A photograph of a ceramic teapot with a serene face caught my attention. Somehow, the reflection of the face on a glossy counter gave me the willies. What if the reflection behaved differently from the solid face? Ah. A story seed!

Originally, the reflection was going to be a dark spirit. But as Tia came to life, it was clear she wanted to be a mentor, a good witch, an adoring aunt kind of presence.

Last thing: while this story is pure fiction, there is a well-known pottery shop on the mountain with a rustic and magical charm. I'll purport that many who frequent it come away with a fluffier spirit, a feeling of groundedness and goodness. Thought it deserved a heartfelt nod.

I dedicate this story to the Women of Sewanee.

Saturday the 14th

The urban legend about the cab driver who picks up a ghost is universal, I suspect. I've heard it in the States, heard it in Japan and have seen it on ghost shows all over the world. The story is a cab driver picks up a ride late at night. Often, it's raining. It's certainly desolate and dreary. The passenger gives a remote address that is either an abandoned house, an asylum or a cemetery. When they arrive at the destination, the passenger disappears, often leaving a wet puddle where he/she was sitting.

With that in mind, I gave it a twist and set it in New York City.

A Fleeting Idea

My neighborhood is dense with trees. We joke that if it's windy in Alabama, our power will go out. And the repair guys come out at all times of the night in the rain to restore our power. They are hard-working, friendly guys and the inspiration for Zap.

I wrote the Zap segments as introductory hints to each story then felt badly about how that ended. Didn't want to end on a downer. This story came to me all at once as a satisfying way to leave the BW&S/Spirited Away.

Grace may be an alter ego; I'd love to work at the Spirited Away though I'd never match her efficiency.

266

The Hoarder House

I dedicate this story to Tally Johnson, Alex Matsuo and James P. Nettles III, fellow panelists at Atomacon. This story came to me all at once after my boyfriend binge-watched episodes of Hoarders and we had a discussion on the fascinating psychology behind hoarding.

The question arose: what if a psychic hoarded ghosts instead of junk?

Thank You

Thank you for reading Uncanny Stout. *If you enjoyed it, please consider a quick review on Amazon and/or Goodreads. Reviews matter! Writing a book isn't the hard part. Sure, it's challenging and takes time, but* **MARKETING** *is the booger! Reviews help a book stay alive and are enormously appreciated. If you liked it, take a second to promote it. Stars really are golden!*

Please visit hedonistichoundpress.com for news about upcoming books and events.

You can also find Hedonistic Hound Press on Facebook:

Best wishes,

Jessica Elliott January 2020

.